THE CALLING

THE CALLING

THE BOOK OF THOMAS JAMES

JACOB ISRAEL

Columbus, Ohio

The Calling The Book Of Thomas James

Published by Gatekeeper Press
2167 Stringtown Rd, Suite 109
Columbus, OH 43123-2989
www.GatekeeperPress.com

The cover design, interior formatting, typesetting, and editorial work for this book are entirely the product of the author. Gatekeeper Press did not participate in and is not responsible for any aspect of these elements.

ISBN (hardcover): 9781662909214
ISBN (paperback): 9781662909221

For my beautiful wife and my amazing children.

You are my dream that came true, and I will always be grateful for you.

I can't wait for what comes next.

They know nothing, they understand nothing. They walk about in darkness; all the foundations of the earth are shaken. I said, "You are gods; you are all sons of the Most High." But you will die like mere men."

—Psalm 82:5–6, KJV

Your life is not what it appears to be.

What will happen when the truth is poured out on a world that is deceived?

Open your eyes and this book may set you free.

—Thomas James

As a child I knew no sin until I was taught by others I was bad to begin.

As I a child I was not ashamed, or easily tamed, I was alive and free.

As a child I was who I was born to be until the ignorant ones got a hold of me.

As a child I was perfect, until tricked into eating of that cursed tree.

—Thomas James

A Child Is Born

September tenth.

Mars hangs closer to the Earth than it has in six thousand years. It appears as a bright orange star in the sky. Like the light that led men from the east to a child in a manger, it could well be a sign of things to come.

Sheets of rain flood the roads leading to the small town of Bethel, and the storm has just begun. What should be the brightest night of the year has become one of the darkest.

The doors of Bethel Memorial Hospital swing open, and a very pregnant nineteen-year-old girl staggers into the emergency room. Her hair is matted from the fierce rain. Droplets of water trickle from her to the floor. A large wet white T-shirt clings to her protruding belly; her teeth chatter. She holds her stomach with one hand and braces herself against the wall with the other.

"Someone…someone…please…please, help me," she gasps before her legs give way, and she falls to the floor.

"We need help here!" yells Lance, a young emergency technician. He charges to her side.

The lights in the hospital flicker. The storm outside breaks the electrical current and forces the generators to take over.

"This girl needs help!" Lance yells again. He cradles her head in his lap.

Her scared eyes flutter until they meet his. "It's happening." Her voice is barely audible, distressed. She grabs Lance's arm tightly. Her hand feels like hot coals to his skin.

A crack of lightning rips through the sky. It startles Lance as the sound of it thunders around them. He flinches just as the young girl loses consciousness.

"Help! We need help!" His screams are more urgent. Her body goes limp in his arms. Nurses and aides swarm the area.

"We'll take it from here," an ER nurse assures.

"On the count of three." They prepare to lift her onto a gurney. "One…two…three!"

In a fluid motion, she is whisked up and away.

Lance stands alone. He is dazed as they rush her to a delivery room. His arm burns where the girl grabbed him. He shakes it frantically, but the pain persists. He pulls back his sleeve. "What the—" His eyes widen in horror.

A glowing imprint of the girl's hand pulses brilliantly on his forearm. He grabs the bottom of his shirt and scrubs the area feverishly until the natural color returns. Now, out of breath, the room circles him. He feels sick.

"What did she do to me?" he cries and runs to the restroom to vomit.

"Make way!" someone shouts as the emergency room team crashes through the delivery room doors.

"Where do you want her?" one nurse asks.

"Right here." Nancy, a heavyset African American with a distinct Southern accent, points. "OB is on the way." She grabs a freshly laundered sheet from the warmer.

They rush the girl into position.

Nancy leans in to tighten the cuff around her arm and adjusts the fetal monitor belt to record contractions. Her eyes are red, as if she has been up for hours. Or maybe she has recently cried.

"Can you hear me, sweetie? Can you hear me?" Nancy looks concerned as she turns the unconscious pregnant girl's face from left to right. "Did anyone get her name?" Nancy says, looking curiously from one person to another.

The group has no answer to give her.

Nancy takes a deep breath and shakes her head. She leans on the table and thinks what to do next.

"Are you sure you're up for this, Nancy?" another nurse asks.

"I'm fine!" Nancy snaps. "Wait, wait, wait..." Nancy quiets the room by raising her pointer finger as the mysterious girl revives.

"Where...where am I?" the pregnant girl asks fearfully.

Nancy straightens. "You're safe, honey. You are about to have a baby. Now, you have to listen very carefully. Do not push. Whatever you do, don't push, not till we tell you to."

The two lock eyes. "My name is Sophia," she says timidly. "Sophia James."

"Sophia, should we call your parents or the father of the child?"

She closes her eyes, shaking her head in disagreement. "I...I don't know who the father is."

Everyone pauses to wonder why the girl would confess such a thing. Even though the times are more liberal than ever before, those in the town of Bethel still frown upon a pregnant woman out of wedlock, especially one as young as Sophia James.

"That doesn't matter now, Sophia," Nancy declares. She takes the girl's hand and tosses a look of caution to the others. "All that matters right now is this baby." Nancy smiles sweetly and turns to the clock on the wall. "Will someone page OB again?"

"You don't understand," Sophia whispers.

"I don't understand what, sweetheart?"

Nervous tears leak from her eyes. "I'm scared...I'm not ready... I'm not—" She swallows her words as labor pains attack her back and legs. "It hurts. It hurts too much!" she cries.

"Just breathe, baby, just breathe."

Sophia reaches up and grabs Nancy's scrubs. "He's coming! He's coming!" she screams, writhing in pain.

Nancy takes her place at the foot of the table. She inspects the mother to be and realizes they are out of time. "The baby is coming with or without the doctor. Are you ready, Sophia?"

"I can't do this!" Sophia cries, bearing down as the pain drives her to push. The baby begins to crown.

"Yes, you can. You can!"

The aide mops Sophia's brow. Her cheeks inflate and then deflate as she huffs, puffs, grunts, and groans.

"The head is almost out...All right, Sophia, we are going to do this together. Now push, two, three, four, five, good... now breathe."

The baby's nose and mouth become visible. Nancy guides the head out gently, and Sophia's breathing becomes shallow.

"You did it, Mom...Okay, now take a second to relax, and we're going to—" Nancy stops speaking as she notices the color drain from the young girl's face. She looks at the monitor. Sophia's blood pressure is falling. Sophia is bleeding out.

"Sophia...Sophia?" Nancy's words trail off in an echo as darkness crowds the young mother's sight.

Her pupils dilate. She relaxes into the table as if asleep.

The sound of those in the room turns into the sound of waves rolling in and out on the seashore.

Sophia's eyes open to a crystal clear sea. "Where am I?" she whispers in a voice that barely sounds like her own. She stands in its ankle-deep water. The sand on the shore behind her shimmers like a million diamonds in the light. Sophia's hair dances from the cool breeze, caressing her. To her amazement, she is no longer pregnant.

"What is this place?"

"Blessed are you above all women," an angel crowned with twelve stars says as he descends from a scarlet-colored cloud.

Sophia falls to her knees.

The angel's feet rest on the sea. He smiles curiously and then walks above its rippling waves toward her.

"A leader your child will be…one who will clear the way for others to see."

"What do you mean?" she asks in confusion.

The angel smiles and says, "Thomas James will be his name, and the words he writes will release a world held captive by ignorant chains."

"I don't understand."

His rainbow-colored eyes begin to glow, and a soft light surrounds him as he tilts his head, almost bowing to her, to say, "Prophets and kings desire to hear the words your son will speak. A writer he will be, one to make way for those in darkness to see."

The angel extends a jeweled hand, which Sophia takes cautiously. He leads her away from the water to the pink-and-blue sand of a new seashore. The corners of his mouth point down as his eyes fill with thought. "Dark days lie ahead for the chosen child."

"What are you saying?" she pleads.

"This world lives in confusion," he says sadly. "But the truth will rise, and those who have scattered will draw near to us again."

Thunder roars, her breath catches, and the heavens open to steal the angel away in its blinding light.

Sophia trembles as she weeps for the child she has not yet held in her arms. She closes her eyes. "God help us," she says as once again the sounds around her change.

"Sophia? S-o-p-h-i-a, can you hear me?"

Sophia's eyes flutter open in response. "Where…am…I?" she struggles to ask.

"You're in a recovery room, sweetheart," Nancy answers.

Sophia squints as the morning sun catches her eye through the window. "I don't understand."

"You had a rough spell. But you're okay now." Dark bags hang heavy under Nancy's eyes. "I've been waiting for you to wake up. I've been here twenty-four hours, actually. I could have been home cleaning. Could have gotten myself some sleep too." She chuckles.

"I'm sorry."

"Sorry? Do not be silly. I was just joking, sweetheart. Besides, it's been twenty years, and I still can't pass up a young mother in need." She presses the intercom. "Ms. James is awake."

"Mother?" Sophia's eyes widen.

"Yes. You scared us for a bit, but you did real well." Nancy takes her hand. "You have a beautiful baby boy."

"Boy? I have a boy?" Tears of joy fill her eyes.

"I just let them know you're awake. They should bring him any minute." Nancy gently pushes back some of Sophia's hair behind her ear. "Before you know it, he'll be in those pretty young arms, and it will feel like everything is right in the world."

"Thank you."

"There is no need to thank me, child. It took more than my help to keep the two of you in this world." She blinks nervously as she lets go of Sophia's hand.

"What do you mean?"

"Never mind that now," Nancy says evasively. "That baby is so beautiful. If I didn't know any better, I would say he was smiling when he was born."

"Here we are." Another nurse wheels the baby into the room. She spies Nancy sitting in a chair next to Sophia; a look of concern falls over her face. "Nancy, shouldn't you be home, taking care of things?"

Nancy shoots her an angry look, one she hides from the patient. "I'm fine."

Sophia sits up in excitement. "Thank you. Thank you so much." She reaches for her newborn but is not strong enough to lift the child on her own. Wrapped in a pure white blanket, the baby almost seems to glow.

"Oh my God, you are so beautiful." Tears slide down her cheek.

Nancy lifts the baby from his bassinet and lays him gently in Sophia's arms.

"Hi there," Sophia says joyfully, drawing the child close to her heart to kiss the top of his head.

"Do you have a name yet?" Nancy asks.

She looks up from her baby curiously. "His name will be Thomas... Thomas James." She pauses to recall her strange dream. "An angel told me to name him that."

"Thomas?" Nancy looks stricken. Her heart pounds as she continues. "An angel told you to name him... Thomas?" She holds her breath.

"Yes, he did."

Nancy takes a few steps back as tears well in her eyes. Sophia stares.

"Are you all right?"

"I'm fine." Nancy gulps down the lump in her throat. "I'll leave you two to get to know each other." With one hand on the door handle and the other clasping her heart, Nancy turns slightly, feigns a smile, and quickly exits.

Sophia takes a moment to let go of her concern for the nurse and gazes once again into her newborn's beautiful blue eyes. "Maybe she doesn't believe me, but that doesn't mean what I am about to say isn't true. You are going to be a writer, Thomas, an important one, for such a time as this," Sophia declares as she gently taps his forehead twice with her index finger. "You're going to make a way for others to see... aren't you?"

From death sprouts life.
Darkness prepares us for the light.
To grow we are stretched.
For great strength our spirit is put to the test.
At our lowest point, the greater our will is to fly.
In our error we find the wisdom to make things right.
When we lose much we find what we are truly grateful for.
There is a reason for all we go through and a purpose for all we endure.

—Thomas James

In Dreams, Heard and Spoken

Twelve Years Later

"Help me!" Thomas screams in the darkness of his bedroom.

His mother, Sophia, wakes in a panic. It is 3:00 a.m. "Tommy?"

The cries of her twelve-year-old son continue as she hurries from her bed down the hall.

"I'm coming, honey." Her heart pounds in her chest. *When will these nightmares end?* "It's just a bad dream, baby." She enters his room in a panic. "It's just a—" She swallows her words at the sight of her son thrashing back and forth in his sleep. He pulls at his collar as if being choked.

Sophia cautiously moves to his side. "Oh, sweetheart—"

In a panic, Thomas sits up, gasping for air. Sweat leaps from his brow as he turns left and right, violently, as if looking for a way to escape his torment.

"Just wake up, honey, just wake up." She gently rests her hand on his to comfort him.

Thomas pushes her away and leaps to the floor. He acts his nightmare out.

"Please...stop...stop...no more...no more..." he whimpers, pacing back and forth like a caged animal.

"What can I do? Honey, what's happening to you?" Sophia asks hopelessly.

Thomas cannot tell his mother about the nightmare haunting him repeatedly. The nightmare began the day he turned twelve years old and has plagued him ever since. He cannot share his belief that there is more to it than just a petrifying dream. He worries this nightmare is a vision of things to come. Moreover, he knows he must keep that a secret.

His mother does all she can to get Thomas help. The night terrors, as the doctors call them, are getting worse. The best advice they give is that Thomas will grow out of it. Sophia knows better. She is the one who watches her son suffer every night. She is the one who finds him when he hides and does not remember doing so.

The doctors are not there when mysterious welts appear on his back. They do not see the tears of blood that fall from his eyes or the bruises that appear from nowhere on his wrists and ankles and disappear just as fast. They offer therapy and drugs instead of giving a solution to the problem.

"Come on, Tommy...wake up." She wants to slap him or shake him from this horrible state, but the doctors warn her never to do so. "When is this going to end?" she asks weakly, looking at the ceiling for answers.

Thomas calmly wakes from his nightmare and turns to find his mother weeping quietly on his bed. "Mom?"

Her red eyes light with joy, and her frown becomes a smile. "You okay, Tommy?" She hugs him and sniffles back some tears.

"I'm fine." Thomas rubs his neck. "I had that dream again," he says quietly.

"I know...but it's over now."

"Is it?"

"Of course it is." She caresses his right cheek.

Thomas looks away.

"You want to talk about it?" Sophia asks sweetly.

His deep-blue eyes meet hers. "Something bad is going to happen."

"No, sweetheart, that's not true."

He stares blankly. "What if it does?"

"Well, then there has to be a very good reason for it. Bad things only happen to prepare us for truly great things."

"How do you know?" he asks.

Sophia touches the tip of his nose and smiles. "I know this because I have faith, honey. More importantly, I have faith in you. One day, all of this will make sense, I promise. There is more to you than you know, sweetheart."

Thomas feigns a smile. *How can a nightmare of being tortured and publically executed as a traitor while the whole world watches ever make sense?*

"Well, you have school in the morning, and I have to get back to bed if I am ever going to wake up for work," she says with a yawn.

"All right…I'll see you tomorrow." Thomas returns to his bed and lies down.

"It's stuffy in here." Sophia walks to the locked window. "Let's open the window. What do you say?"

Thomas sits up fearfully. "Keep it closed, Mom. I…I don't like it open."

She turns curiously. "Why?"

No answer is given. Instead, Thomas looks at the window, troubled.

There are nights he hears whispers coming from outside. These eerie voices call him from the wind. They howl through the branches of the trees, losing their leaves while glowing red eyes peer in his window in the dark of night. Whether his imagination or not, frightful things wait for Thomas outside the protection of his room, and he does not want to chance it.

"Well, why don't you want it open?" Sophia asks again.

How can Thomas answer? His mother has so much to deal with already—cutbacks at work, his ailing grandmother. Does she really need to hear of the monsters he believes are waiting for him outside his room?

"How about I keep it open just a crack, Tommy?"

"Fine." Thomas clenches his jaw.

"Good night, sweetheart." Sophia flips the light switch on the wall and disappears into the hallway of their low-income apartment.

Thomas pulls the sheets tightly over his head. "Please, God, let me sleep, let me sleep," he prays quietly.

The sound of dead leaves rustling together outside are no comfort. He covers his ears, but the sound still creeps in. For what seems like hours, he tosses back and forth, trying to sleep, until he hears a ghoulish whispered voice call for him. "Thomas... James..."

"Who's there?" He sits up immediately, his teeth chattering as he turns on his light to scan the room. *The coast is clear.* He takes a deep breath and exhales to build his courage.

"It's my imagination, just my imagination," he tells himself, all the while worrying what he heard may be real. He cautiously gets out of bed and walks slowly to his window. The hair on the back of his neck stands erect, and his bottom lip quivers. He cannot find the strength to close it.

"Close the window, Tommy, close the window. It's just the wind."

He quickly grabs the top of the window, and the wind squeals past him as he slams it shut. He turns the latch to ensure his safety. He once again scans the room to make sure there is no one there. He returns to his bed and reaches for the light. Before his fingers touch the switch, the bulb burns out, stealing the light from the room.

"What?" Scared, he jiggles the bulb to bring it to life, but to no avail.

The air chills instantly, and he begins to shiver in the darkness.

"There is nothing to be scared of, Thomas... It is just your imagination," he assures himself again as his heart pounds in his chest. With his breath held, he reaches for the small wooden bat next to his bed. He raises the bat in the air, readying himself if need be.

A sudden gust of wind screams past his ears, sucking the bat from his hands inexplicably. He feels hot breath on the back of his neck.

"Mom!" Thomas screams as he runs from his room, never looking behind. Thomas reaches the door at the end of the hall and pounds on it.

"Let me in! Let me in! Let me in!"

The door slowly opens, and to his surprise, he finds his grandmother rocking in her wooden chair. In his panic, he accidently ran to his grandmother's door instead.

"Nanny?" The smell of mildew and roses permeates the air as he enters the safety of her room.

"Come here, Tommy." She taps her knee. "What's wrong, my beautiful boy?" Her Italian accent calms him.

The old wooden floor creaks as he approaches to rest on the end of her bed.

"In fearing the dark, you give it strength, Tommy, remember that," she says mysteriously.

"Okay, Nan," he answers without a clue to her meaning. Her words of wisdom seem more like a spiritual riddle than advice. It reminds Thomas of his grandmother's devoted past.

She had studied to become a nun. While in the convent, a gardener caught her eye, and the two fell instantly in love. She left her pursuit of religion for a relationship with the gardener instead. Nevertheless, she continued her studies and spent a good portion of her life trying to unlock the mysteries of holy books, like the Bible, on her own.

Many called Nanny eccentric, but Thomas knows her to be wise, even if at this moment he doesn't understand her advice.

There is nothing false about Nanny. She is the glue that holds the family together. Now that she is old and cancer is quickly stealing her life, she can no longer care for them the way she once did. That torch she will pass to her eldest daughter, Thomas's mother. Still, no one sees Nanny upset, and there is never a time she will not fight to put others above herself, especially her Thomas James.

"I will tell you a secret, Tommy." She places her wrinkled hand on his knee. "It doesn't matter how scared you get. It does not matter how weak you think you are. Evil will never overcome you because you will overcome evil with good." Her smile grows large with pride.

"If you say so, Nan." Thomas yawns, forgetting his troubles.

"Do you remember the story of when you were born, my beautiful boy?"

She rocks faster in her chair, excited to tell the tale. Thomas relaxes into her bed.

"You were a miracle, a gift from God. You came into this world with a great light in your heart, and it was your voice that brought your mother back from the dead. You were born to give life where others had selfishly taken it..."

His eyes grow heavy as she speaks.

"They tried everything to bring her back from where she'd gone, but the hands of men weren't strong enough. It took more than what is in this world to save her. It was you that brought her back from the abyss. A miracle, Tommy. That's what you are."

Thomas drifts off to sleep as she speaks. Her loving voice leads Thomas to the doors of a dream. "There is a reason you have visions in the night, Tommy." Her soothing voice echoes around him as he enters the vision of a long tunnel with a pulsing white light at its end.

"You are lit from above," Nanny's words trail off in the distance as Thomas reaches the end of the tunnel. He finds a golden puzzle box floating eye level before him. There is a burning in his right hand. Thomas looks down after opening his hand, and to his surprise, an old jeweled key rests there. Putting two and two together, Thomas understands the burning key is meant to unlock the puzzle box.

Thomas uses the ancient key, which had always been within his grasp, to open the iron lock on the large puzzle box. As Thomas turns the key, the golden box opens, and it unfolds itself, growing into the size of a great hall. Thomas finds himself in the center of it all. He stands on the cold and dirty marble floor. Looking to his right and his left, he finds four large waterfalls that close him in.

Thomas realizes that he is covered in dust. He slaps it away. The dirt leaps from him. The particles in the air sting his throat as he inhales them. He begins to cough. As the cloud settles, he quickly breathes freely again. Only his feet remain littered with the dry earth covering the magnificent floor.

Thomas raises his eyes in horror.

"Six thousand years!" a defiant black king roars directly across from him. The black king pounds his bloodied chest plate. "For six thousand years I have ruled. Who dares make war with me?" Behind the king, a foul and mighty army gathers. The black king and his army stand tall. They pound their shields with their swords and scream, "Forsaken, forsaken, forsaken!"

Thomas shakes from fear. As he trembles, he notices twelve laborers dressed in white on either side of him.

Where did they come from? Thomas questions. *How can they make a difference at all? They have no weapons. They do not appear to be violent. They are like gardeners, nothing more. They have but a few rakes, a shovel, a hoe, and bags of seed hanging from their belts. How could they overcome such a dark force?*

From above, a loud trumpet sounds.

Thomas looks up and sees a white king, purer than the driven snow. The king flies high on a white horse in the clouds above. The white king raises a book high into the air and shouts, "The day is at hand! Let the book finally be opened by all!"

Instantly, the twelve laborers become white kings themselves. They each grab a single seed from their bags. The seed becomes a double-edged sword in their hands. The dark army scatters as the white kings begin their march toward them. They trample the enemies' black swords and black shields under their feet.

The black king cries, "There is none like me! There is none like me!"

The twelve white kings surround him. They raise their swords high in the air. The swords catch fire as they slowly lower their blades toward their enemies.

A shining white queen appears from the raging seawall behind Thomas.

"Where did you come from?" Thomas asks the queen, his heart pounding. No answer is given.

The queen holds a newborn wrapped in pure white linen in her arms. She points Thomas's amazed stare to the one who had tormented him and the laborers for so long. The mirror on which the black king appears shatters, allowing Thomas to witness the black king's destruction firsthand.

"Without me you are nothing!" the black king cries as the twelve white kings overcome him. They make their enemy their footstool and raise their hands in victory.

The black king's crown falls from his head. It rolls to the center of the great hall and crumbles into the dust from where it came.

"Dust to dust, spirit to spirit, the prison no longer holds sway," the white king, flying above, declares. His words signal the white army of twelve to join him above. They collectively nod to Thomas and float toward the first king, disappearing together into a cloud.

There is silence in the heavens. There is quiet in the hall. Nevertheless, there is trouble in Thomas's heart.

The queen's gentle footsteps startle Thomas. She approaches, rocking the infant in her arms. She bends her knee, smiles sweetly, and places the babe at Thomas's feet.

"Who are you?" he asks curiously.

The mouth of the queen opens to speak. Her teeth are like that of a lion—as sharp as they are sparkling white.

"As you are, so are we," she says softly in his grandmother's voice. "The first shall be last, and the last shall be first. You must die to live. It is then you will help others to see."

Thomas shakes his head with an equal measure of fear and confusion. Her words make no sense to him, and her arrival is not the comfort he had hoped it would be.

"Fear is the death of mankind, son," the queen says in disappointment. Her head tilts back as she stretches her arms toward the sky. Large white wings stretch from the queen's back with a span that never seems to end. A bright light shoots from her eyes. The skin of her face peels away and falls like pieces of a mask to the ground. The head of a strong eagle is revealed. Her feet turn to talons of gold. She flaps her glorious wings and takes flight. She soars toward the sun, out of Thomas's sight.

Thomas looks to his feet. This is where the queen left the child wrapped in white linen. He bends down carefully for a closer look. Slowly, he moves the white blanket away, one corner at a time. A tiny hand reaches out and grabs Thomas's index finger. As he removes the last corner, he sees the face of a baby.

Thomas jumps back. "My God!"

The baby's face is his own, the face of Thomas James where the newborn's face should be.

The baby's eyes are Thomas's eyes, and they turn bloodred. Next the hair of the child becomes white as wool. His skin turns to the color of fine-polished brass. His grip on Thomas tightens.

The child pulls Thomas closer and screams, "Wake up! Wake up! Wake up!"

The bright morning sun flooding his grandmother's room wakes Thomas from sleep. He slowly opens his eyes. *That was a terri-*

ble dream, but a different dream than the usual nightmare, Thomas recalls as his eyes painfully adjust to the bright light.

"Nanny, are you here?" He gets off her bed and fixes the quilt he ruffled in his sleep. "Nan, where are you?" He looks at the clock on her dresser. It is 7:00 a.m. "I'm going to be late for school!"

Usually the house fills with the sound of his mother talking and laughing while she smokes her cigarette and drinks her morning coffee. Today there is only silence.

"Hello?" Thomas enters the hallway. "I need to get to school."

He approaches the kitchen. The smell of fresh bacon, cheese eggs, and brewing coffee is not in the air. This morning is different from the rest.

"What is going on? Where is everyone?"

The back door is open. Thomas curiously walks over to close it.

"Mom?"

He receives no answer.

The low sound of a busy signal gets his attention. He turns to the wall to find the receiver dangling from its dirty vanilla cord.

"Is anyone here?" A lump of fear gathers in Thomas's throat.

He hangs the phone up and walks to his mother's room. "Mom?" He knocks on her door. "Mom? Nanny? Anyone in there?"

Slowly he opens it. The room is a mess. Not like his mother to leave it that way. Something is wrong. He worries as he turns for the bathroom. Thomas knocks three times quickly on the bathroom door.

"Nanny, are you in there?" He knocks again, harder than before. "Is anyone in the bathroom? Mom? Nan?"

He jiggles the handle. The locked door will not open from this side. Pressing his thumb firmly against its slit lock, Thomas unlocks the door as if his thumb is a key.

"I'm coming in." He opens the door slowly and peers into the room with squinted eyes. Through blurry vision, he sees someone is on the ground in the corner next to the toilet. He blinks his eyes, allowing the room to come into focus.

"Nanny? No!" he screams.

His grandmother moans softly on the floor.

Thomas is frozen. *What do I do?*

With every bit of the strength she has left, his grandmother reaches for him.

He knows she wants him to hold her one last time. Fearfully he wraps his arms around her. "I love you, Nanny. I love you so much!" he says with tears filling his eyes. "You're going to be okay…I'll get help!"

She shakes her head in disagreement and holds Thomas tighter. "You brought me peace," she says quietly, spraying saliva and blood on his shirt.

"Someone help!" Thomas screams, and in that instant, the pipes rattle and crack as the light in the bathroom ceiling bursts, as if Thomas's voice alone instigated both. A spark from the light's broken current ignites gas fumes leaking from the now-cracked gas main nearby. Tiny shards of the glass from the bulb fall to the floor as fire begins to shoot from the cracked pipe like a flame-thrower. The gas pipe rattles more, fighting to break free from its ceiling clamps. It spits fire wildly above the two.

Thomas tries to drag his grandmother from the scene. He is too weak and cannot move her.

Joseph, the off-duty firefighter who lives next door, rushes into the bathroom. "I found him. He's in the bathroom with your mother, Sophia!" he shouts into the hallway after finding Thomas and quickly evaluating the scene.

Sophia appears frantic behind Joseph in the hall, holding her chest. "Tommy?" She sees the fire. "Jesus!" She lunges for her son.

"We have to get out of here now!" Joseph demands, shielding his face from the heat.

"Let her go, Tommy." Sophia fights to pull her son from her unconscious mother.

"No, No, I won't leave her…I won't leave her!" Thomas demands, pulling his arm from his mother.

The fiery pipe breaks free from the ceiling clamps holding it in place.

"Tommy, let her go now!" his mother demands.

Joseph grabs Thomas violently and pries him away.

Nanny's body falls to the bathroom floor as they leap to the safety of the hall. The pipe bursts with the sound of cannon fire.

Sophia pulls her son's head to her bosom and covers his ears. Thomas spies, through the space of her fingers, the fire hailing down upon his grandmother. Her gown and hair catch fire. She raises her head, and their eyes meet for a moment.

"Don't be scared, m-my b-boy," Nanny says and collapses as the fire consumes her.

"No!" Sophia cries.

Sirens scream outside as emergency workers arrive at the scene.

The expression on Sophia's face disappears. Her tight hold on Thomas relaxes.

"What's happening? What's happening, Mom?" Thomas looks into her blank stare.

"She's, she's…gone." Sophia drops her arms and sits motionless, as if giving up the will to live herself.

"Mom?"

"Come on!" Joseph yanks Thomas from Sophia and drags him down the hall away from the fire. "You stay right here," he demands.

The fire attacks the ceiling of the hallway outside the bathroom. Joseph cautiously makes his way back to Sophia. She stands to her feet in a daze and says, "I can't leave her…I can't."

Thomas's eyes widen in horror as he watches his mother slowly walk toward the flames engulfing the room. "Mom… don't…" he says with his heart in his throat. Tears streak his ash-covered cheeks.

"You stay right where you are, Sophia! Don't you move," Joseph instructs. He grabs her by the elbow and spins her around to face him. "You have to listen to me. You can't do anything for her. She's gone."

"That's not true!" Sophia screams like a madwoman.

"I'm not leaving without you." Joseph grabs her wrist.

"Let me go!" She slaps him.

Joseph wraps his arms around her in a bear hug.

Sophia kicks and screams desperately. "Leave me alone!" She stamps her heel into the top of his foot. Joseph lets go. She tries running into the bathroom to save her mother, but Joseph reaches out and stops her again. She flails her arms violently and catches Joseph's right eye with her nail, ripping his eye apart. He buckles over and falls to the floor, holding his eye in its socket. He screams in agony as the smoke makes the air poisonous.

Sophia covers her mouth and prepares to enter the bathroom.

"Mom, what are you doing? Please, please don't!" Thomas screams.

Sophia hears her son's pleas. Her reason returns. She stops and realizes there is nothing she can do. She turns to Thomas and smiles. "It's going to be okay. I'm coming, baby."

As she steps toward Thomas, smoke shoots up from the floor and attacks her nostrils. It rushes into her as if the smoke has a will of its own. Sophia is frozen, dazed by it. Her eyes turn completely black as the evil smoke possesses her. Her countenance changes, and her arms fall to her side. An eerie smile grows toward her ears. The woman Thomas calls Mom is gone.

"There's nothing you can do," she says in a strange voice.

"It's not her!" Thomas screams. "It's not her, it's not her!"

Sophia straightens. She turns to the bathroom. She keeps her black eyes fixed on her son as she walks purposely to her death.

Joseph stumbles toward Thomas as part of the hallway ceiling collapses. There is no saving Sophia now.

"No!" Thomas desperately cries. "We have to help her!" He runs to save her, but Joseph catches him and carries the twelve-year-old away from the scene in a daze.

Paramedics arrive. They lead Joseph and Thomas outside.

Thomas weeps as they carry him away from his childhood home.

"It's going to be okay," The paramedic assures, but Thomas knows better.

"You don't understand...something took my mother. Something killed my mother. We need to help her. We have to—"

A strange vision quiets him. Thomas notices the curious movement of the smoke billowing out from the entrance. Like the smoke that possessed his mother, this too begins to move as if it has a will of its own. The smoke begins to take on a monstrous shape. Curious, Thomas stares at the aberration of smoke as it takes form.

"Everything will be okay, son," the paramedic assures again. He is ignorant of the smoke-filled monster coming to life behind them.

"Can you see it?" Thomas asks, pointing at it in fear.

The smoke continues to gather, forming the head of a giant bat-like creature. Its red eyes open—two large rubies from the pit of hell. Thomas has seen these eyes before. The same red eyes forever staring into his bedroom window each night.

"It can't be." Thomas's lips quiver. "Can't you see that?"

The paramedics ignore him. At the ambulance, they shove an oxygen mask in his face.

Thomas breathes deep as he stares at the terrifying vision before him. "Why is no one answering me? Can't you see it?" Thomas points and yells. "It's right there! It's right there!"

The dark creature spreads its black wings, as if stretching after a long sleep. Its arms reach toward the heavens as if they can drag them down. The monster's actions remind Thomas of the black king that terrified him in his dream.

The entire roof of his apartment catches fire. In the distance, more sirens scream through the air.

"We need to stop it! It's going to destroy everything!" Thomas yells.

"Everything is going to be all right, son, just...just relax." The man opens a white medical box and takes out a needle filled with tranquilizer.

"You don't understand. I know what did this. I know what this is. I know what it wants!" he pleads.

The creature of smoke whips its head toward Thomas, pinning him beneath his burning red eyes. The child sees what no one in six thousand years has seen before. The monster lets out a shriek.

Thomas trembles uncontrollably from the terror it inspires. "It sees me! It sees me! It sees me!" he screams, fighting to get away as they restrain him.

"This is going to make you feel better, son," the paramedic says as he puts the needle into Thomas's arm and releases its contents into his vein.

"No, no, you don't understand. We have to stop...we...have... to..." Thomas's words are lost as he falls into sleep. One thought runs through his mind. Now that he sees the evil hiding in plain sight, and the evil knows that he sees it for what it is, he may just be running from it for the rest of his life.

The trees didn't mourn the loss of their leaves.

When the flowers dried, the grass didn't cry, nor did the birds grieve.

When the snow came, the fields didn't blame the clouds.

When the snow began to melt, the snow never cursed the sun.

Change touches everything and everyone.

—Thomas James

Life Becomes Death

A light rain falls as Thomas sits alone on the cold steps of his childhood church. He watches the driver of the hearse make the final preparations for the long sad ride to the cemetery. Soon they will lay his mother and grandmother to rest. For Thomas there is only sorrow. He is numb. His mind is clouded by grief. He convinces himself that the vision of the dark creature he saw just two days prior is imagination. Hiding away beneath his grief though, there is a great fear Thomas is not yet ready to address.

The driver winks at him as he arranges small bundles of silk flowers in the corners of the hearse window. He shuts the curtains behind, leaving the floral display for all to see. He exits and steps back to admire the work of his hands. "Not bad, huh?" He smiles with satisfaction, closes the hearse back door, and activates the car alarm.

Thomas shrugs with a frown. Why a person would ever think to steal such a depressing automobile evades him.

The driver removes his hat as he approaches. "I'm very sorry about your loss, son."

Thomas shrugs again, pretending not to care.

After a sympathetic pat to his shoulder, the driver climbs the stairs to enter the church. "Things will get better soon," he says, leaving Thomas to his thoughts.

"If you say so." Thomas rolls his eyes and notices his distorted reflection in the wet doors of the hearse. His matted hair, bags under his eyes, and rain-stained gray suit mirror his broken spirit.

He had never known the grave, but in that moment, the grave becomes home. A hollow feeling fills his chest. His head is heavy. He wants to cry, but his tears are all but spent.

Two people quickly exit the church. The funeral service has just begun.

Who can that be? Thomas wonders as he turns to see.

"Ugh, I hate these things," Beth, one of Sophia's cousins, says, opening her black umbrella. She grimaces at the dark-gray clouds above.

Thomas has not seen her in years, but he knows Beth and her story. His mother had explained how the love of money could change people and replace a warm heart with a cold one.

"I'm so glad we left," she continues heartlessly.

Her husband, Daniel, glances at his gold Rolex and grits his teeth. "You don't want to go to the cemetery, do you?"

"Of course not," she says. The two rush down the stairs.

Thomas's nostrils flare.

Beth is surprised. "Hey, Tommy, what are you doing out here?" she asks, forcing pity into her eyes.

"Waiting."

"For who...Godot?" Daniel laughs alone. His joke is better suited for someone in the theater district.

"Honey, you're all wet." She takes out a handkerchief and dangles it in front of him.

Thomas looks away. He will not take her charity. She has never offered any before.

Beth puts the handkerchief away with a huff. "Well, honey, if you need anything, just call us, okay?"

"Keep that chin up, champ," Daniel falsely encourages while mussing Thomas's hair. They cross the street to their new Mercedes and disappear around the bend.

"Jerks," Thomas says, fixing his hair. He stomps his right foot on the stair beneath him in anger. A flash of lightning and thunderous boom startle Thomas the instant he does so. He looks to the sky as if it could fall at any minute. The rain lets up, yet above him everything becomes black. A larger storm is to come.

"Why did you take them, God?" he asks pitifully. His stomach pains him. What is he to do now? Where will he go? Who will ever love him the way his mother and grandmother did?

"I want my family back," Thomas begs, desperate to hear his grandmother's laugh or the encouraging words of his mom again.

No one comforts him. No one takes the time to hold his hand. No one is there for Thomas. No one at all.

"I want my family back!" he demands.

Eternity has begun for the two.

Thomas does not know what that means. If he were to tell the priest how his mother died, he would say there is no hope for her. He would not believe the story Thomas had to tell. Why should he? Evil smoke possessing someone to take their own life sounds foolish. The priest would believe she killed herself. He would overlook what possessed her to do so. He would ignore the pain that opened her up to do such a thing. He then would go on to explain that there is a special place in hell reserved for those that commit suicide.

This, Thomas cannot accept. "She never hurt anybody!" he cries, shaking his fist in the air, remembering the last time he and the priest spoke.

Six Months Prior

"Why would God send most of his creation to a place of endless suffering for not believing?" Thomas asked the priest sincerely.

"His ways are beyond ours, Thomas," the priest replied in his strong Irish accent.

"That doesn't make any sense. You don't punish someone for not knowing any better. You teach them."

"God is just, Tommy. He cannot force people to accept his gift of salvation. He gives everyone a chance."

"Why can't he force people? It's better than the alternative. And if salvation is a gift, why do we have to do anything to receive it?"

"You have to open a present to find out what it is."

"And what is it we are saved from? The future? What about being saved in the here and now? And why would any father send their child to a place where they are burned endlessly? That doesn't make sense. What, because they didn't know any better? I don't know, Father John. I just wouldn't do that to my kids."

"Well, it's a good thing you're not God then, Thomas!" The priest had enough.

"How can he be the Savior of the world without saving the whole world?"

The Irishman stood angrily. His belly protruded as he looked down his nose at Thomas. With an extended bloated finger, he jabs the top of Thomas's chest, saying, "He saves those that come to him. The rest will be sorry they never became part of his Church."

"So God will burn and torture forever those that aren't Catholic? Sure sounds like a God of love to me," Thomas said sarcastically.

"God is love, young man!" the priest yelled and slapped his hands on the desk.

Thomas is taken aback by the priest's actions. In that moment he saw the devil. As if the devil was not some creature outside of everyone ruling this place called hell, reserved for non-Catholics everywhere, as the priest had taught everyone. Thomas saw the devil as if it was simply the lust for power and control within the heart of man.

"And I am supposed to take your word for it?"

"That's enough!" The priest grabbed Thomas by his ear.

"Ow!"

"Your smart mouth is going to get you in a lot of trouble if you're not careful. Hell is a very real place," the priest threatened as he escorted Thomas to the door. "And if you are not careful in the things you say, you might find out how very real hell is. Good day, young man!"

He slammed the door in Thomas's face and left him to walk home in tears.

The priest's threats, like a poison-tipped dart, did just enough damage to allow Thomas to begin to question whether or not his feelings about God were false. That fear quickly spread. He began to worry that if he didn't begin to see things the way the priest did, perhaps there was a hell and, worse still, that he would end up in it.

It was not until later that night that his mind was set at rest.

"The gospel is good news, Tommy," his Nanny assured. "Jesus was never meant to become the idol he has become today. He is symbol of us, Tommy, in our awakened state. The firstborn of many. As he is, so are we to be in this world."

Thomas's eyes glossed over as she continued. Much of what Nanny said felt right but made no sense at all. In any event, it did not matter for as she continued, his fear began to disappear.

"Jesus is our pattern, not some grumpy ignorant priest. He is the pattern, son. His message was love, and love does not condemn or threaten, Thomas. Love is gentle and meek. Love does not hold account of past wrongs. Love never fails and never gives up. And that kind of love, the love that Jesus shared back in the old days, made the ignorant ones so mad they wanted Jesus dead long before he ever died on that cross."

"Why?"

"Because he showed them how much they actually hate. People want to feel like they know more. They want to feel like they are better and that they alone have the answers. People want control, and they literally sell their soul to greed and corruption so others will look to them as if they are God themselves. This is the trick of their ego, which fights to keep them ignorant of the very truth that could set them free."

"What truth, Nanny?"

Nanny smiled. "No one can tell you the truth, Tommy, no matter how persuasive they seem. Not me, not that priest, not anyone. The truth can only be revealed from within."

"From what?"

"From within each individual. From God, Tommy, from God. And God is love. So the only real hell there is, is that ignorant place in the heart of hate that made that priest act the way he did earlier today...But I don't have to tell you that because you already know that, don't you?"

Thomas agreed.

"Remember, Tommy, no one is too wicked to be forgiven, and no one is too lost to be found. God will not let his children be lost forever, my baby boy."

"I don't understand."

"Don't doubt what's in your heart, Tommy. It's the heart that God gave you, and that is where He speaks to you from. It is that heart that should lead you, not some grumpy old priest."

Present

Nanny was right. What does it matter where the priest would say his mother is? What does it matter what anyone would say? She was not bad. She did nothing wrong. She was sad, that is all. She was hurting; that is why the evil took her. You do not punish someone because their pain is too great that they cannot go on. If anything, you show them more love. If Thomas knows this, God most surely does as well, or at least that is what his heart tells him.

Thomas reaches for the locket his mother gave him. His skinny fingers pry at the latch. He opens it delicately. It reveals a small picture of Thomas and his mother on opposite sides of it.

Thomas sniffs the cold air and exhales sadly as he looks at her picture. He misses her so. He had acted so childish when she had given it to him.

Last Year

"Try it on, Tommy." Sophia's eyes filled with joy as she held the heart-shaped locket in her hands.

"They'll make fun of me if I wear that," he said disrespectfully.

"You shouldn't care what people think, Tommy. Because no matter how hard you try to please everyone, no matter how hard you try to fit in, there will always be someone fighting to bring you down. So don't let them." She placed the locket in his hand. "It doesn't matter if you wear it or not. I just want you to have it. So you know that my heart will always be with yours."

Present

Thomas shakes his head and the memory away. He will wear what fear kept him from wearing before.

"I don't care if they make fun of me!" he says, bravely closing the locket. He gently wraps the chain around his neck and fastens it. His mother's heart will always hang above his own.

"But what am I going to do now, Mom?" he cries, driving his knuckles into the stone steps. "What am I going to do?" he begs the dark sky above.

"If the answers are found up there in the clouds, the birds will find them before you do," a strange-looking man says, approaching from what seemed like thin air. He wears a long dirty-brown trench coat and a tattered baseball cap embroidered with the letter *A*. His hands are dirty. His fingers are long and swollen. His eyes are as blue as Thomas's own eyes, and there is a familiar feeling about this strange man.

Thomas prepares himself to run, just in case.

The stranger smiles curiously and crouches down. He winks at Thomas once he is on his level. "I'm sorry about your mother. She was a remarkable woman," he says in a sweet voice while tilting his head curiously.

"How...how did you know about...Wait, did you know my mother?" Thomas asks, slowly backing away.

The stranger scratches his scraggly beard, and as he avoids Thomas's question, his eyes light with compassion. "You don't have to be scared of me, son," he says sincerely.

His ragged appearance frightens Thomas nonetheless. *Is he homeless? Is he crazy? Is he a killer?*

The stranger raises his eyes to a small clearing in the clouds. It makes way for a single beam of light to shower down upon the man alone. "I have a message for you," he says as everything around him becomes bright.

"You have what?" Thomas squints. It hurts to look at him. This light, this amazing beam of light, seems to grow brighter by the second. "Who...who are you?" Thomas asks, shielding his eyes. The stranger smiles and leans toward him, as if to tell Thomas a secret.

"If we hope for what we see not, then we do with patience wait for it, Thomas."

"How do you know my name?"

"You are a breaker, Thomas. The ground is dry and hard, but you are set to open it with words given to you from above...These words you will write for all to see."

Thomas backs away in fear and accidentally stumbles on a step. The stranger, catching him by his wrist, keeps Thomas from falling. "Careful," he says with a smile.

"Thanks," Thomas replies as the man gently raises him to his feet again.

"This is for you." The stranger takes out a folded piece of yellow paper from his inside jacket pocket.

"I don't understand," Thomas stutters nervously as he takes it from him.

"You will," the stranger says, turning and walking away with a curious smile. "Remember, Thomas," he says without facing him, "in fearing the dark, you give it strength."

Thomas is frozen. His jaw slacks. They are his grandmother's words.

How can it be? Thomas inspects the note left behind. The burnt edges and coarse texture give it an ancient feel.

"What is this, mister?" he calls out, but the stranger is gone as quickly as he arrived. *Where did he go?* Thomas wonders as he runs to the bottom of the stairs. He looks left and right, but the man is nowhere. "Impossible!" Thomas throws his hands into the air.

He looks again at the paper given to him. "What is this?" he asks audibly and slowly opens it. His fingers become dirty from its burnt edges. With great care, he opens the last fold and sees, written in black calligraphy on the top of the page,

The Kingdom is at Hand

"What does that mean?" he questions in a fearful whisper.

A signature in the lower right hand corner of the page catches his attention.

Immanuel

What Kingdom? Who is Immanuel? Thomas wonders as he runs into the empty streets to look for the stranger. The streets are empty. They are quiet and damp. *Where did he go?*

Bethel is a small town. Thomas knows almost everyone in it, but not this man.

He looks to his watch. There is little time until the service lets out. Shall he tell someone about the stranger and about this mysterious note? If he does, who would believe him? Will it be as it has always been before? They might say he is looking for attention. Behind his back they might mock him, call him a freak, an oddball, and a loser—like many of his peers say to his face.

Popular is not the word to describe Thomas. Different, yes, different is what he is, and that is why there is no one he can share this information with now that his mother and grandmother are gone. He certainly cannot share this visit with someone inside the church.

He will not find acceptance or any comfort there. Inside this church, there is misery, confusion, laughter, cries, cheers, songs, and praise. There are recitals and prayers, smoke from a waving silver ball, and two altar boys on their knees. The pews fill with mourners wearing black gowns, black suits, black hats, and black shades. Horrific statues and paintings litter the church walls. Prominently displayed in the front of them all is a life-size statue of Jesus. The statue is naked, beaten, and dying on a cross of pure gold. This statue shines brighter than the rest.

Everywhere there is defeat and suffering in this church. How can Thomas share this chance encounter with, or get advice from, anyone found inside such a depressing place?

He half hopes the clouds will part, as they seemed to do for the strange messenger, and angels would give him the answers he longs for. But that is not his reality. Thomas must find a way to be strong on his own merit, with his own strength.

The church bell rings, shaking Thomas from his sad thoughts. The service has come to its end. The loud gong echoes for a mile. Those waiting for the annual Bethel Day Parade to begin on Main Street can even hear the sound of this bell.

Looking at the clock tower, Thomas notices the hands of this great timepiece. It is 11:11 p.m. This is a time that haunts him. It is a time that has haunted him for years. As if these numbers are trying to tell him something. However peculiar the time, the bell tolls because the end of the funeral service is near.

Thomas notices two mourning doves flying above the clock tower. They float above the church, riding the wind as their wave. While staring at them, Thomas smiles. In the midst of the dark clouds and thunder, he sees peace flying without fear. How he wishes he could be those birds.

The large carved church doors open with a dull thud. The uneasy feeling in Thomas's stomach is gone. He knows his time is short. He must slip inside before Aunt Leah, his new caretaker, yells at him for leaving the service early.

Trying not to draw attention to himself, he enters quietly and positions himself in the corner of the small lobby. He rests his elbow on the ceramic bowl holding the holy water in its place and searches the crowd for his flamboyant aunt.

"How are you holding up, son?" A deacon surprises Thomas as he raises a red velvet rope to section off the stairs leading to the highest point of the church.

"I'm all right, thanks."

"It was a nice service for your mom and grandmother, wasn't it?"

"If you say so."

"Don't be rude, Tommy!" The heavy hand of his aunt slaps the back of Thomas's head. His elbow accidentally dips into the water blessed by the priest.

"Thanks." Thomas shakes his arm angrily.

"Don't act like such a baby," she says in her heavy Long Island accent. "Take this." She hands Thomas a couple of used tissues from her purse.

"That's gross." He flicks them away.

"Oh, as if it matters...You're drenched from being outside already. And I'm not going to tell you again to watch that tone. You're in God's house." She flicks his ear.

"Leah, how are you holding up?"

Thomas glances up at the desire in the deacon's voice.

"I'm doing just fine, Dom. Will you excuse us?" She wraps her arm around Thomas's neck and leads him outside. "Tommy, what were you doing?"

"What do you mean?"

"You were gone for the whole service. What were you doing?"

"Thinking."

"And what were you thinking about?"

Thomas has no answer to give. Leah primps her bushy blonde hair, waiting for an answer. She gives up. "Well, do you want to go to the cemetery with us or what?"

"I don't...I don't know." Cemeteries seem foolish to Thomas. What is the point of honoring someone in death if you did not do it in life? This is what his mother taught him. He knows she will not care if he does not come to a field of rotting flesh and bones to honor her or not. It does not matter where their bodies rest. It is where their spirit is that Thomas cares to know, and he will never find that by looking at a carved piece of stone.

"You don't know what? It is simple. Either you're coming, sweetie, or you're not."

"I...I don't know."

"Look, Tommy, baby, we really have to get going. We are in the lead car, grumpy. It will not look good if we get there last."

If there is a moment for Thomas to gather his thoughts, then a decision could be made. Her pressuring him is not helping any. What does he really want to do?

"Why don't you come with me and Uncle Pete?"

"Uncle? You're not even married," Thomas argues.

His outburst catches the eye of the priest as he says his good-byes. He gives Thomas a fake smile and returns to his depressed flock.

Leah's face turns red from embarrassment. She squeezes Thomas's hand like a vise. "Come with me!" she demands, leading him down the steps for some privacy. "I know this is probably hard on you, but this isn't a walk in the park for me, you know. I lost my mother and my sister, do not forget about that. On top of that, now I have to look after you. You think I want to be stuck with a twelve-year-old kid who acts like he's thirty?" Leah waits for his reply.

"No?"

"No, is right, Tommy. But I'm the only family you have left. So cut me and your uncle Pete some slack. You should be grateful your mother's life insurance is enough to take care of both of us, or you'd probably be in some home right now. So do me a favor and act like you love me, at least until the funeral is over, okay?"

The loud car horn snaps her to attention. Leah fumbles through her purse for some makeup. "That's your uncle Pete. Are you coming or what?"

An old yellow Mustang races around the corner, screeching to a stop in front of the two. It is Peter. He pulls down his mirror sunglasses and gives Leah an angry look. He rolls down the window and flicks his cigarette to the street. "Let's go," he commands.

"Tommy, we don't have all day." Leah's impatience is clear from her perturbed look.

"I don't know what to do." Thomas is so lost.

"All right, fine...Look, maybe you shouldn't go." She walks away as a mother would a spoiled child.

"Wait...I...I...." Thomas fumbles.

"You what, Tommy? You what?" She stands next to Pete's car, tapping her left foot.

"Come on," Peter huffs and turns up Led Zeppelin playing on his radio. "Why don't you go to Main Street and find a job? It will keep you busy after school while we're both at work. Get your mind off things."

Leah walks to Thomas and gives him a superficial hug. "Maybe you can still catch the parade if you hurry, honey. Aren't your friends supposed to be there?"

"The parade?" Thomas had all but forgotten about the Bethel day parade. Everyone will be there—including the one person Thomas knows will understand.

Peter jams his hand down on the horn again. "So what's it going to be?"

"You go ahead. I'll meet you at the house later." Thomas hopes she will wrap her arms around him and tell him everything is going to be okay. To assure him that he will never be a burden to her—that he will be a son.

Instead, she says, "That sounds good." She turns her back to him to enter Peter's car.

Thomas waves sadly as they drive off. He thinks about the one person who can put a smile back on his face.

"Betty," he whispers like a student with a crush.

His friend Betty will be at the parade. They've grown up together as neighbors. They are in the same grade, and both started junior high earlier this year.

Betty is a beautiful girl. She is one of those girls that everyone knows or wants to know. To Thomas, Betty is the closest friend and only friend he has ever had. For six years, they were insepa-rable. They got chicken pox together, walked to school together, and shared everything. Recently, the two seem to be drifting apart. Thomas misses her, but he knows she is just too busy with their new school and the many clubs she is a part of.

Betty will be at the parade that starts at noon. This explains why she did not come to the funeral. She is a new cheerleader. It is her duty to support the Wildcats football team. They are one of the parade's greatest attractions.

Thomas knows to find her on Main Street. The first stop will be his aunt's apartment. He needs to change his clothes and get his bike. Then he will ride and find the only person he believes cares enough just to listen, the only one who might possibly bring some peace to his troubled heart.

As Thomas walks to his new home, he takes out the folded piece of yellow paper that the stranger had given him.

The Kingdom is at Hand

Immanuel

What does it mean? he wonders.

A loud crack of thunder sounds directly above him. Thomas falls to the ground and covers his head in fear. He waits for lightning to strike. The silence that follows makes his skin crawl.

Thomas raises his eyes to the dark storm clouds as they pull away like a retreating tide.

The sun pierces through the darkness of the day and shines on him. The gray sky turns blue. Thomas slowly stands to his feet and wipes the dirt from his clothes.

Can this be a sign of good things to come, or will the storm get worse as he makes his way back home?

I've asked why...I've questioned how long...

I've wondered when things would be easier and when peace would come along.

I've cried, I've lied, I've shouted, I've pouted, I've mourned, and I've longed,

I've been angry, I've been hurt, I've been lost, and I've been dead wrong.

And yet these, I now see, were keys to unlocking life's love song.

—Thomas James

When Hearts Are Broken

It is a moment before twelve. Thomas rides his old Huffy bicycle to the corner of Tulip and Rose. He passes McCardles Flower Shop and admires the neatly landscaped lawns on his way to Main Street. The bushes are in perfect shapes, squares, and rectangles. The marigolds bloom like tiny suns. The flowering cabbages and chrysanthemum flowers pave the way, as if leading to a magical place.

Thomas stops at his usual spot. In thirty or so paces, he will stand on the famous avenue known for overpriced shopping.

"Made it," he says, catching his breath, and not a minute too soon. The parade is about to begin. The crowd will be great, and it will be hard to find Betty once the parade begins.

For the first time, Thomas chains his bike to a parking meter. Now that his mother is gone, the sad-looking bike with tattered red-and-green flares hanging from the handlebars means more to him. The irony of this realization is great. Just five days ago, this bike, which he now cherishes, was the subject of the last fight he had with his mom.

Five Days Ago

"What do you mean, 'I don't need a new one'?"

"The one you have is fine, Tommy. You don't need another one," his mother said patiently as she made dinner.

"How would you know?"

She turned to him and laid the soup ladle down. "Plenty of children don't even have what you have. I did not raise a spoiled child, and you are acting like one right now." She punctuated her words with an extended finger pointing at his forehead.

"How do you expect me to fit in when everyone around me makes fun of all my secondhand junk?"

"Junk?" she threw a dish towel in his face. "Your bike is junk?" She shook her head.

Thomas felt her disappointment like a knife in his chest.

"I scrubbed toilets for three weeks to get that bike for you, and it's junk?"

"I didn't mean it like that," he mumbled.

"Out of the abundance of your heart your words are spoken, Tommy. You need to take responsibility for the things you say." She turned away from her son, held back tears, and stared out the window to gather composure.

This forced Thomas to act. "I'm sorry, Mom."

She took a deep breath and turned to him. "Tommy, your road may not be an easy one, but one day you'll realize just how blessed you are. You may even regret saying what you just said. You will learn that there are more precious things in life than things themselves. And when you do, sweetheart"—she leaned in farther to muss his hair—"try not to be too hard on yourself." Sophia smiled and returned to the meal she was preparing.

Present

How selfish, Thomas thinks. *How ungrateful I was to the one woman who would give me the world if it were in her power.*

Words are like toothpaste, he believes. Once they leave your mouth, you cannot force them back in. How he wishes he could take back what he said that night.

"I'm sorry, Mom," he says, swallowing the lump of regret in his throat. He takes a deep breath and presses on to find Betty.

The hooded sweatshirt he wears is a gift from his mother as well. She gave it to him a year ago, last Christmas. He wears this sweatshirt often. The deep hood offers refuge from the judgmental stares of those around him. Whenever he feels insecure, he simply hides his face away inside it, as if becoming invisible to the world.

"Don't hide who you are, Tommy," his mother used to say. "Never hide who you are from this world. You wouldn't put a candle under a bucket, would you?"

She would say these things, never waiting for a response.

"No, Tommy," she would continue. "You would put a candle in the very center of any room so everyone can see it. Let them see you, Tommy. Do not hide that light of yours. Let it shine, and be glad that it is. Because one day, who you are may just be what this world needs to find everything they've lost. And besides that, why on earth would you hide those pretty blue eyes?"

If only her soft words were here to encourage him now.

His belly fills with what feels like a thousand butterflies at war inside him. It is likely everyone from his school is here. That means there may also be those who take pleasure in causing him pain. The bullies.

Every town has them, but in Bethel, they are the worst. Those that are strong systematically tear down the weak, and there is none weaker in Bethel than Thomas James.

Will today be different from the rest? Will the widely spread news of the fire and his loss keep him from being picked on if found today? *Why take the chance?* he thinks. His sweatshirt will come in handy after all. He raises his hood as he approaches the great crowd lining Main Street.

The cars honk their horns in unison. There are cheers and shouts for the parade to begin. Everyone is out on this frigid October day. Children are running with balloons in their hands, attacking each other with cans of foam spray. Parents wear mittens and gloves. They sip coffee and hot chocolate and speak of the football season sure to bring victory to the town of Bethel this year. Street vendors yell for their patrons, knowing that this day, they will make more than ever before.

The parade begins on time as always. It is high noon. There will be the same people, the same clubs, and the same marching bands playing the same dreadful music.

The uneasy feeling Thomas has gets worse. *How selfish to celebrate on a day like today,* he thinks.

He does not like being in crowds, especially this one. The amount of people is not what bothers him so much as it is the quality of the people themselves. The feeling he gets when looking into their eyes almost makes him sick.

Mainly inhabited by the privileged, Bethel is a town of movers and shakers in business and heirs to family fortunes. The residents are very different from the humble pioneers who founded the place many years ago. With a bloated image of themselves, they are aloof in every sense of the word. They have their own clubs, their own cliques, and their own laws. They look down on those beneath their financial medium. They believe that only they and their offspring are destined for greatness; that's what their checkbooks tell them. They bow down to no man or woman, unless their wealth exceeds their own.

A pack of wolves is what they are in Thomas's eyes. Whether it is a position at the country club or an elevated seat on the PTA, keeping up with the Joneses is their way of life.

Thomas is not ashamed of his lower middle-class roots. As hard as it is to grow up in such a wealthy town with not much at all, it offers a wisdom few in Bethel will ever possess—to be content with what you have and never want more than you need.

Everyone sandwiches in to get a better view of the parade. It is hard for Thomas to get anywhere. How will he find Betty in such a crowd?

"Watch it!" an old woman shouts, bumping Thomas back a few feet. She will not lose her place to him.

"Sorry." As Thomas retreats, he hears the sound of a beautiful laugh. Like that of a child being tickled. *That has to be her*, he thinks. His eyes widen with excitement. It is Betty's laugh. He pushes his way through the fur-covered crowd. *Where is she? Where is that laugh coming from?* "Betty," he calls out as he gets a place on the curb. He scans the crowd.

The Boys' Club marching band passes him in their neatly pressed blue-and-red uniforms. The bandleader screams, "Halt!" The entire six- through twelve-year-old marching band stops dead in their tracks. They raise their instruments into the air, waiting for the leader's next command.

Three clicks of drumsticks and a trumpet blast signals the beginning of their demonstration. The bandleader marches around in a circle, and the band plays the same song they have played for the last ten years.

"Company march," he commands, and they descend the avenue in unison. The proud tears of their parents, looking on, streak their cheeks.

The pounding drums, crashing cymbals, and trumpet calls drown out Betty's sweet laugh.

Frantic, Thomas begins walking up and down the street, looking at every face across from him. Behind a group of drunken men, a strange old man peers through the crowd, staring directly at him.

What the heck? Thomas pauses to wonder if the man is indeed looking at him.

The old man's strange eyes are dark, and his skin is pale and blotched from the stains of age. He tilts his head curiously and smiles.

Thomas looks away in hopes that he will stop. "Betty?" he calls out, trying to ignore his curiosity. He glances again across the street, but the old man is not where he once was. He is not gone at all though; now the old man stands in front of the crowd he was once many feet behind.

"It's not possible," Thomas whispers to himself. No one is that quick.

Thomas tries to walk away from the mad-scientist stare, but the old man's eyes follow him. "What's with that guy?"

The old man's head turns slowly, following his every step.

Thomas walks faster without looking in front of him. "Weirdo!" He crashes into a three-hundred-pound man, knocking his cup of hot chocolate to the ground.

"Hey! What's wrong with you?" the giant says angrily.

"I'm sorry, sir." Thomas quickly picks up the now half-empty disposable cup and hands it back to the man. He looks fearfully back across the street to see if the mysterious old man is still watching him, but he is gone.

"Just leave it alone, kid," the rotund man says, shoving the container back into Thomas's face.

"Okay, I really am sorry, sir," Thomas says, taking the cup with him. As he continues his search for Betty, he wrestles with whether or not he should drop the cup to the ground. The people of Bethel do not care what trash they leave behind. But Thomas is different. Instead of adding to the mess already littering the streets, he decides to look for the proper place to dispose of it.

Midget sports cars with men wearing champagne buckets on their heads race by, almost hitting Thomas. He trips over his feet to get out of the way and falls to the ground, spilling the rest of the hot chocolate on his sweatshirt.

"This is just great!"

"You okay?" an onlooker asks, biting his lip to hold back laughter.

"I'm fine!" Thomas gets up in embarrassment. He wipes the oval chocolate stain with his sleeve but fails to clean it away. "Shoot!" *Why does this always happen to me?* Thomas thinks sadly. He sees a trash can nearby. He picks the cup up and throws it away as many look on.

A spectacle is what he is. Some hide their laughter, some pretend not to see, but most point and stare at him like a freak at a sideshow.

Thomas shakes his head as the pressure of tears mounts behind his eyes. He grabs the sides of his hood, flipping it back into place. "Jerks!" he yells.

Once again, he hears that wonderful laugh. He jogs toward it. With each step, his anticipation builds, as does the sound of her laugh.

He sees her finally, not twenty-five feet from where he is, the only friend he has in the world. Thomas runs for her.

"Hey, watch it!" an old woman yells as Thomas brushes past her.

"Betty!" he screams and waves his hand back and forth high in the air to get her attention.

She stands with four of her new friends; each wear a cheerleader outfit. Their hair is in pigtails, their skirts are too short for their age, and their looks are sour.

"Betty, it's me!" he yells louder and waves his hands higher, finally catching her eye.

She waves back uncomfortably. Her friends give her a disapproving look.

Thomas quickly pulls down his sweatshirt hood and fixes his hair while Betty makes her way toward him. Her friends follow close behind. They mumble to each other and roll their eyes.

The palms of his hands begin to sweat. A childhood crush puts lightly how he feels about her, his first true love.

As she gets close, Thomas smacks his mouth open, as it seems to fill with cotton. "Hi," he says with a squeak.

"Hey, Tommy." There is concern in her eyes. It is not the concern Thomas is looking for.

"I, uh…I'm uh…" No words, only nerves. *Say something,* Thomas's mind prompts.

"I'm really sorry about your family, Tommy." Betty places a heavy hand on his shoulder. An electric tickle shoots through him.

"It's all right. I will…I'll be fine," he says bravely. "So you were in the parade, huh?"

"No, I wasn't. Why would you think that? I just came to watch with a couple of friends."

His heart drops. "Oh, I thought you would have…ah, forget it…" He fumbles.

"You thought what?"

Her friends giggle wickedly behind her. Their message is clear. Betty cannot be friends with someone like Thomas if she wants to be friends with them.

"I thought you would have come to the funeral. I thought you didn't come because you had to be in the parade," he says with disappointment.

Betty shakes her head as if Thomas does not get it. "Well, I still had to be here even if I wasn't in the parade!"

Betty's friends make it clear they are bored with the conversation.

Thomas continues timidly, "Well, it doesn't matter. It would have been nice if you were there. But it…it doesn't matter." He looks to his feet. Where is his courage to speak? He needs his friend. He wants support. Betty is all he has now. Where is the strength to tell her this?

"Well…" She nods uncomfortably. "It was good seeing you, Tommy." She turns quickly to leave.

Do something, Tommy! His heart cries as he sticks to the mud of inhibition.

Betty and company walk away.

He stands motionless. If he does not act now, he will never get this chance again.

"Wait!" Thomas cries.

Betty turns to him, confused. "What is it?" she asks awkwardly. Her friends stare on in judgment.

"I just...I just wanted...." He knows what he wants to say. Why is it so hard for him to do so?

She takes a few cautious steps toward him. "Is everything all right, Tommy?"

"Yeah, I'm, I'm fine...it's just..." His heart pounds in his chest.

"It's just what?" Betty is annoyed. She seems to care more about what her new friends think than for the true friend she has had her whole life. Where is concern for the hurting friend standing in front of her?

"Let's go," Brittney, the short blonde, commands, wrapping her arm around Betty to escort her off. "Bye, whoever you are," she says heartlessly.

"Maybe I'll talk to you tomorrow." Betty turns and follows.

"Why you can't you talk to me now?" Thomas asks, walking behind her like a sad puppy who does not want his master to go.

"Listen, Tommy, I don't think I can—" Betty struggles with her words. "You know what? Maybe you should just let me go." Her friends snicker as she dodges his questions.

Betty has news to deliver, bad news, but she does not want to share this with him today of all days.

"You don't think you can what?" Thomas asks pathetically.

"Oh, please. She's busy, okay?" The leader and dark-haired dragon of the bunch, Mary, makes her feelings clear.

"Mind your own business!" Thomas fires, out of character.

"You have problems, whoever you are!" She turns to Betty. "So do you if you stay with him. I'm gone, girl, gone!" Mary leaves with an annoyed flip of her hair.

Betty gets right in Thomas's face. Anger replaces the concern from before. "What is it, Tommy? Can't you see you are embarrassing me?" she says softly, so the queen bee Mary will not hear.

"Why are you acting like this?" he begs.

Betty's eyes drop to the ground. "Acting like what?" She dodges his question.

"Maybe you two lovebirds should work this out after all," Brittney cautions with a fake smile. "Oh, and when you're done slumming, Betty, maybe you can catch up with us. Ta." Brittney skips away.

Betty stomps her feet. "You see what you did?" She huffs and shakes her head. "Why do you always have to act like such a victim, Thomas? It's pathetic!"

"What did I do?" The color drains from his face.

"You just keep pushing and pushing and pushing, Tommy. Take a hint once in a while, will you?"

"Why don't you just tell me what it is I'm doing wrong so I don't do it anymore?"

"Just leave it alone, Tommy. Let me go with my friends." She turns to go, but Thomas stops her again.

"Stop doing that!" Betty pulls her arm away.

"Tell me what I'm doing wrong so I can fix it. Please, please don't leave me."

Betty's eyes roll in disgust.

"I thought we were friends." He pauses to worry. "We are friends, aren't we?"

Betty looks to the ground. "You don't understand, Tommy."

"I don't understand what?"

"Look…no one likes you, okay? No one, Tommy! Are you happy now?"

"Why would that make me happy?" he asks with the eyes of an abused puppy.

"I'm sorry…but everyone thinks you're a freak. Can't you see that?"

Tears finally fill his eyes. What is he supposed to say? He stands there, his heart growing empty.

"Look, I'm sorry. But I have to go."

"How can you say that to me? What did I do?"

"You didn't do anything, it's me…It's me, its not you. Okay? I just can't."

"You can't what?"

"Enough!" Betty demands. "Can't you see I want to be alone? I'm not like you, Tommy, and I don't want to be."

"Not like me? We've been friends for years. How can you say that? We were two peas in a pod, remember?"

"You see, Tommy...I mean, grow up. Two peas in a pod? Huh! That was like three years ago."

"Aren't we friends?"

The question hits home. Betty has no answer to give.

"Why won't you answer me? Answer me, Betty. Aren't we?"

Her eyes roll up from her feet, but she cannot look Thomas in the eye. "No. We're not friends, Tommy. Not anymore."

As if dropped from the heights of a roller coaster, his stomach churns with unbelief. "Why?"

Betty offers no reason. She just gives a cold stare, as if he had it coming.

"Why?" he cries louder. His tears blur his vision.

It is like a nightmare. They got to her. The town, the clique, they got to her. Now she is lost, and Thomas is truly alone in the world.

"But you're my best friend, Betty. You are my only friend. Without you, I have nothing!"

"I'm sorry." She walks away without saying good-bye.

"Please? Please, Betty, don't do this."

She just shakes her head and never looks back. She continues to place one foot in front of the other. The decision is no longer hers to make. Bethel's hooks are deep inside Betty's heart. What little compassion she has will make way for the pride of popularity and status.

The spirit of the town seems to corrupt the most beautiful of spirits. The lust for money and power finds its way into the hearts of all Bethel's children. They are taught only the strong survive, it is a dog-eat-dog world, and the early bird gets the worm if it beats down all others that are hungry.

Betty swallowed their invisible poison and must have become part of this ignorant herd long before this altercation. She is no longer who Thomas remembers. There was a time Betty didn't care what anyone thought. That time has passed her by. Now, she will be what everyone wants her to be. No longer choosing her friends, they will be chosen for her, as well as her enemies. She will only seek praise from those around her; it will not matter at what cost this praise comes.

Thomas watches Betty disappear into the crowd from where he had found her. "Good-bye," he says in a broken voice. Thomas backs away from the avenue and those surrounding it as he allows his tears to fall.

The Bethel crowd is too busy watching the parade to notice his pain.

In this moment of despair, John—the Goliath of the schoolyard whose awesome presence makes preteen-agers across the world shiver from fear—snaps Thomas out of his misery with a hard slap to the back of his head.

"Hey, Tommy, Tom-Tom...where's your bike?" John asks as his gang laughs hysterically.

"My...my...bike?" Thomas's vision becomes blurry. His head feels light.

As John and his lackeys laugh, everything seems to slow. Thomas sees a vision of the group vandalizing his bike moments ago.

How can this be? he wonders.

He shakes his head, trying to rid himself of the strange sights and sounds. The boys appear as animals in this vision, wild and relentless. They kick his bike, spit on it, and as John slashes the tires, his friends dance around it in victory.

John gives Thomas a shove, snapping him to attention. "So where is it, James? Where's that Kmart-special bike of yours?"

Thomas steps back. He tries making sense of what he pictured in his mind. "What did you do to my bike?" Thomas asks, rubbing his temples with his forefingers.

The question surprises John. "What was that?" he asks, confused.

"I said..." Thomas pauses, looking directly into John's bewildered eyes. "What did you do to my bike?"

His gang looks at each other in shock. "Are you accusing me of something?" John makes a tight fist and raises it in the air to demand an apology from Thomas.

It must be true, Thomas thinks as they react like convicted children caught with their hands in the proverbial cookie jar. *Is it even possible to know such a thing?*

"I asked you a question!" John shoves Thomas against the brick wall of the Trust Family Bank in anger.

Thomas's head bounces off it painfully. His neck twists.

John raises his pudgy finger and presses it firmly against the end of Thomas's nose. "If you're accusing me of something, you better have the proof to back it up, loser!"

Thomas is stunned. He cannot stop picturing what they had just done, as if he was there himself, watching the terrible scene.

"I asked you a question." John grabs the collar of Thomas's shirt and raises his large fist high into the air, ready to strike. "You accusing me of something, freak?"

A confidence comes over Thomas that he has never known. He begins to speak. It is beyond his control. "I saw what you did." he proclaims.

John releases his collar. Thomas called his bluff. "You saw what exactly?" John laughs. It doesn't matter if he saw what they did or not.

"You all wrecked my bike. I saw what you did!" Thomas scans the group, looking directly into each of their eyes. His stare forces their eyes away.

"Knock this kid out," John's pint-sized partner in crime, Pat, says while lighting a Marlboro cigarette.

Thomas returns to John. "And you ruin my bike the day my mother and grandmother are buried." Thomas stares into John's confused eyes. "Why?"

John's smile disappears from his face. "You better shut up, freak! I forgot about the funeral. You're lucky. Come on, guys, let's get away from this loser." John turns to leave, but Thomas stops him.

"Why do you hurt people?" he asks in a daze.

John crinkles his forehead. His gang looks to him for retribution for Thomas's accusation. But John is confused. Never has Thomas spoken this way. Never has anyone like Thomas stood up to John before. He merely stares at the boy he's picked on for many years.

"You gonna let this punk talk to you like that?" Pat flicks his cigarette at Thomas's feet and eggs the schoolyard general on.

John snaps out of it. He turns with a snarl. He grabs Thomas by the collar of his shirt again.

What feels like a great surge of electricity takes Thomas by surprise. He becomes nauseas. His body quivers.

"What's wrong with you?" John asks, noticing Thomas's eyes roll to the back of his head.

Thomas braces himself against the wall of the bank. He has another vision. This time it is the darkest hours of John's life. John's memories have somehow become his own. Thomas convulses as the bully's painful past plays out before him.

"What's wrong with the freak?" Pat asks, backing away.

John's pain, his suffering, and his loneliness are more than Thomas can handle. "No, no, no, no," he cries as he falls to his knees.

John backs away, unaware that Thomas is reliving the worst moments of his life, the sleepless nights, the tear-soaked pillows, the blood, the bruises, the welts, and the broken bones. John has secrets that Thomas now knows. His father abuses him, beats him down physically and verbally, whips him, and tells him he is no good.

No wonder John hurts those that are different, Thomas thinks.

"Cut it out, freak!" John screams.

Thomas snaps out of his vision. Thomas straightens himself, his red eyes blinking to focus on his adversary. The vision passes, but a lifetime of John's memories have somehow become part of Thomas as well.

"What the hell is wrong with him?" Pat lights another cigarette nervously.

Thomas no longer gives John an accusing look. He looks at this giant of a child with pity and love. John is not a monster. He only believes this because his father tells him so. How Thomas can see into the boy's past is a mystery to him, but he does not question it. He knows it is true.

"I'm outta here. You're messed up, James." John flicks Thomas's ear and turns again to leave.

"You hate it when your father picks on you. So why do you do it to me?" Thomas declares with a voice that, to Thomas, barely sounds like his own.

"What did you just say?" John turns to him with a nervous bottom lip.

"You hate being told you're nothing. So why do you tell others they are nothing?"

"You better shut up." John positions himself in front of Thomas. His chest begins to heave from embarrassment and anger.

"Being hurt doesn't give you the right to hurt others, John."

"I'm warning you!" the great bully says like a volcano about to burst.

Thomas continues without fear. "No, I am warning you. If you don't stop, you'll end up being worse than the very thing you hate the most—your father," Thomas finishes with authority.

"I'll kill you!" John lunges for him. He slams Thomas into the wall of the bank. He grabs him by the ears and throws him to the ground. Pinning Thomas's arms with his knees, he sits on his chest and slams his head repeatedly into the sidewalk as he screams, "I hate you! I hate you! I hate you!"

John's gang runs away in panic. The monster of Bethel has snapped, and no one is brave enough to intervene.

"Leave the boy alone," the peculiar old man from earlier demands. He pulls the crazed teenager off Thomas with ease and throws him back six feet.

John is shocked by the old man's strength.

"Touch not his hand," the old man demands in his distinct Romanian accent.

John fearfully backs away from the scene. "You're dead, freak. You are dead. Do you hear me? At school tomorrow, you're dead!"

Thomas does all he can to keep his eyes from closing as he fights the urge to sleep.

The old man shakes his head sadly as he watches John run off in tears. "Are you okay, child?" the old man says softly.

Thomas looks around him. Everything is blurry. He wipes blood from his upper lip onto the sleeve of his sweatshirt. He is woozy, dazed. "What happened?"

The old man raises Thomas to his feet. "This is why we fall, child. So we can pick ourselves back up again."

"I don't…I don't understand what happened," Thomas mumbles, touching the wounds on his face. He feels a large lump forming on the back of his head and remembers his visions.

Thomas has seen things about people before in his mind, but he always figures they are childhood daydreams and nothing more. What he saw about John, John's father, and even what the gang had done to his bike was different than anything he had conjured in his mind before. These visions had to be real.

Thomas rubs the back of his neck. "Why did I say those things?" he worries. Things will be worse for him at school now.

"There is always darkness before it becomes bright. I am telling you the truth. All things will work together for good." The old man draws Thomas close to him. He allows Thomas to rest his head on his bony shoulder.

Thomas begins to weep. The man pats him gently on his back. It is the first time Thomas is comforted since his family was taken from him.

"You need not cry, child. You need not shed a tear for yourself. There will be plenty of time to cry for those around you. They are the ones your tears are for," the old man encourages. "Be strong.

You are not like them. Don't expect them to be like you," he whispers softly in his ear.

The entire universe ceases to exist as the old man speaks. All Thomas can do is focus on his strong, kind voice. It draws him in like a sailor to the song of a siren. It is mesmerizing, as if the man speaks directly to his very soul. Thomas cries no more. Whoever the old man is, he must be right, because his advice is exactly what Thomas needs to hear.

"Now pick yourself up and walk, if that's what you want." The old man lets go of Thomas, allowing him to wipe the wet tears from his cheeks and take a deep breath.

Thomas knows he has to be strong. He slowly stands. He locks eyes with the man who has helped him.

"There you are… much better now, aren't you?" The old man brushes some dirt from Thomas's shoulders. "You are strong. I can see the strength in your eyes."

Thomas remembers the man. He stared at Thomas from across the street when he searched for Betty. The old man's eyes are a deep dark brown. They are completely dilated; the pupil hides the iris. His face is pale and pasty, his skin almost transparent. Dark, thick, pulsing green veins run down either side of his forehead. His nose is long and bony. It has a hook shape. White hairs sprouts from his chin, entangling it into a five-inch forest of a beard.

Thomas is numb. Chills race down his back and neck as he continues to stare into the old man's frightening eyes. He cannot move, but not because of his fear.

Around the old man, there is an aura-like warm glow. Thomas does not know if he is seeing it or feeling it. After taking a deep breath, the man says fourteen words that Thomas is not able to comprehend. "Unto you it is given to know the mysteries of the Kingdom of God," The old man says, lifting his right hand. He extends two of his elongated fingers and taps Thomas on his forehead twice. This is exactly what the strange homeless man had done to him on the steps of the church not two hours ago. "Soon, the truth will rise," the old man says with a sweet smile.

"What?" Thomas fearfully backs away.

"You've been asleep, Thomas, but the day is coming, and behold, the day is here when those that sleep will rise from their beds and the world will know the Lord is near. They will know it is God who sent you, Thomas." The man places his hand over Thomas's heart. "Rest. All will be well." He takes his hand away.

Thomas melts back against the wall of the bank for support. His eyes close as all his troubles fade away. He feels like he is floating in the calm waters of a warm bath. "How did you do that?" Thomas slowly opens his eyes.

The old man is gone.

"What? Where did he go?"

A vendor nearby spits tobacco into an empty soda can. He stares at Thomas as he looks around. He snickers while making an inflatable toad hanging from a stick and string dance for potential sales.

Thomas pushes away from the wall. The old man has vanished, just like the homeless man before him. He is gone, as is the sorrow that filled Thomas's heart. The old man took it with him.

Thomas walks to the vendor. "Where did the old man go?" he asks quietly.

"What old man, kid?" the vendor replies uncomfortably in his Brooklyn accent.

"The old man, you know...Where is he?"

"What?" he replies, surveying the area for customers in an attempt to hide the fact that Thomas is making him uncomfortable.

"The old man...the guy who picked me up and talked to me."

"Who are you talking about, kid? I didn't see any old man."

"The old man, I know you saw him. Everyone had to see him. What are you, blind?"

"Hey, kid, I don't know what the heck you're talking about." He pushes Thomas back from his cart. "Balloons here."

Thomas looks into his eyes and begs for an answer. "You had to see what happened. You were, like, six feet away. You probably saw me get beat up, and you didn't do anything about it. If it wasn't for that old man, who knows what would have happened to me. So just tell me where he is...please?"

Hearing the urgency in Thomas's words, the vendor leans in, calling for his ear. "I'm sorry to say this, kid. I did see what happened, but I didn't want to get involved. I saw you get beat up, and then that kid ran off...on his own. Then I saw you stand up, and it was like..." Confusion rises in the vendor's eyes.

"It was like what? What are you talking about? Just tell me where he is!" Thomas demands.

"You stopped crying, you stood up, brushed yourself off, and... you started talking to yourself, kid," the vendor does all he can to spare Thomas from the truth of what he had seen.

"Talking to myself? What?" His words shake Thomas to the very core.

"There was no old man. That's the truth, kid."

"What are you saying?"

"It's like you had an imaginary friend or something. Kid, you really freaked out a lot of people. If I were you, I would not do that in public anymore. Balloons here! Get your balloons and blowers!" Without even a pause, the vendor goes back to his work.

Thomas does not move. He notices the crowd pointing and staring. *What if the vendor is right? What if there is no old man?* Thomas worries. "What's happening to me?" he says to himself as he slowly makes his journey back home.

The crowd parts for the beaten child as he walks. He looks into the sky for an answer to his problems. But he now knows, if the answers are up there, the birds will have them before he does.

His head sinks as he arrives at his bike. As he suspects, John and his gang had destroyed it. His tires are slashed, his rims are bent, and the chain is snapped in two. It is beyond repair. His vision was real after all.

"How?" he mumbles in disbelief. How did he know what happened to his bike? How did he know what they had done? Could Thomas somehow be special? Does he have a gift that few, if any, have had before? Is this why he was visited by the strange men that he now believes no one but Thomas can see? Is this why everyone hates him?

These dark days have left Thomas with no family, no friends, and now the school bully waits to beat him within an inch of his pathetic life. Yet Thomas continues on with a peculiar feeling stirring inside him. Perhaps there is more to this story than Thomas is aware.

He leaves his broken bike behind and raises his head high with the hope that the end of his journey will be greater than the journey itself.

Without the dark, the light wouldn't be as bright.
Without tears, a smile would never feel right.
Without death, no one would appreciate life.
Without the naughty, how would we know the nice?
Without the blind, there would be no desire for sight
Compassion is birthed out of another's plight.
Be encouraged, for every wrong helps us to embrace what is right.

—Thomas James

IN SCHOOL THERE IS NO REST

The school bell rings; it is two thirty. The sounds of books closing and shuffling papers fill the air. The class celebrates the end of the day's lessons by shouting and pushing each other in jest. There is an added excitement in the air.

"Fight, fight, fight," some repeat in barely audible voices so the teacher cannot hear. Learning is not what is on their minds this day. This day, Thomas James pays for his crimes against the popular crowd.

The great bully, John, waits somewhere for Thomas outside the protection of his classroom. He is ready to make an example of the poor boy.

Thomas's eyes scan the classroom nervously. The desks are in rows of six and ten. The floor is speckled black and white, and there are stains from soda and cemented chewing gum all around. The classroom is not as dirty as it is aged. Paint peels from the corners in the ceiling, and cobwebs line the heating vents.

The school is as old as Bethel itself. Built atop a filled-in marsh, the rumor is the town will soon tear it down and rebuild; each year the school recedes at least one-half inch into the miry earth. There are also days, like today, that the smells of the old marsh bubble to the surface. If you did not know any better, you would think that someone or something has died under the school.

Faculty tells the children to ignore the smell. They say it is harmless. Eventually, those inured to it forget the stench. But this is not what concerns Thomas. The fear of what John will do to him if he is caught plagues his thoughts.

"Don't forget to study for your test tomorrow, everyone," Mr. Brooks demands from his large wooden desk. He places his reading glasses on and takes no notice of the group of children pointing and mocking Thomas as they leave.

Brooks is a short handsome African American man in his early forties. He has a thick, bushy black mustache and perfectly formed hair. Every day he stands out wearing his neatly pressed suits. However, he is infamous for his withered right hand. In private and in the hidden corners of the school, the children mock the stern teacher by calling him "hook" or "the claw." They share tales of a withered hand that possesses supernatural strength. They claim he uses it to choke the life out of those who do not turn in their homework on time. If only Thomas could have that power today.

Mr. Brooks is not a man to fear. He is someone to admire. He is a moral and just man who does not believe in violence. If Brooks knew of what Thomas faces because of his actions at the parade, John and his cronies would have to pay. The irony is Thomas would rather be beaten than tell on his tormentors. This is Thomas's fight, one he plans on avoiding.

All day he does an amazing job of keeping himself hidden from the group that threatens his life. He knows John does not use idle words. His gang will not let him forget how Thomas brought him to tears.

A reckoning is coming. The whole school knows this. If Thomas does not face John and his gang head-on, he will never be free from the looming threat of being beaten to a bloody pulp.

"He's so dead," whispers Yang, the pudgy Chinese boy in the class.

Thomas tries to ignore this as he slowly zips his backpack and swallows down the lump of fear in his throat. He sinks in his chair and buries his head in his arms until the last of his classmates leave.

His seat is in the back row. It is next to a cracked window overlooking the infamous woods that lead to the town dump. Frequently, Thomas gazes out this window, dreaming of the world and his place in it. Today, he only looks out this window to formulate his escape.

There is but twenty minutes until the last bus leaves. This is his only hope for survival.

John and his friends cannot miss this bus. They will give up their wait by then, and Thomas will be free, if brave enough, to walk home through those woods. Something Thomas has never done before.

As he looks to the clock, he wills its hands to move faster. The seconds seem to pass in minutes. The entire day feels longer than the rest. Perhaps the rumors of Thomas's demise drag it down.

The students interview John repeatedly, all with one question to ask: "What are you going to do to him?"

John's answer is always the same. "I'm going to kill him."

Thomas is the latest gossip. Every child wants to hear, talk, or laugh about him. Most do this to his face. They mock him as he eats his lunch alone in the corner of the cafeteria; some throw french fries at him while others tip his milk and take his only dessert. As Betty said, "Thomas is Bethel Junior High's biggest joke, and his new name is Dead Meat."

These children have no compassion. They have no remorse. They act like heartless beasts. Monsters—monsters is what they are. Nonetheless, Thomas never raises his voice against them. He never curses or tells. Instead, he prays they will change.

Thomas does not understand the delicacies of playground fighting. The unwritten law at Bethel Junior High is that once a dispute is manifest, the combatants have but twenty-four hours to settle their differences off school grounds. If either party refuses, then all bets are off, and the defaulting party will face a more severe punishment on school grounds.

Kids can be the most horrible of enemies if not taught better. John is the greatest of them all.

As he walks one block away from the school to the Judges Park playground, thirty children follow, wishing to gain his approval by cheering him on. The playground hides behind overgrown shrubbery and is the perfect place for a fight.

Thomas purposely wastes as much time as possible in Mr. Brook's classroom, hoping it will go away.

Seventeen minutes are left. His eyes focus on the clock until the sound of a throat clearing in the hall distracts him. It is John's gang. Three rough-looking boys stand, ready to escort Thomas to his place of correction. They are the SIN gang, meaning Strength in Numbers. If you are not friends with them or if you do not listen to them, you are not one of them. They will come after you until you do whatever they say.

Pat is the largest of the three. He is John's right hand. He wears black all the time and a cap that displays a skull and crossbones patch. Pat is the craziest of the crew. Rumors of his brutality are legend. They say he takes pleasure in blowing up frogs, cats, and other small animals with an M-80 and a match. Many wonder how long it will be before someone sends Pat to juvenile hall or to the place troubled teens go for treatment, Legirion Psychiatric.

When looking into Pat's eyes, it is hard for Thomas to see anything but a vicious thirteen-year-old child. His hard look and fierce eyes make the hairs on the back of Thomas's neck stand on end.

Pat positions himself outside the classroom door. Thomas alone can see him. His two friends laugh as Pat slowly drags his thumbnail under his neck. Their intention is clear. Thomas is going to pay.

"Just leave me alone, please, please." Thomas worries to himself. "Why are they doing this to me?"

Pat pulls back his jean jacket and reaches into his inside pocket. He pulls out a retractable knife. He opens it dramatically.

Thomas's skin crawls. Pat smiles as the blade shimmers in the fluorescent lights of the hall. Thomas wants to look away, but fear freezes him.

Mr. Brooks catches on. "Thomas?" Brooks looks to the hallway.

Pat quickly shoves the knife back into his pocket. The other two change their frightening looks to innocent ones.

Realizing what is going on, the teacher takes action. "Go home!" Brooks yells, slamming his book on the table in dramatic disapproval.

Two of the SIN gang runs off, but Pat is defiant.

"Do we have a problem here, Mr. Pirro?"

Pat exhales his answer. "Pssst, whatever, Brooks."

"Excuse me?" Mr. Brooks stands in disbelief.

Pat's chest deflates as the fiery teacher walks to him, a lion about to pounce his prey.

"I'll repeat the question. Perhaps you did not hear me the first time. I said, is there a problem, Mr. Pirro?"

Pat grimaces as the spit from Brook's mouth showers his face. "No, no problem"—he rolls his eyes—"sir."

Brooks forces the student to make eye contact. Pat does so arrogantly. "I don't know what's going on here. But if you are not out of my sight by the time I sit back down at my desk, and if I find out that you're up to something no good, not only will you be spending every afternoon with me in detention for the rest of the year, I will do everything in my power to make sure it's two years in a row." Brooks pauses. He searches every inch of the student, staring into his very soul. Pat's shoulders slouch. His eyes droop to the floor. "Are we clear, Mr. Pirro?" Brooks asks with authority.

"Yeah…we're clear," Pat mumbles.

Mr. Brooks lifts the bottom of Pat's chin once again, forcing the gang member to make eye contact again. "Excuse me?"

"I mean, yes, sir. I understand." Pat's arrogant look and pride-filled words are gone.

"So then get!" Brooks points toward the exit sign and then turns to enter his classroom again.

Behind him, Pat mouths the words, "You're dead." He raises his hand as if it is a gun and mocks shooting Thomas in the head.

Thomas closes his eyes tight, hoping for everything to end.

The door to the classroom shuts behind Brooks. "You can open your eyes now. They're gone." Brooks walks to his desk and leans against it. He folds his arms and clears his throat. "Hmm, mmm!"

"Sir?" Thomas's eyes shoot up.

Brooks motions with his fingers for Thomas to come forward and sit in the front center desk.

He slowly rises out of his chair. He worries that if Brooks asks about Pat and why they are waiting for him, things could get worse.

"Take Henry's seat, son." Brooks taps the desk three times.

In sitting, Thomas notices a worksheet Henry left behind. What strikes Thomas as odd is how Henry wrote his name. It reads "Inri Cutler."

Is Inri *Henry's real name? Is it a spelling mistake? If Inri is his real name, why does everyone call him Henry? Why wouldn't he want people to know what his real name is? And why does Brooks want me to take his seat?* Thomas wonders, feeling like he is somehow taking Inri's place in the classroom.

Brooks snaps Thomas out of it. "You know, you're not the first person to be picked on for being different, Tommy," he says with concern.

"I'm sorry, sir?" Thomas plays coy.

"I have eyes, son. I see all you go through, and it breaks my heart. But it is how I see you handle it that impresses me so."

"I don't...I don't know what you're talking about, Mr. Brooks."

"Look, you've been through a lot lately. I just want to let you know, it will get better. It does get better. You have to have faith, son."

"Okay." Thomas brushes his comments off. Brooks has no idea of his predicament.

"You know, my father led a small congregation in Alabama. We did not have much growing up, and people made fun of us because of what we believed. You see, my pop taught that God has a plan for all of us, that all of us would one day understand this plan, and that in God's timing, everyone, even the worst, would see the error of their ways and change—because they will understand that God has forgiven them and that their experiences had molded them into thinking they were bad, when they were always God's beloved."

"You believed this?" Thomas's ears perk up.

"That's hard for anyone to believe, Thomas. That's why they said my father was a liar. They called our church a cult, and then one day the leaders of the other congregations came after our Sunday service and burned the entire church to the ground." Mr. Brooks looks up as he remembers the day.

"That's horrible," Thomas replies.

"People don't hate because it's the right thing to do, Tommy. They hate because they do not know any better. And the only way they will ever learn to change is if they see an example of someone who truly loves and forgives, no matter what the cost. Like my father...like you."

"What do you mean like me?"

"It's just your nature, Tommy. I see how you act. It is a blessing, not a curse. There is strength in being weak. Remember that."

"But what if that doesn't change a thing?" Thomas asks with sad eyes.

"Oh, it will. It just may take time. For my father, there was no cursing the vandals or even dwelling on the tragedy. No, my father gathered family and friends together to pray for those who destroyed the church. Would you believe that one week later, the congregation got together, and within one month that church was rebuilt to twice its original size?" Brooks says with a smile. "So you see, even in our darkest hour, there is a plan. This is why we must never give up hope." There is concern in Brooks's eyes. He rests his good hand on Thomas's shoulder and feigns a smile.

Thomas is curious. "Is there something you want to talk about, sir?"

"Yes, yes there is." Brooks walks behind his desk. He pulls out a large dark-brown envelope and unravels the string holding its many papers inside.

"Did I do something wrong?"

"No, you didn't, son." He takes out a paper from the pile and places it facedown on the desk. He pauses for a moment to gather his thoughts, puffing his top lip out. "I'm worried about you, Tommy."

"I'm fine."

"I'm not just talking about your mom and grandmother passing, son."

"So what do you mean?" His voice sounds small in the large classroom.

"You're a very good student, and I am quite fond of you. I say this, Mr. James, because I want you to know that whatever you say here stays here, unless I tell you different. A man's word should be one that is trusted, and my word is my bond because of whom I represent."

"Whom do you represent?" Thomas laughs uncomfortably.

Brooks face is stone. "Someone who will hold me to what I say. But that's beside the point."

"Okay." Thomas fidgets in his seat.

"What's going on with you?" Brooks is as direct as a heat-seeking missile.

How can Thomas answer? He cannot tell on John and his gang. If he becomes a rat, it will be worse than any supposed crime committed before it. There is a code, and even if Thomas is not part of the school's social system, he knows he must be wise enough to play by their rules.

"Nothing, sir, everything is fine. I'm just very tired."

Blaming lack of sleep is his trademark excuse. His sleepless nights always leave dark bags under his eyes as evidence.

"And how did you get those bruises, Tommy?"

Thomas bites his bottom lip and lies. "Fell off my bike, sir."

An uncomfortable pause lasts a few seconds as Brooks stares at him curiously. It feels like a lifetime.

Thomas breaks the silence. "Is this about…my accident, sir?"

Brooks exhales his heavy answer. "No, son, it's about the essay you turned in last week."

"My paper?"

"Yes, your paper. Or I should say the content of it."

"What's wrong with it?"

"How can I put this?" His eyes find the ceiling. His bottom lip overtakes the upper in thought.

"Any way you want. I can take it, Mr. Brooks."

"Well, Tommy, your paper is…it's bleak. The content is worrisome. I was going to bring this to a social worker first, but I thought the best course of action was to speak with you."

"A social worker?" Thomas stands, upset.

"Now calm down, son."

"It was just an essay for creative writing," he insists.

"The world is coming to an end, Tommy?" He hands his student the paper to inspect. A large red *F* appears on the upper left-hand side of his paper. Thomas has never received a failing grade until now.

"An F?" Thomas needs this as much as he needs the hole John wants to put in his head.

"The assignment was to describe where you see yourself in the future. And yours was…well, Tommy…son…your paper…It is frightening. And to be quite honest, I don't understand why you wrote what you did."

"It wasn't meant to be scary." Thomas folds the paper up and places it in his book bag. "What did you expect?"

"What did I expect?" Mr. Brooks paces back and forth. "Well, I didn't expect all of humanity turning on each other like cannibals in the streets. I was not expecting your depiction of rape and murder as sport. I mean, come on, son. Blood being shed on every street corner?" Brooks stops his pacing to look directly into Thomas's eyes. "The assignment was to describe where you see yourself in the future. I was expecting a paper about you becoming a doctor, a lawyer, or an astronaut. Not about you becoming some martyr ushering in a new age." Brooks places his hands on the desk and raises his eyebrow, waiting for Thomas's response.

"I'm sorry." Thomas deflates back into his chair.

"I don't want an apology, son. I want to understand why you wrote what you wrote?"

"I wrote about the future, just not one that you would expect, that's all."

"So you're telling me that you actually believe this?"

Thomas needs to make a choice. Mr. Brooks wants to hear an explanation. He wants to hear what everyone wants to hear, that everything is going to be perfect. That is not how Thomas sees things.

The nightmare that taunts him each night convinces him that things are going to get worse before they get better. Like the strange messengers who visited him the day of the funeral said, it always gets darkest right before the light breaks through.

Thomas sees his teacher's concern. If he tells Brooks that not only does he have dreams of a world turned over completely to darkness, but that he believes these perverse days are soon to come, he might find himself carted off to Legirion and locked away with the other crazies there.

Thomas loves his teacher and trusts he would never try to do him any harm. He also knows that Mr. Brooks won't understand or believe what Thomas tells him is true.

"What does that mean, Tommy? A future I wouldn't expect?" Brooks makes his intentions clear by rounding the table to get the answer he seeks. "I want an answer, young man. I know things are hard for you right now. However, if you believe there is no hope...then, Tommy, we need to get someone for you to talk with. Someone who can show you there is."

"I never said there wasn't any hope. Didn't you read the end? Everything goes back to the way it was supposed to be. There is a point to it all, the suffering, the hate, the pain...It is all part of something bigger. I know there is hope, Mr. Brooks. I'm not some…some problem kid who needs a shrink. It was just a paper. I was…I was just being creative. It *is* creative writing, isn't it?"

What else is Thomas to say? Shall he say that based on his experience, he does not see hope for people the way they are? That he sees more things wrong with this world than right? That he cannot imagine anything getting better until it gets so bad that people have no choice but to change? The world Thomas sees is lost. Humanity must wake from this nightmare if there is ever to be hope for the future.

"I didn't say you were a problem kid, Tommy. I just want you to talk to me. Help me understand why you wrote what you wrote."

Brooks does not know that Thomas simply found a way to share with others what he has kept private for so long. It is the first time he has shared the intimate details of his dream. Thomas does not know if doing this will accomplish anything at all. However, disguising it as fiction and not the fact he believes it to be is clever for sure.

After realizing Mr. Brooks has dissected his paper like some mystic on a crystal ball, he knows there is only one thing to do. His vision must remain a clever story for those who do not have eyes to see the truth.

"Fiction…it's just fiction," Thomas answers plainly.

"Excuse me?" Brooks stops his foot from tapping.

"I just felt like doing something different. I'm sorry you took it the way you did. I didn't mean to worry you."

"You did more than worry me, Tommy. You presented yourself as a martyr who is put to death in front of millions watching around the world because of a book you wrote."

"Like I said, it's just fiction." Thomas winks and delivers a smile.

Brooks exhales in relief. "So this was all just made up? It's just a story?"

"Would you believe it if I told you it was true?" Thomas asks.

"Of course I wouldn't."

"Well then, why are you asking me if I believe it? I just wrote what I felt like writing. I'm sorry it worried you."

Thomas wraps his backpack around his arms and readies himself to leave before Brooks decides to question him more.

"Well, I have to tell you, young man. You are a great writer. Your description of everything is haunting, and at such a young age. You really have a gift. I felt more like I was reading an important novel instead of a class paper."

"Well, I did work hard on it. Maybe you can rethink that F then?" Thomas smiles again.

"We'll see." Brooks chuckles. "You know, the funny thing is, your paper kept me up all night thinking. To think that this world means nothing, that it is a clever trap, a testing ground, an illusion. That nothing that is seen is real, and everything that is not seen is real..."

As Brooks continues to speak, Thomas gets lost in the memory of his nightmare. As if he is transported there himself.

Near Future

"Burn! Burn! Burn!" the people shout as another layer of ash blankets the ground. The light from the enormous inferno splashes an eerie shade of red on the crowd's anxious faces. I watch in agony as they throw page after page of my book into this mountain of flames.

The air fills with the bitter smell of smoke. My eyes water. My throat swells. I stand here helpless for all to see. I am beaten and confused. My name is Thomas James, and I am doomed to die by the hands of hate because I have written words inspired by love.

"Death to Thomas! Death to Thomas!" the angry mob shouts as I quietly weep. They gather to watch the silencing of a voice that says a new day is about to rise.

I cry not for my life; I know I will lose it. Instead, I cry for those lost to the great darkness covering the land.

A wicked spirit spread its wings, and man has become vicious, filled with lust and pride. He commits unspeakable acts against others as well as to himself.

This is why I am here. I was told to pick up my cross as the one before me. By my death, people will hear the words of my book. By my blood, they will finally understand the mystery of our existence.

The Book of Thomas James—my book, which they burn before me, is not a work of fiction, as some will say. It is a fiery truth cast into the sea of deception mankind calls life.

I speak not of revolution in the world but of a revolutionized thinking. This is my calling, my purpose, and my tears are for those who call me traitor.

I remember how things were. The world is not what it once was. The courts changed when the Leader gathered the nations into one. The accused no longer can speak to their defense. Men who never knew me chose my fate. Things I said openly were twisted. People who once loved me claimed they never did, and everything I stand for they now call a lie.

The crowd cheers. The trumpet sounds. The guards cinch my restraints as the High Counselor of Dominion approaches. She is the reason for the shackles on my wrists and ankles. She is the cause for my many beatings.

She catches my eye as her guards lead her through the crowd toward me. Her cocky look fills with contempt. Today my blood will pay for the hours she spent manipulating the truth.

Stepping directly into the spotlight, she waves to the thousands in attendance. They roar as she points at me to turn her thumb upside down in what she believes is victory. The moment her thumb lowers, I alone see who she is and what she is—a host caught unaware by a clever parasitic enemy. I can see the devils hiding behind her eyes, using her as they see fit.

"Death to Thomas James!" the spoiled woman cries. The crowd erupts. She spits on the ground in my direction and licks her lips seductively. Chills race down my back, leaving every hair on my body erect. My time has come. My final moments in this world are here.

"That's the man everyone fears?" she asks in her arrogant British accent. "Doesn't look like much standing there...does he?"

She flips back her shoulder-length blonde hair and straightens her form-fitting, dark-navy jacket. Her low-cut sheer white blouse frames her large round breasts. The skirt of her business suit rides the top of her thighs as she walks toward me with the polish of a runway model. Her plump inviting lips are painted red, and I know behind them is the poison of asps.

Men in the audience stare with carnal desire as she is led up the carved stone stairs to where I stand. A guard grabs my hair and pulls my head back to get me to stand at attention.

The woman grabs the microphone from the black podium next to me. Prominently displayed on its front is the insignia of the Leader. This symbol now covers the world.

Tapping the top of the microphone three times, she quiets the crowd with a feedback squeal. She spits again in my direction, following her saliva with the same eerie smile as before. Our eyes meet. I know my moments in this world will soon be over.

"The traitor dies this night," she says calmly and confidently as the blackness of her sins swallows her eyes.

I alone can hear the demons cackling inside her as she does their bidding. The spirits that feast on her soul are like many I have seen before, but never so many in one host. Their sheer number makes the devils strong. She welcomes them for power, fame, and fortune, but does not know at what cost it will come.

She points to me, and the crowd stretches to see and hear more. "This man is not of a prophet. He is a liar," she declares, and they follow her words with nods of agreement. "There are still many that believe what he has written is true, after all we have done."

The crowd boos.

"He has convinced thousands into denying our glorious Leader, and in doing so they and their families are dead. We offer a life of peace, and Thomas tells you not to take from our giving hand. This man is a traitor!"

Their hate overwhelms me. It is hard to breathe.

She points like a cleaver chopping meat. "His lies kept food from children and medicine from the sick. His words came at a great price, and tonight, Thomas James pays that price for all!"

The crowd erupts in cheers.

My thoughts run wild. I knew this day would come. I knew those who stood with me would run, and those who hated me would try and silence what they could not understand to begin with. In this age, I was one of the first to wake from the deep sleep put on humanity. I am one of the Chosen. One of those called to bring light to darkness. To manifest truth to those who only know lies. They declare me their enemy as opposed to the liberator I was born again to be.

"Down with Thomas!" an older man cries.

"Death to Thomas!" yells a poor woman and her child.

This chant spreads like a cancer through the courtyard until it seems to echo for miles. Their thunderous screams make my teeth chatter as their blood boils over.

The High Counselor turns to me only to wink and raise her microphone a final time. "This liar wanted the spotlight and didn't care at what cost. So tonight we give him the spotlight he so truly deserves." She motions to the men stationed on the two towers above me. Immediately, spotlights shower the area for all to see.

As the lights focus directly on me, I am blinded to the people chanting, "Down with Thomas!" on the dried ground of Dominion's court below me.

"Let those still drunk from this man's foul wine know that tonight, his lies die with him. Death to Thomas!" She stands back to marvel at the crowd she possesses.

As my eyes adjust, I alone see her skin crawl from the seductive slithering of the demons in her flesh. They pleasure her with pride, and her reward is a sea of misguided puppets.

The final tide has turned, and the evil I had tried to fight with words has once again confused the world. On this night, I am condemned as a criminal, and they worship evil as a king. Nevertheless, I can remain silent no more.

"Stop this!" I shout, hoping they will listen. Their ears are far from me.

The woman turns her head toward me like a threatened snake. Her black eyes are cold. With disgust on her face, she motions for the guards to silence me.

The younger of the two takes an electric cattle prod and jams it into my ribs. My entire body convulses as the surge of its heat shoots through me like a hot knife. I fall to my knees and raise my head in confusion after biting through part of my tongue.

"Take me to him," she whispers with a devious grin.

As she approaches, the blood sliding down my throat makes me nauseous as it settles in my empty stomach. An anticipating fear grows inside me the closer she gets.

A putrid, stinging stench attacks my nostrils, causing my eyes to water. I alone can smell her. It smells like rotting garbage that has been baking in the sun for days. The devils inside her are foul and angry.

She parades her long legs in front of me. The guards pull the ropes again, restraining me further. Tied from my neck to my wrists, they choke me into submission. The woman leans mere inches from me, polluting me with her bile-scented breath.

"Years of silence, and now you speak?" She pauses only to slap my cheek with her diamond-covered hand. "You are going to die, and no one will remember you, you pathetic man. Even your family denies you. Poor Thomas, where is this great God you speak of when you need him the most?" She slaps me again, harder this time. Her heavy hand cups my ear and causes it to ring.

She moves in closer and licks the side of my face, caressing my thigh to arouse me. "You could have had it all." She rams her knee into my groin. I gasp for air as she spits directly into my right eye. "You're going to hang over the very flames your precious book has burned in."

As she laughs, the demons' repulsive faces come to the surface of her skin to startle me. Six heads grow where one should be, and on each of the heads a name of blasphemy. I grow itchy all over. My body temperature rises, and my throat begins to close.

"Your suffering has just begun," one demon says, splitting her tongue down the middle.

"Who will save you now?" another asks without her knowledge.

I try to answer, but my mouth fills with a rancid taste.

The crowd erupts in anger. "Kill him! Kill him!"

I look into the eyes of the beast hiding in the politician's womanly frame. "Greater is he that is in me than he that is of the world! Greater is he that is in me than he that is of the world."

This evil can take my flesh, but it cannot rule my spirit. It can take my life's work and burn it with fire, but it cannot take from me the life I have already laid down willingly.

"You have no power over me," I barely whisper, and the guards choke me back.

I fight to keep air in my lungs as they pull the rope tight around my neck. Its coarse hairs sting like a hundred bees as it rips into my skin and squeezes against my jaw like a vise.

"Kill him already!" a man screams from the crowd and throws a rock. It hits me in the leg. This gives others in the crowd the courage to find ways to do similar. Many push against the human perimeter keeping us separate.

"Guards, attend the crowd!" the Counselor demands. Quickly, what appears to be hundreds of uniformed men take their place.

"Look! The whole world hates you, Thomas." She purses her lips and mocks a kiss of betrayal. "Take him to the gallows!" she demands.

Patriotic music plays loudly; it comforts the crowd. The Leader himself will arrive at his high post to witness my death. Those in attendance feel an added excitement because of it.

The guards grab me violently and lead me through the courtyard like an animal to slaughter. The gallows are located directly above the bonfire built with thousands of copies of my condemned book. In the center of Dominion's Court is where I will hang.

Getting me to the gallows will take time. The multitude crowds the noose. They want their part in punishing me as well. As they lead me through the angry mob, I am slapped, spit at, and urinated on. I am cut with small blades, and a group of young children throw animal waste in my face from buckets their parents prepared for them. They hate me so deeply. They don't even know why.

As if in slow motion, the nightmarish images of those around me—hurting me, screaming for my blood—brings an unfamiliar voice to my head, one that makes me question, *Was I wrong? Have I made a mistake?*

My purpose, many said, was my delusion. Not truth. They called it evil conjuring, not the knowledge of God.

I shake my head. *Stop thinking, Thomas. Stop thinking!*

I believed I was born to change the world with words given to me from above. I dreamed about it, prayed on it, and finally set out to do it. I wanted to share a great truth that could set everyone free. I wanted to change the world with a single book. The very book they burn this day. The one I always knew would cost me my life.

We reach the tower. The guards quickly move me into position. They place me where a noose hangs quietly in the center of a grand stage. Spotlights from the surrounding posts illuminate it.

I stand a yard away from television cameras broadcasting to the farthest reaches of the world. The noose slips over my head and tightens slowly around my neck. The crowd cheers for more. I feel alone for the first time in so very long.

The guards attach the chains between my feet to a hook mounted on the metal trapdoor beneath me. The hatch heats from the books burning below it. My prison-issued rubber galoshes melt. The soles of my feet cook. The pain is hard to ignore. I move from one foot to another, trying to accommodate the pain surging up my legs and attacking my groin.

"Father, help me!" I cry as the guards laugh at my tears, joining the others in formation just six feet away from me.

It is the first time I am left alone since my arrest. I raise my eyes to the third tower across from me. It was built in honor of the Leader himself. The largest tower in the courtyard, it stands eighteen stories tall. The tower is sectioned in three groups. The top six are lined with pure gold, the middle six are lined with silver, and the bottom six are completely covered in iron. It will be in this great tower that I see the enemy in his greatest human form. I am terrified to do so.

The fanfare sounds the Leader's arrival. A dead silence falls upon the crowd. Large drums beat like a racing heart. A golden light showers his tower.

The large man, dressed in black, walks out from behind the four glass pillars filled with the smoke of those he burns as his enemies. He takes his seat on his ivory throne and waves to the thousands below.

A thunderous applause welcomes him. He shrugs off his black leather cape and exposes his chest, proudly displaying a coat of arms unique only to him: the face of a golden dragon engraved into a platinum shield of fire. This image is now the world's symbol of strength. Many say it can be seen wherever a man stands.

The Leader hushes the crowd with his black-gloved hands. His true name is Eilas Livedeht (pronounced, Elias Liv-dot), yet many have forgotten it because it was blasphemous to say his name out loud, unless one did so while looking in the mirror. Today he is simply known as the Leader, and he has come to watch me die because I speak against everything Livedeht, and those in his kingdom, believe.

His past is as mysterious as his rise to power. There is no record of his birth, no known family. It is as if he never existed at all. However, his entrepreneurial ventures brought him more power than the kings of old.

His armies won the last war, and now the world crowns him king. His reach of power extends over every inch of the globe. Those that worship him he rewards. Those that oppose him he kills. He ended poverty, famine, and now war, but man does not know that his victory is only found in their defeat.

The Leader holds one of the last copies of my book above his head. He displays it to the left and the right as he looks down upon his people.

The crowd screams, "Lies! Lies! Lies!"

He raises his fist toward me. He extends his thumb up and turns his hand upside down, as the High Counselor of Dominion had done earlier.

The crowd cheers.

He throws my book high into the air, farther, it seems, than what is possible by human strength. It lands in the bonfire beneath my feet.

"Livedeht, Livedeht, Livedeht," the crowd chants.

The High Counselor of Dominion licks her lips. Her face and the top of her chest become red with excitement.

The Leader smiles at his worshipers and rises to his feet.

He is a giant among men. His presence brings great kings to their knees. His words can convince a man to kill his own son, yet the crowd loves him so.

He approaches a group of microphones to give his much-awaited address.

"Today is victory," he boldly declares. "Today you stand with your bellies filled, pockets lined, and you are free from disease. Ten years ago, war raged. All fought for many reasons, and none resulted in peace. However, today there is peace, my friends. One goal leads to victory!"

The members of the overwhelmed crowd throw their hands into the air as if God himself speaks.

"We must put mankind above everything else. Are we to continue looking above for answers? Or are we ready to look to ourselves?"

If a pin were to drop in the crowd, all would hear it. They wait for his words as a homeless man would a bed in a shelter.

"We are the answer! Religion is not. Millions have died because of religion! God is not the answer. Millions more have killed in his name. We, my friends, we are the beginning and the end." He scans the crowd to make his point clear.

"We don't need promises of hope. We need promises that are kept!" A confident applause follows.

The Leader pauses to take pleasure in the effect his poisoned words have on the crowd. Folklore has it that he can convince men to take their own lives or to gouge out their own eyes.

"Today is victory. Today the promise of prosperity is at hand. Today we lay hold of a life that has no boundaries and let go of the suffering that faith and religion brings."

He motions for the members of the Coalition to file in behind him. They form a semicircle around his throne. They applaud the man who gives each of them a kingdom of their own to rule, under the laws Livedeht creates, of course.

"Today we boldly leap into a new era, an era where we live for man and not for man's God." The Leader pulls a large lever that brings to life one hundred more spotlights pointing in my direction. My execution is a message for those who search for life and truth outside the rule of Livedeht.

"Livedeht, Livedeht," the High Counselor chants from her seat.

The guards join in. "Livedeht, Livedeht."

"There can be no holy war if we fight for the same cause! There can be no holy war if we can claim there is no God to defend!" He slams his gloved fists into the podium to punctuate his sobering news.

I use every ounce of my strength to show Livedeht the soul he has no power over. I raise my beaten face, open my swollen eyes, and stare directly at his throne. My eyes meet his, and time seems to melt. Everything stops; there is no sound, no movement but ours—a moment outside of our gaze seems to pass in an hour.

A whispered voice rings in my ears. "I am your punishment."

I alone see the Leader grab the sides of his face and pull the flesh away to reveal the head of a serpent beneath it.

He blasts fire and black smoke from his nostrils, and my clothes burn away. I cannot breathe. I stand naked and burned before him.

"You cannot look into your God's eyes!" The serpent's booming voice drains the fluid from the drums of my ears, leaving me in muffled silence. A sense of falling comes over me.

"Pledge yourself to me." His words now force thick bloody mucus to ooze from my nose. There is no escaping the sound resonating in my head.

It is a nightmare from which I cannot wake. One I had dreamed before this moment came to be. One I did not know was a nightmare to begin with.

"No!" I scream in fear.

He pulls aside his coat of arms and rips a black heart from his chest. He places the heart above the council members' heads and squeezes. The black blood spills on them. They reach for it with an addict's lust as they hand Livedeht a black key from their blood-soaked hands. These keys will unlock the gates to the true kingdom of Livedeht.

"See no more!" The serpent roars, and my eyes melt from their sockets.

I try to behold the beast that is and is not and yet is—but I am blind. The crowd's muffled chants close in on me. "Kill Thomas! Kill Thomas! Kill Thomas!"

I can't block it out. The pain is too much to bear. My feet cook from the fire below, my flesh is ripped apart, the noose strangles me, and my naked body is exposed for all to see. The Leader casts me into a realm of complete torment, a place of darkness, and the murmured screams of those who want me dead.

"Father, why have you forsaken me?" I cry out, facing death as a man who cannot find his faith. I am so scared.

"Help me! Help me! Someone help me!" I shout as my thoughts run wild.

Where am I? What is real? What is not? Am I in hell?

I want this nightmare to end, but I don't know how to wake from it.

"Someone please…please…Help me."

Present

"Tommy?" Mr. Brooks snaps Thomas out of his dark thoughts.

"Yeah, no, I'm sorry. Go on." Thomas exhales heavily.

Brooks chuckles with relief. "I have to admit, I mean, your paper made me think. Are we all somehow sleepwalking through life, prisoners to a dark force, blinding us to the truth of who we all really are? Tommy, it is deep in there. More than I would expect from a normal twelve-year-old."

"I'm going to be thirteen soon. Does that help?" Thomas inches toward the door. He has got to get out of there.

"Next paper, let's try something a bit brighter, shall we?" Brooks extends his left hand for Thomas to shake as a way of sealing the deal presented to him.

"Sure." Thomas extends his right hand instead of his left.

Brooks is surprised. Never before has someone offered to embrace his deformity. He pulls back his left and offers his withered right. "You're a good boy, Tommy," Brooks says with a proud look in his eyes.

As the two shake in silence, Thomas decides that from this day forward, he will keep the truth to himself. He will hide it away as a clever story, a parable. Until something, or someone, tells him different.

As an empty cup cannot help those that thirst, a selfish deed makes things worse.

As it is difficult to find rest without a bed, you will never know peace with thoughts of anger in your head.

As the one who plants receives the fruit of their labor, those who help others will always find great favor.

Consider not the bad, but look always for the good.

Do not do what others ignorantly do, do what you should.

—Thomas James

Between Life and Death

The door to Mr. Brooks's classroom swings open. Thomas exits quickly. He stops for a moment in the hall to see if the coast is clear. There is no one to his left, no one to his right. He spies the stairs leading to his locker on the third floor.

If he can get to his locker, drop off his books, and grab his coat without John's gang seeing him, he might have a chance to hide in the janitor's closet in the basement.

"Please, God, don't let them be at my locker," Thomas whispers as he runs to the stairs. His time is short to escape. With most of the teachers leaving for the day, not much can stand in the SIN gang's way.

As John's minions patrol the school waiting for Thomas, John waits for his victim at Judges Park.

Thomas knows they won't think to look for him in the janitor's closet. It is the one place no one will look. Few know where it is to begin with.

There, amidst the dirty hanging mops and the smell of chlorine, is a small clock radio hanging from a dirty chain on the wall. Thomas knows this because it will not be his first time hiding there. He will listen to the radio as he waits for it to be safe to go home. Then Thomas will do what he has never done before—he will bravely make his way home through the woods next to the garbage dump. The smell in the school is nothing compared to the stench of the manure and rotting food filling the air there. But this is the least of his concerns.

Few venture into the woods after dark, which is why Thomas chooses this dangerous path to find his way home. Not even the great bully, John, will enter without the protection of sunlight.

Many say a ghost of a man found dead in the center of the small forest years ago haunts the woods. He was found hanging from a large willow tree, slowly swaying back and forth above the now-polluted stream that runs through the woods and eventually makes its way to Lake Bethel, the town's water supply. The dead man's eyes, ears, and tongue were all missing, as were his hands and feet. The slightest trace of blood eluded those searching for the truth. He was drained dry, swinging from the sad tree above the waters, and his blood poured out for all those in the town to drink. The man's death was easily ruled a homicide, although no evidence was found. His name remains a mystery, while the cause of his death is now a frightening story to tell.

Many claim to hear the sounds of weeping and wailing coming from inside the seventy-acre forest on many a cold night. Frightened children run from the woods screaming that they came face-to-face with the man whose death, they say, soured the waters.

Thomas, like many others, is scared to enter the woods after dark. But on this day, what other choice does he have?

He can only imagine what evil waits for him inside the bowels of what was once called Lyons Belt. It was a place known for romance and discovery. Lovers met there and carved their names into the beautiful green trees after walking hand in hand through a place that seemed almost magical.

Now the trees are gray; their branches are black and barren. The path through the woods is littered with papers, cans, and cigarette butts. The carved names of lovers in the trees succumb to the sprayed paint of prejudice, hate, and pride. Where children once walked to collect fallen leaves blanketing the ground with gold, red, green, and yellow, now dealers of drugs from the neighboring towns wait to entice the young to enter the woods for different reasons. The pure water of yesterday is muddied with tires, oils, garbage, and sludge. Perhaps the man's death did bring change to Lyons Belt. The woods chose to die with him that day.

Thomas will enter, regardless, to find safety by traveling through a place that is not safe at all.

He reaches the third floor in a flash. Thomas throws aside the impressive steel door with the strength of ten men, or so he believes.

Coast is clear! No one is in the hall. He fantasizes that they took pity on him and hopes he can avoid his journey into the haunted woods. Reaching his locker, the reality sets in. They most certainly will not.

"I can't believe this." His heart sinks. "Why won't they leave me alone?" His eyes fill with tears and his stomach with the crashing waves of fear. Written in crimson permanent marker on his locker are three very large letters.

DIE

"They want me to die?" Thomas cries, slapping the locker with his right hand. He looks down the hall at the other lockers; not one is marked as his. It is the work of John or Pat. Their message is clear, and if Thomas does not do something about it, everyone will see the scarlet letters, and tomorrow will be worse than today.

Quickly, he hurries to the bathroom. He will wash away the stains placed there by his peers. Once they are gone, no written reminder of how much they hate him will remain. He enters the boys' room to the smell of urine and stale cigarettes. It tickles his nose and causes him to gag. His eyes tear as he lifts the neck of his cotton shirt and raises it above the bridge of his nose.

He cautiously walks to the back, looking under each stall door to ensure he is alone. A toilet overflows at the very end. He cringes at the sight of the soiled soggy paper gathering around the legs of the stall door.

"Gross."

He winces and carefully maneuvers through the large pool of dark water flooding the area. He tiptoes through it to the paper towels hanging on the back wall. His cotton shirt can no longer hide the smell. He hikes up his jeans, trying to keep his garments clean.

"This is nasty!" he says as the percussive beat of the last faucet drips behind him.

He straddles the worst part of the puddle and slowly takes towels from the dispenser. Then with a bunch in hand, he moves his front foot back in a careful retreat from the scene.

Careful, Tommy, careful.

He takes his last step, and his foot slips. He fights to balance himself, but to no avail. Thomas crashes instantly into the disgusting toilet water below.

"Great!"

He picks himself up and flicks the foul water from his hands. It drenches his sleeves and blackens his faded blue jeans.

"I knew this was going to happen!"

In his anger, he kicks the stall door next to him. It bounces back and slams into his shoulder.

"Ow!"

The foul odor now covers him completely. There is no need to worry about getting dirty now. He is in the thick of it.

"This is disgusting!" He gags. His mouth fills with saliva, anticipating the vomit that may soon come. He swallows and calms himself as he returns to the towel dispenser to grab another handful.

Wet footprints follow him as his shoes squeak and squish with every step he takes toward the leaking faucet. He looks at the metallic dispenser where the pink liquid soap is stored. Thinking of how large the letters are, he knows it will take lots of soap and water to do the job.

As he pulls the lever on the dispenser, the soap squirts onto the towels, and the brown paper becomes pink in the process.

That will do, he thinks and places his hands on the dirty porcelain knobs of the sink to turn the water on. The knobs' rusty metal resists Thomas as he squeezes and twists. Something snaps, and the water rushes out as if open to high blast.

"It's about time." He places the soapy pink towels under the water briefly and then lays them on the adjoining sink to turn the faucet off. He turns the knobs round and round, but the water remains fierce. The faucet is broken.

"You have to be kidding me."

The sink also clogs. The water level is rapidly rising. Frantically, he begins to turn the knobs again. The harder he tries to tighten the knobs down, the looser they seem to get.

"Great! This is perfect!"

The water spills to the ground. Worried he will be in trouble for breaking the faucet, Thomas decides to tighten the loose knobs, come hell or high water. Literally. He grabs the dirty porcelain knob in his hands as tight as he can. Positioning his body above the sink, he uses his weight to force the knob back down into its groove. He places his left foot on the adjoining sink for leverage and begins to pull and squeeze. His fingers act like a vise. Slowly the knob gives way. His face is red. His knuckles are white. Under his stretched skin, the veins in his arms fill like the branches of a tree.

"Almost there..."

Thomas becomes weak. If he does not beat the knob soon, it will most surely beat him. He takes a final breath, gets a better grip, and counts. "One."

He makes the position of his feet secure.

"Two."

He leans back, getting ready to lunge forward as fast as he can to tighten the knob down.

"Three!"

With everything he has, he throws his entire body forward. The knob snaps off completely. It happens so fast, Thomas does not have a chance to react. The momentum pulls him violently forward, into the mirror above the sink.

The sound of the knob snapping in two is mild in comparison to the loud dull thud of his head crashing into the mirror on the wall. Mirror glass shattering only adds to the sound of Thomas screaming as he falls to the floor. His head slams as he lands, cracking a floor tile in the process.

A large spiderweb crack is in the center of the mirror. Small amounts of Thomas's blood left from the impact seeps into it.

In a daze, he lifts his head from the floor.

"What happened?"

Slowly he rises. His head feels like a hot iron is searing it. The sensation of a warm thick liquid runs down the side of his face. Believing it to be the water from the sink, he ignores it.

In getting to his feet, his stomach twists as if he is falling from the pinnacle of a roller coaster. Thomas straightens himself but continues to feel woozy. He is unaware of the blood pouring from his right temple. He makes his way to the sink. The blood oozes into his eyes, forcing him to squint and reach for the sink like a blind man.

Finding the overflowing basin, he submerges his hands into the water and begins to splash a good deal of it on his face and head. The blood washes down from his wound into his mouth. He spits it out, not knowing what the metallic taste is. Slowly, he opens his eyes. The room blurs in and out of focus.

Water shoots straight up from where the knob broke off.

"Oh no."

Fear overcomes him the instant he sees the severity of his injury. Blood covers his face and stains his shirt. From his temple the blood squirts out, pulsing with each beat of his heart.

"Oh no…oh no…oh no…what do I do, what do I do?"

He is frozen. Searching for options, he finds none. He tires quickly; even raising his hand to hold the blood back becomes a difficult task.

"Oh no, oh no," he whimpers as his legs turn to jelly and his head becomes heavy.

His breath shortens. His hands finally fall to his side, allowing the blood to flow freely. His knees wobble back and forth. Thomas knows he is in trouble. He tries to cry out but cannot find the voice.

The room circles him. Slowly, he lowers himself to the ground, wanting now just to rest, if only for a moment. If he rests, soon he will sleep. However, Thomas doesn't know that if he sleeps, he may never wake again.

Thomas tries to speak. He cannot find the strength. He can only whisper, "Help, someone, help…"

A mighty wind rushes into the room with a squeal from the window overlooking the dead woods. The floor seems to shake below him as darkness crowds his sight.

It feels like an army of butterflies flap their wings inside his stomach. His eyes roll into the back of his head.

Thomas relaxes into the floor.

Sharp pains attack his body. His muscles constrict. He convulses uncontrollably, yet his mind processes everything as it happens. His body flails around like a great fish taken from the waters of a raging sea.

In this place, between life and death, he hears a sweet voice.

"Let go." The voice is his grandmother's. "Let go, child. Let go."

His body continues to shake violently. He is scared to die. He does not want to give up the only life he has ever known, even as pathetic as his life is. He still feels the need to hold on as long as he can.

"Let go, Tommy," his grandmother begs again. "In fearing the dark, you give it strength."

Her words trail off, and finally it happens. Thomas lets go.

There is silence. His body stops convulsing. His pain is gone, as is his fear, and Thomas is still alive.

How can this be? Am I dead? No, can't be, he thinks. *A panic attack. That is what it must be. It wasn't as bad as I thought.*

Thomas opens his eyes and gets to his feet. The room seems brighter than before. The foul smell of it is gone.

"That's weird," he thinks as he looks around.

Everything is the same, but it feels different. He reaches for his head and cannot feel the cut that was there moments ago. He looks to the ground. What he sees seems unreal.

On the flooded floor beneath him, Thomas sees himself. His body lies in a pool of dirty water and blood. His eyes are rolled into the back of his head, and vomit covers his chapped lips.

How is it possible?

He bends down curiously and studies the empty shell of what he once was. He reaches out his right hand to touch the broken frame. He notices the new color of his arm. He studies his new flesh in amazement. It is so bright. It glows. He holds his hand in front of his face and marvels at its beauty. It is pure and soft. It is radiant. There is not a hair on it—smooth as a baby's skin and the color of pure milk.

He inspects the rest of his body. Sinewy muscles cover his once-frail frame. His genitalia is gone. He has become androgynous. However strange it seems, what Thomas is now is no bother to him. It excites him.

Hovering above his once-childish body, he takes pity on it. Oh, how lost the soul of Thomas was. He never knew he had always been perfect inside. Understanding dawns. He was never the fleshy shell lying on the floor in a mess of blood, vomit, and waste. He was not the boy John and others taunted, or the child who lost his family and only friend. He was not who he thought he was at all. Yet he and this poor boy are the same.

No longer a child or an adult, Thomas just *is*. Like waking from a nightmare and finding the comfort of his true reality, Thomas feels alive for the very first time.

He turns to the cracked mirror. The glass fuses together and catches his glorified image. It reflects a bright light in all directions. His presence fills the room and steals the darkness of this place away.

He examines himself in the mirror. His eyes are piercing blue with no pupils. There are no wrinkles, blemishes, or scars. His movement is poetic. He takes a step. His feet never touch the ground. It is not like walking at all, actually. He glides now. Gliding above the foul waters where his old body lies.

"Who am I?" Thomas says in a voice unfamiliar to him. It is a voice that sounds like many in one. The beautiful harmonies of his words echo around him.

The world he once knew seems foreign to him to now. None of it makes sense. It is tragic, really, to never know the beauty of what hides away inside of humanity. Like a treasure hidden in earthen vessels. The visible world is more like a trap than reality, more like hell than the paradise many believe it to be.

Thomas cries. He is so grateful. *Did I have to die to truly live?* he wonders, no longer feeling the pain and suffering of his past.

He now knows nothing exists but love. Love is the only constant. Love is the only truth and only reality. His tears gather and float in the air before him. They dance, forming a large, round, powder blue orb. It rises to the ceiling of the bathroom.

Thomas stretches out his entire being and lets the waters empty from his once-blind eyes. Like a crystal water balloon, it fills. The orb grows with his joyful tears until Thomas stops, only to watch it float like a graceful jellyfish above him.

He softly runs his fingers through the orb down the middle. Two perfect halves remain. They are mirror images of the other.

One floats above while its twin sinks below. Apart from each other, they will never be whole. Thomas grabs both halves and places them in his hands. He links the waters together and throws it above his head. A bright rainbow explodes in its place. The wonder of this moment is stolen away by the sound of police sirens. Thomas turns to the entrance of the bathroom. He had not seen the janitor who found Thomas's body after water spilt into the hall.

The janitor points to Thomas's lifeless body on the floor and says, "He's in here...the boy is in here. This is where I found him. He's hurt bad."

Thomas stands in front of the frantic man in his glorified form. He slowly waves but the janitor sees right through him. Thomas can no longer be seen, or heard, by the eyes or ears of mankind.

Time passes in an instant.

The room fills with people working hard to save the flesh body on the bathroom floor. Thomas watches curiously as paramedics quickly load the body on a gurney while forcing air into its lungs.

A crack of lightning steals his stare away. Looking up, the ceiling tiles fall one after another to the ground. They pop like popcorn from above and shatter around everyone below, and no one but Thomas is the wiser.

The ceiling cracks down the middle and separates, as if being peeled away. Behind it, a new sky appears. The bricks of the walls vanish, as does the rest of the foul bathroom. Those in the room crumble to dust. A strong wind blows it all away. Thomas is left alone to gaze into the tremendous sky above him, one that no artist could render.

It is rich, like emeralds shimmering in a field of colored light. It moves back and forth like the tide. Never still, it seems more like an ocean.

"Amazing," he says, titling his head like a child looking at a skyscraper for the very first time.

A trumpet sounds. From the many-colored waves appears glorious beings swimming in and out of them. The creatures are like Thomas—different yet somehow the same. Each has the face of a man. They all hold rods of iron and wear golden crowns. This is what makes them different from Thomas. He has no crown to speak of yet. They seem to dance back and forth in celebration above him. They smile as they look at him, as a mother would a newborn babe.

"How can I join you?" Thomas asks.

Their celebration suddenly ends.

"Can't I join you?" he begs.

They float in silence and slowly shake their heads.

"Why?" Thomas cries as he hears another crack of thunder. This time it is louder and closer.

Thomas feels a pull from deep inside him. Like a moth drawn to a flame, he follows it away from his brothers and sisters in the sky.

In the twinkling of an eye, he is caught away into a dense forest filled with thickets and thorns. His feet land on the muddy earth. He is trapped in the center of this dangerous place. The razor-sharp trees close in around him. The bright light slowly turns to the gloom of night.

"Where am I?" Thomas fearfully asks, his glorious body beginning to return to his original fleshly form.

"You're lost, Thomas," a kind voice answers from deep within the woods.

The voice sounds as if it came from his mind. It is more like a whisper, like a thought—his thought—yet it is not him.

He walks deeper into the woods, cutting himself on the many thorns in his way.

"Come to me," the soft voice continues.

Where will he find this voice in the dead woods? "Where are you?" Thomas asks.

"I am, Thomas," the voice thunders back. "Look up!"

The forest shakes as the words thunder around him. Thomas raises his eyes to find a waterfall made up of twelve different waters from twelve different mountains. They are the reason for the clearing in which he stands.

"See me!" the voice booms.

"What do you want me to do?"

"Lead." He hears the voice in every direction. The word is like a fire searing his tongue. Thomas realizes the word has come from his own mouth. He is the one who spoke it.

"I don't understand! I don't know what's happening!"

His head becomes light. It is too much to comprehend. He becomes dizzy. The woods seem to spin around him. He tries to brace himself, but there is nothing for Thomas to hold. He presses his hands against the sides of his face and cries, "What's happening to me?"

"You are blind, Thomas." The answer is given. Once again these words come from deep within him. Thomas is answering his own questions with a voice he is not familiar with. Slowly the flesh of his youth returns. It begins to cover every inch of his glorified new body. Thomas tries to shake it away but cannot.

"What's happening to me?" Thomas cries again, not wanting to return to the body that once trapped him. "I don't want to go back!" he screams, trying to tear the skin away as it crawls up him.

"You have chosen sleep, but soon you will wake, and you will be my witness."

"Please, please, I don't want to go back," Thomas begs as the prison of his youthful flesh seals the very last part of his glorified body. "No!" He falls to his knees in shame. Thomas looks above to find a way out of his suffering. Instead, he sees the waters cut off from the land and the mountains cast to the ground beside him. Only a decaying forest remains.

Dead trees everywhere he looks, trees like withering men with eyes that can't see, ears that can't hear, hands that won't stretch forth, and scales that will never fall away. Dead trees that remind him of the dead man found hanging in the center of Lyons Belt.

"What's happening? What's happening?" he cries and shuts his eyes as tight as he can.

"Lead," the voice demands, using Thomas's tongue again. Fire shoots from Thomas's mouth, clearing a small straight path through the dead woods.

In the distance in front of him is paradise. Behind him is a wasteland.

All Thomas needs to do now is open his eyes and let others see what he sees. If he does this, he will prepare the way for others to hear the great voice sleeping inside them all.

Awake, oh sleeper, why continue to rest your head?

From eternity you fell, deep into a hell where nothing is perfect and you live as if dead.

Arise, arise, oh sleeper, why continue to cry and lament?

If you only knew what was true, you'd create new worlds with your thoughts and words that are said.

You are more, you are more, the center of everything, the beginning and the end.

From you, your dreams can come true, but your dreams to this world you do not lend.

Yours is the tale of the brokenhearted, yet all along your victorious song has been hidden deep within your sleepy head.

So awake, awake, oh sleeper, and rise from the dead.

—Thomas James

Until Eyes Are Open

Six Years Later

June sixth. Police guard the entrance to the Bethel Memorial Coma Ward. An uncomfortable silence filters through the hall.

Lauren—the fit blonde twenty-six-year-old nurse—stares blankly at the clock on her station desk, lazily hunched over in her chair. *It is only 11:00 a.m.?* she questions as she unrolls her shoulders and look around the nurses' station to make sure no one can hear her. "Just one hour, and he's dead," Lauren whispers quietly to herself before taking a large bite of her tuna fish sandwich. She chews with her mouth open and rolls her eyes to one of Thomas's monitoring screens.

"What the—" she screams, spitting tuna and bread into the air.

"What is it?" Nancy, the sixty-two-year-old African American nurse, yells back as she pulls fresh linens from the closet.

Lauren stands slowly in amazement. "It's Thomas James. He's…he's…"

Nancy turns to her. "I don't have all day, darling."

The color drains from Lauren's face. "He's waking up."

"He's what?" Nancy's heart sinks. She quickly walks over to Lauren to see if what Lauren says is true.

"Look." Lauren points her shaking limp right hand at the screen.

Nancy looks closely and finds a frail and sickly Thomas James lying in a hospital bed. Attached to multiple machines, he is no longer an awkward twelve-year-old boy. Thomas is eighteen. He is disturbingly thin, skeleton-like. His hair is long, shoulder length. It looks like it has not been cut or combed in months. His complexion is fairer than fair. His fingers twitch and his eyelids flutter as if he is waking from a bad dream.

"It's not possible." Lauren drops her sandwich to the floor, and her jaw slacks.

A chill comes over Nancy. She shudders from it. She walks closer to the monitor slowly; her eyes widen as she fixes them on the screen.

No one believed Nancy when she explained to the doctors and staff that she knew in her heart this day would come. Nancy knew Thomas would wake. More importantly, she also knew when. Those she told had said her faith was in vain. Nancy had not told them why she believed such a thing. Nancy never told them about her strange visitation.

If Thomas is awake, then what Nancy saw and heard not three weeks prior is real. And if it is real, then she knows everything is about to change.

"See?" Lauren moves aside to give Nancy a better view.

Thomas's eyes open. His head slowly turns toward the camera monitoring him. He stares into its lens.

"Holy Jesus." Nancy drops the linens from her hands. They gently float to the ground and blanket her feet. She reaches for her face and cups her cheeks with her pudgy hands. It is as if Thomas is staring directly at her.

"What are the odds of this happening now?" Lauren asks, backing away from the desk.

In less than one hour, the state is free from its obligation to keep the comatose boy alive. In less than an hour, Thomas is supposed to die after they pull his proverbial plug.

"The press is going to go bananas!" Lauren laughs. "This is crazy." Lauren runs to the phone and presses the page button.

"What does this mean, Lord?" Nancy says in a barely audible voice. Her eyes fill with tears. She reaches for the monitor and gently caresses the image of the boy she has been caring for these many years.

"Dr. Adams to room 222M immediately...I repeat, Dr. Adams to room 222M immediately." Her page echoes throughout Bethel Memorial Hospital.

"I knew it...I knew it....but I never really believed." Nancy's voice cracks. Reaching inside her blouse, she pulls out the gold crucifix that hides between her large breasts. She rubs the gold cross between her thumb and forefinger. "It's a miracle. He's alive. My god, my god, he's alive!"

The halls immediately come to life. The silence is gone. Doctors, nurses, and interns rush to the scene. Police fight to hold the press back at the entrance. Flashes of light from their cameras illuminate the halls. Everyone is frantic, everyone except Nancy.

She stands still with tears of joy rolling down her cheeks. "They didn't believe you, Lord," Nancy says with a smile and closes her eyes. "They'll believe you now."

The child ran into the backwoods and ducked under the tree his parents planted to hide.

"Who am I?" the child cried.

"Who am I? Who am I? Am I really bad, or did my parents lie? What must be done so I may again have fun and rid myself of this sad feeling inside?"

He grabbed an overripened piece of fruit dangling from the tree, wondering if he'd grow up to be, as his parents wandering around in a world of misery.

That thought alone made the child want to scream, "Am I doomed because I've been groomed to believe everything people say about me? Or is there a way I can escape this agony?"

It was then the sunlight broke free from the sky, prompting him quickly to wipe away the tears he cried.

In that moment, in that twinkling of his eye, he heard a new voice called Wisdom inside.

"Perhaps you are more, perhaps you can be more, perhaps you always were more," this voice began to cry.

It was then the child put down the overripened piece of fruit, recognizing it as a voice of truth inside, and promised never again to choose his parents' tree to hide.

—Thomas James

Yet There Is Hope

Three Weeks Prior

Nancy hums an old-fashioned gospel song as she washes her hands in the bathroom of her studio apartment. She faintly hears the preacher on the television set in the bedroom. "What's that man saying now?" she asks with a chuckle as she grabs a towel from the wall. She dries her hands. Curiosity motivates her to walk to the edge of her bed and look on.

On the television, she sees a fancy-dressed preacher speaking to what looks like a sea of people. "The Lord wants to bless you," the preacher says. "There is no need to suffer. You can have that new car. You can afford that new home. There is no disease God cannot heal. There is no problem too big for the Lord to solve!"

The crowd cheers as the preacher pauses for effect. He waits a moment until the crowd settles. He reaches out his hand, extending a finger toward them. From one side of the auditorium to the other, he slowly points to everyone in attendance. A dead silence follows. A small smile creeps unto the preacher's face.

"Hook, line, and sinker," Nancy whispers as she shakes her head in disapproval.

The preacher raises the microphone to speak. "But you need faith. And you must show that faith by giving all you can give to receive the harvest that God has waiting for you."

Nancy leans forward and fixes her eyes on the crowd.

The thousands there begin to wail. Some cry, others cheer, but almost all raise their hands and wave as if God himself speaks.

"Look at all those people, Lord," Nancy says in disbelief.

The music swells. Like a sorcerer or some master puppeteer, the preacher beckons those that are sick and hurting on to the stage. They crowd the altar. One by one, his sharply dressed staff parades the weak in front of him so he can lay his hand on their heads.

"Be whole in the name of...Jeeeeeeesussssss!" he cries, sending each of them to the floor as if unconscious, only so they can be picked up again by his staff and sent away with the hope that this day their miracle is found.

Nancy turns off the television sadly. "I just don't know why things are the way they are, Lord." She takes out her gold cross and rubs it nervously with her thumb and forefinger. "I don't even know what to believe anymore," Nancy says, placing her necklace back in her shirt and kicking off her worn slippers.

She pulls back the covers of her bed and sits, takes a deeply refreshing breath, and lets out a sigh. Nancy grabs a small picture from her nightstand and smiles at the image of a young man inside the frame.

"I miss you, son," she says in a pained voice and holds the picture close to her heart.

The lights flicker. She tenses. She places the picture back on the nightstand as a whispered voice from inside the bathroom startles her.

"Child," the strange voice says in a distinct Romanian accent.

Nancy stands in terror. "Who...who's there?"

"Child," the voice calls again.

Her hands quiver. Her shoulders shake. She takes a cautious step toward the bathroom and sees the reflection of an old man in her mirror. He pins her under his stare.

"Child," the old man whispers a third time. He beckons her to come close with his aged hand.

"Help me!" Nancy screams as she runs for the door. She grabs the handle and pulls it in a panic, but it will not budge.

"Do not fear," the old man assures as he slowly approaches.

Frantic, Nancy kicks the door and slams into it with her shoulder. "Someone, help me! There is a man in here! Help me! Help me!"

The old man stops briefly to watch her. Pity is in his eyes.

She runs to the window. Her fingers lock onto its lip. With all her might, she tries opening the window, but like the door, it will not move. "Please, Lord. Please!" Nancy cries. She grabs a chair from her desk. She swings it at the window with all her strength, but it bounces off the glass as if steel.

"Help me! Help me! Someone help me!"

The old man bows his head as Nancy tires. Her weakness forces her to release the chair. "Please, please, don't hurt me," she whimpers in between heavy breaths. With no fight left in her, she rests her back against the wall and slides to the floor.

The strange old man takes his place above her. He lowers his face so his eyes can meet hers.

"Please, please don't hurt me…take…take…take what you want…" Nancy barely says. His dark eyes are as haunting as his voice. She covers her face with her hands and weeps.

"Fear not, child," the old man says, now standing directly above her. "You are highly favored, and you are loved." His voice echoes in the room pleasantly.

Nancy cannot help taking her hands away to look up at him.

He smiles sweetly at her and then looks above. He turns his palms upward and vanishes away into what appears to be a soft glowing white cloud the size of a large fist.

Nancy holds her hands defensively in front of her face.

The small cloud hovers in front of her. The old man's voice continues from inside it. "One and twenty days he will be born. One and twenty days that which sleeps will sleep no more. One and twenty days. He will make strong what has been weak. One and twenty days, Thomas James will begin to speak."

The voice is like a trumpet in her ears. Nancy's eyes widen as the cloud grows and finally bursts into what seems like a million tiny stars. It showers the area with so great a light, it steals Nancy's sight.

"I can't see!" she screams, shivering in fear. "I'm blind, I'm blind."

"Faith, Nancy. Have faith." These are the last words Nancy hears.

For one hour, she sits in this darkness, wondering not only if the aberration has gone, but what will happen in twenty-one days and what part Thomas will play, if any at all.

She hears a mourning dove begin a new song outside her window. Nancy tries to open her eyes again. Her sight returns. She focuses on the room and straightens in amazement.

"What?"

No longer is she sitting up against the wall as she had been when the old man turned cloud spoke with her.

"A dream?" she asks in disbelief from under the covers in her bed. "It can't be. It was so real." She rubs her eyes and looks again. Nancy had been in her bed asleep the entire time...or had she?

Daylight is come. The night has been spent. Nancy rises from her bed. She looks around her apartment with suspecting eyes.

"One and twenty days, Lord? What does that mean?" she asks with a strange feeling gnawing away inside her mind. "It can't be," she says, trying to convince herself it is not what she fears it may mean.

She walks to her front door and unlocks it. She takes a deep breath, worrying that the door still will not open for her. It opens with ease.

Her eyes widen and her breath catches. "It can't be."

On the cover of the morning newspaper, in bold print, the caption reads, "Twenty-One Days, Thomas James Dies."

"He's going to wake up, Lord, isn't he?" Nancy questions with tears of joy leaking from her eyes.

In twenty-one days, Thomas's doctors are supposed to take him off life support. If Nancy's vision or dream or whatever it was is true, then in one and twenty days, Thomas is going to live again.

Those who suffer much find a compassionate touch.
The lower we go, the greater the capacity to grow.
The heavier the weight, the more we learn to appreciate.
The harder the times, the more strength we find.
The more we endure, the greater the reward.
We learn to pick ourselves up because we first fall.
There's a plan, one day you'll understand, after all.

—Thomas James

For the Brokenhearted

Present

Bethel Memorial Hospital is buzzing with the miraculous news. After six long years in a coma, Thomas James is awake. Reporters from all over the world camp at the hospital. They wait for public confirmation from the very same doctors who said such a feat is impossible.

For years, the name *Thomas James* created a stir in the town of Bethel. Different groups came to the comatose boy's aid after his aunt was suspected of wanting Thomas off life support for a further payment from their family life insurance plan.

Local charities, churches, and pro-life organizations raised hundreds of thousands of dollars to create awareness of his situation. This news spread fast.

A large law firm from the neighboring city of Salem took legal action pro bono, knowing a victory in what quickly became the highest-profile cases of euthanasia would garner millions for them down the road.

The state claimed it was cruel to prolong the inevitable, but the many experts the Salem law firm brought in disagree. As if arguing for something greater than the life of one child, the lawyers fought like never before. For months, then years, victories and defeats visited each side. Because of this, as Thomas turned into a young man, all parties involved became famous.

Eventually, this epic battle landed itself in the middle of the Supreme Court of the United States. After six months of testimonies and expert witnesses, they passed the sobering judgment. If Thomas was unable to sustain life without the aid of life support, he would die.

The defeat sends shock waves throughout the world. Protesters held candlelight vigils on the Supreme Court steps. Many petitioned heads of state and foreign consulates.

Thomas's story became fodder for talk shows, debates, and late-night television. His face was seen on multiple network broadcasts, newspapers, and magazines around the world. The title of the latest *Time* read "Is There Truly Life When You Seem Dead?" It proudly displayed a picture of the gaunt Thomas on the cover. This edition became the third-highest selling in the periodical's history.

How Thomas's story made its way around the world to become such a point of interest is a question no one asked. His star rose while he slept. With each day that passed, more and more felt a connection to him.

The hospital parking lot fills with people from all over Bethel and surrounding areas. Police barricade each entrance to keep the anxious crowd at bay.

"Is it true?" an elderly woman asks an officer sectioning off a yellow-lined perimeter.

"Whatever happened, lady, they can't explain it. But I'm glad he's awake," the officer says with a smile and looks to the sky, as if searching for the one who makes it possible.

The older woman makes the sign of the cross and begins to weep quietly. "It's a miracle," she says in her Italian accent. "A miracle, everyone. He is alive, alive. Thomas James is alive!"

"It can't be," a thin woman declares, exhaling smoke from her Capri cigarette. "It's not possible...the timing...It's unreal."

"Well, it is real, lady, so deal with it," the officer replies. "People today, huh!"

"Alive? I cannot believe it. It is true! It is true! Thomas is alive!" a frail bearded man yells as he jumps up and down. He drops his protest sign to the ground. The many people pressing in trample it underfoot.

The large crowd erupts joyfully as the news spreads like wildfire through the parking lot. There is dancing, singing, and praise. People who never knew each other hold hands. Some cry and pray, while others hug the one to their left and kiss the one to their right. This day they all have one thing in common—the rebirth of Thomas James.

He has been in their homes on television, in their prayers, on the radios in their cars, and in the papers on the steps at their doors. Everyone relates to him. Everyone worries for him. For the content in life, for the brokenhearted, and for those who refuse to give up hope, whether wanting to keep Thomas alive or begging to let him die, almost all love and know the silent child who defied logic and science this day.

"They are calling it a miracle. The miracle of Thomas James," spouts a handsome reporter, shielding his eyes from the sun. "Just one hour before the time the US Supreme Court had ruled Thomas James was to be taken off life support, Thomas James began to show signs of movement. Rumors that the president will put a hold on the Court's decision is no longer relevant. After six long years of what seems to be the longest recorded recovery from a vegetative state, Thomas James is now awake. I repeat, Thomas James has woken from a six-year coma, doing the impossible on the day the courts decided he should die."

The reporter walks in front of the enormous crowd pressing against the guarded perimeter to continue. "I'm here outside Bethel Memorial Hospital, and as you can see, where once there was great sadness, now there is great joy. Today is a good day indeed!"

Phone lines jam around the country as people call others to spread the good news. This unique story interrupts all scheduled programming.

It remains a mystery as to why Thomas is the source of so much interest. No one remembers when he or she first heard of him, or why Thomas became as famous as he did without ever saying a word. The truth is, no one really thinks about this anymore.

Thomas is awake. Now all that matters to those celebrating his return is what Thomas will soon have to say, if Thomas can say anything at all.

Whatever a person looks for, they find, whether truth or lie.

You will always experience what you believe, whether joy or misery.

Many are so used to pain they forgot how to feel anything but the same.

They look for all that is wrong, and all that is wrong comes along.

And yet if they looked for all that is right, wrong would disappears from sight.

Whatever a person looks for, they will find every time.

—Thomas James

There Is Good News

A team of doctors, nurses, and aides are in and out of Thomas's hospital room all day. They stick him with needles, check his reflexes, and cart him off for x-rays, PET scans, and magnetic resonance imaging. They ask him many questions to which they receive no answer for Thomas does not yet speak.

He sits in his bed, calmly staring out the window. He is unresponsive and seemingly uninterested in the goings-on around him.

Dr. Felicia Adams walks into his room with purpose. She nervously scans the area. Nurse Lauren fixes the sheets to Thomas's bed. As Thomas's lead doctor and the best neurologist at Bethel Memorial, if not in the world, her presence snaps Lauren to attention.

"Any change?" Felicia asks pointedly.

"Not yet, Doctor. He's been staring like this all day," Lauren answers while taking his chart from the wall to hand to her.

Felicia raises her right eyebrow. The soft glow she notices around Thomas's shoulders and head puzzle her. "That's strange," she whispers to herself.

"What was that, Doctor?" Lauren hands her his chart.

"Nothing." Felicia opens his chart, but her piercing dark eyes do not find its contents. She flips her long brown hair back and unbuttons her lab coat, which reveals a slender build from many years of competitive running. She grabs the pager hiding away on her belt beneath it and looks at its blank screen. "Still no word," she says to herself with a sigh and a disappointed shake of her head.

"I heard there is a problem with his films," Lauren pries.

Felicia's head turns toward her like a threatened snake. "Who told you that?" she asks directly.

Lauren is worried by her obvious anger. "Just…just overheard it in passing,"

"Well, everything is going to be cleared up very shortly. Thanks for asking," Felicia says abruptly. She buries her head into Thomas's file, motivating Lauren to leave.

Lauren scurries out of the room, knowing the doctor is not telling her something about the patient.

Felicia is hiding something. Something that even she does not yet understand, something that a wall filled with accolades, achievements, and even a prestigious career cannot explain. Something is wrong with Thomas's films, and Felicia needs to find the underlying cause of it before this information gets to the press.

She nervously licks the tip of her thumb and gently uses it to turn the pages of his chart. She composes herself by taking a deep breath, acting like there is nothing wrong. Her nerves give it away the instant her dry mouth smacks open to speak.

"Well, there is good news and bad news, Thomas. So let's end on a high note, what do you say?" She puts her nose back into the chart and takes a few steps to read on.

Thomas inches his head toward her. There is no expression on his face, but the sun reflects like a fire in his eyes. He watches her curiously as she paces back and forth, unaware of his peculiar gaze. His severe eyes soften; he rolls his head around his shoulders, as if releasing a burden of some kind, waiting for her judgment.

"You're going to have to relearn everything, Thomas. From speaking to walking and eating, to learning how to read, write, and even tying your shoes. Your body is going to need rehab as well. Muscles fatigue"—she pauses to make eye contact—"especially after six years."

The corners of Thomas's lips curl upward curiously, as if he finds amusement in her prognosis, but does not find her words worth the attention he paid to them. His smile fades as he directs his gaze toward the window, but more importantly away from Felicia.

"There is good news, however." She realizes her words might have been too much for the child to bear. "Your physical condition is better than any other before. That is a miracle in itself. We can thank Dr. Striphe for that," she says with a reminiscent smile.

Felicia closes the chart and looks at him. She gets lost for a moment in the angelic soft glow that surrounds Thomas. He looks peaceful to her as he sits there, staring outside from within. She wonders for a moment what peace would feel like to someone like Thomas, who lost so very much and had so very little idea of what was to come. And yet in that moment of wonder, something extraordinary happens. Felicia feels something. A sudden peace comes over her, like sinking slowly into a pool of warm water. Her arms relax to her sides. She stands there silently, lost in this feeling.

"What was… huh!" Felicia shakes her head and snaps out of the strange and sudden comfort. "I'm sorry, I was zoning for a second." She follows her words with an uncomfortable giggle and looks for a place to sit to explain further.

"Dr. Striphe is an orthopedic surgeon and nerve specialist," she continues as she pulls the companion chair behind her and sits. "You're the first test subject of a cutting-edge new therapy for paraplegics, Thomas. That's why you're in the shape you're in right now."

Thomas takes a deep breath and exhales slowly. Felicia sits up and leans in to him. There is still no expression on his face.

"It's called EPS, electro penetrating stimulation. With your results so far, it is going to transform the therapies in place today. Now that you are awake, it is your choice whether to continue in the trial. So I'm just going to go over what you will expect if you do."

Felicia places his chart on the floor next to her. She locks her fingers together and rests her hands on the foot of his bed.

"Tiny leads have been surgically attached to multiple muscle groups in your body, Thomas. They are very small and cannot harm you. We send waves of electricity to these sites to trick each muscle into contracting and releasing. It's not painful, but it can be uncomfortable." Felicia stops, realizing Thomas is not even acknowledging her words. Her head sinks to her clasped hands.

From the hall, Lauren looks in the room quickly while passing. To her, it looks as if Dr. Adams is praying over Thomas in his bed. She shakes her head and walks away confused, believing it cannot be what it looks like.

"You don't even know what I'm saying, do you?" Felicia straightens up and pulls her hands away. She waits for any kind of response from Thomas, but he fixes his gaze on the green leaves twinkling on the trees from the sun.

"Well, we'll get to the bottom of all this soon, Thomas. It will be sooner than you think." Felicia stands and is startled by the loud buzzing of her pager. She unclips it from her belt and raises it just under her nose. Her eyes widen. She immediately places it back on her waist.

"Possibly sooner than I thought." She grabs his chart and places it back on the wall. "We'll see if they fixed that glitch and your films are back to normal." Felicia walks toward the door. She stops, turns, and once again looks at the curious glow surrounding Thomas.

"Either it's a glitch, or you, Thomas, have more activity in your brain than anyone else in recorded history."

She takes a deep breath and walks out of the room with butterflies gathering in her belly and a nervous lump in her throat. There is something different about this young man, something very different indeed.

A boy came home angrier than before, explained to his father what his anger was for.

"I was cheated and lost the game. I've been angry about it all day."

The father handed him a weight and challenged him, saying he couldn't hold it for long.

The boy struggled to prove Father wrong.

But his arms began to hurt so much; his strength he could no longer show.

The father smiled. "Remember this lesson, son, it always feels better to let things go."

—Thomas James

To Share and to Protect

Thomas's films snap in place on the lit wall of the x-ray viewing room. Felicia stands back so the doctors behind her can see the anomalies for themselves.

"Good lord," Dr. Colin Striphe exclaims with a slacked jaw. He is a handsome man in his late thirties with shaggy light-brown hair, a perpetual five o'clock shadow, hazel eyes, and an athletic build. He scratches the side of his cheek to make sense of what he sees.

"We found these on the scans taken one hour ago," Felicia says, pointing to large starburst-like clusters of activity on the films of Thomas's brain.

"Unbelievable," Colin whispers as he moves forward slowly and bites the corner of his mouth.

Felicia reaches into a large folder and takes out another film. She takes a deep breath and places the scan next to the ones already in place. There is a stark difference between them.

"This was taken one month ago. There's almost no activity at all." She steps away, and her eyes roll nervously from the lit scans to those in attendance. "It doesn't make any sense," she says as her left hand twitches anxiously at her side.

Dr. Natal, the chief of staff of the hospital and an outspoken member of the board of directors, shakes his head. The scowl on the old man's face is a warning to those around him. His words are as sharp as his wits, and like his bedside manner, his social skills leave much to be desired.

"How does someone in a vegetative state with extensive brain damage recover and then show more activity than anyone we have ever seen?" Natal asks impatiently.

"I don't know," Felicia responds.

Dr. Natal's face becomes flush. "They don't, Felicia!"

The door to the viewing room opens abruptly. Felicia's jaw clenches. The large wing-tipped shoes of the unexpected guest click on the off-white speckled tile as he enters ominously. His hat hides his face in shadow as he places a large black umbrella in the corner of the room. Felicia bites her tongue the instant she realizes who this mysterious man is.

"Sorry I'm late," Dr. Vince Manus says with a sinister smile. "Good to see you, Frank." He takes off his dark fedora, revealing his matted hair. He clears his throat and surveys the room.

Manus pins Felicia under his pompous stare. "Is there somewhere I can rest my hat?" He licks his chapped lips and brushes away the dandruff that peppers the shoulders of his tweed jacket.

"What's he doing here?" Felicia asks with knuckles growing white from her tightening fists.

"I asked Dr. Manus for a consult. As chief of Legirion Psychiatric, I'm sure he can offer some insight, considering you, Felicia, are at a loss."

Felicia's head sinks. She closes her eyes to gain composure. "I never said I was at a loss, Frank. I said I've never seen results like these."

"Nor have I." Manus holds out his bifocal glasses to inspect the films. "This could be history, gentlemen. We need to share this with the world. Can you imagine what secrets are hidden away in that boy's mind if these films are correct?" Manus licks his lips again and snaps his teeth together.

Felicia sneaks a look of concern to Colin. He shrugs and shakes his head because there is nothing he can do.

"I would very much like to meet with this young man," Manus declares, puffing his chest out while sucking the air out of the room through his nostrils.

"That's a good idea, Vince. Maybe together we can figure this out. In the meantime, no one says anything to anyone." Natal looks at his watch. "Now, if you'll excuse me."

"Wait!" Felicia demands.

Natal turns to her impatiently. "Yes?"

"Seeing Thomas isn't going to be possible without consent," she declares as she rips the scans from the wall and places them in a private charting file.

Manus turns to her quickly. "Now how am I supposed to get consent from someone who isn't even speaking, Felicia?"

"It's Dr. Adams, and I will not subject my patient to your medieval practices!"

"Enough!" Natal shouts, and Felicia backs away. "Whatever differences the two of you may have is in the past. Right now, we need to get to the bottom of this. Run the tests again!"

"This is the third set we've run, Frank. They all come out the same." She nervously picks at the right pocket of her lab coat.

"I don't want to hear it. Just do it." Dr. Natal storms out of the room. The door slams shut behind him, and silence follows.

Manus places his hat back on and smiles. "I'm looking forward to working with you again…Felicia." He snatches his umbrella from the corner and catches Colin's shin with it in the process. "Sorry, pal."

Colin's nostrils flare.

"My office will ring you when I'm available to see the boy," Manus says with a cocky look. "Good day."

Manus leaves Felicia and Colin alone with the foul odor of his body still thick in the air.

Felicia slaps the wall.

"Look, Manus may be a jerk, but he's helped a lot of people."

"What about those who never leave that place, Colin? What about those, like Elizabeth, who are still suffering there? What about those that never get well, like her, despite his care?"

"It won't be like that, Felicia." Colin chooses his words carefully. "You did everything you could for Elizabeth. Her parents made that decision, not you. It's not your fault."

"She's my niece, Colin...and I'm not even allowed to visit her. So you tell me how I'm supposed to trust that man?"

Colin's eyes find his shoes. He has no answer for her.

Felicia holds back her tears. "We need to protect that boy."

Control is what the ignorant ones are after. Control is what everyone is paying for.

Ancient civilizations have used the twisting and hiding of information so the truth of who we are we wouldn't explore.

Dumbing down each and every generation with a steady diet of fear, lust, greed, pride, narcissism, and more.

Intimidation, degradation, censoring, and manipulating education, control takes many forms.

Control wants you to remain in chains with your heart feeling like it is being stomped on the floor.

Control is the devil, and it's time for its lies to be leveled so the light of love, liberty, and truth the controlled can no longer ignore.

—Thomas James

Be Not Afraid

Nurse Nancy quietly enters Thomas's hospital room. She gently closes the door behind her and takes a moment to acknowledge the silence that follows. The faint smell of roses tickles her nose. She enters curiously after it. Her eyebrows meet as she looks for flowers but finds none.

"That's strange," she says in a barely audible voice.

Thomas lies peacefully on his bed. His eyes are closed. His breathing is steady. He is dressed in white, matching the color of the sheets. He is clean and shaved. His skin is smooth, the color of a newly shined pearl. The pleasant look on his face takes Nancy by surprise. She stares at him for a moment, and a calm feeling comes over her.

He's like an angel, she thinks. A smile inches toward her ears.

The light in the room is dim. Strangely, Thomas seems to be the brightest part of it.

Nancy spies the heavy brown curtains keeping the dawning sun at bay. She approaches them with a light feeling rising in her heart. She grabs the curtains by their hem and begins to hum.

"Let there be light," she jests. She slides the curtains back dramatically. Sunlight floods the room as the stirred-up dust from the curtains seems to dance in the air. Nancy stretches and takes a long deep breath as the warmth of the sun kisses her skin. How strangely calm she is, like waking from a long nap on a lazy summer afternoon. She feels refreshed and does not know why. "Today is a good day," she says joyfully and looks out the window.

In the parking lot below, television trucks and people from all around crowd the hospital. It is a strange sight, a sea of people gazing up at Thomas's window, as if the answer to their prayers waits for them there.

Nancy would be lying if she said she does not feel like there is something very special about the young man as well. This is not because of her strange dream or the timing of his coming to. It is the way she feels every time she is near him. That is what makes her believe this.

She grabs the water pitcher off the window ledge carefully, takes a short plastic cup in hand, and pours water into it. She places the pitcher back on its tray and raises the filled cup to eye level. It will be the first drink of water Thomas has on his own in six years. Water poured from her own hand. She does not know why this seems so significant. Nevertheless, there is no denying the profound connection between her and this mysterious boy.

As she turns to place the cup at his side, the hairs on the back of her neck stand tall. "Good night!" she screams and drops the cup from her hand. Water splashes on the ground against her feet.

Thomas is wide-awake, sitting up calmly as if he's been that way the entire time.

"You're awake." Nancy holds her racing heart. "I thought you were asleep."

Thomas shows no emotion. He stares at her as she speaks, as if studying her.

"How did you sit up like that? Did someone prop you up when I wasn't looking?" Nancy asks with a nervous chuckle.

How Thomas has the strength to sit up on his own is beyond her. She tries to put the thought out of her mind by pouring another cup of water.

Thomas follows her with his eyes as she does so.

Nancy can feel his stare. "Well, it's nice to finally see you up." She makes small talk as she places the cup next to him on the companion table.

"My name is Nancy, Nancy Hearst. But those close to me call me Momma. And seeing as I've been taking care of you for the last six years, you feel free to do the same."

Nancy sits on the edge of his bed. His eyes are so blue, but that is not what strikes her. She cannot see any sadness in them or confusion. This is strange to her. How can there be such peace in the eyes of someone who has been gone for so long?

"Now, I know you might not know what's going on here, child. You may even be scared. But everything will be fine."

Thomas looks away from her. He is not interested in what she has to say. He does not seem to need her encouragement, or perhaps he does not understand what she says, Nancy wonders.

As he focuses his attention out the window, Nancy gets the feeling that she should do the same.

"What's got your attention, son?" she asks. To her surprise, she witnesses another strange sight.

One by one, mourning doves from the clouds above descend on the ledge outside his window. Eight in total face the room as they perch. Their eyes seem to focus on Thomas.

Nancy slowly rises to her feet. "Will you look at that," she says, walking to the window, hardly believing her eyes. "They said I was crazy when I told them about that dream I had. But here you are wide-awake, just like I said you would be."

Nancy looks past the doves to the crowd below. They are from all walks of life. Some are rich, some poor, but all seem to have a stake in the welfare of this young man. In an age where miracles have all but disappeared, Thomas James offers them hope that there is more to life than what they have experienced so far.

Who is Thomas really? Is there more to him than meets the eye? Is he special? These questions and more run through Nancy's mind as she tries to make sense of the strange events following her vision that night.

Nancy turns to him. The sunlight reflects off his eyes and flickers around his pupils like a fire dancing above burning wood. Immediately, the doves fly away. She trembles.

Thomas tilts his head toward her. His expression softens, and Nancy is at ease. She leans in to him as if to share a secret. "It's like you found something out in that darkness you were hiding in, isn't it?"

He does not blink. His eyes are so kind.

"I had a son, you know. He was about your age when he passed. It was a car accident." She shakes her head, composing herself before she continues. "His name was Thomas too... Maybe that's why the Lord brought us together." Her eyes widen as she remembers her son. "It's funny. If I didn't lose him, I'd still be delivering babies instead of tending to you."

Tears well in her eyes. One spills down her cheek. She clasps her hands together and takes a deep breath through her nose. "You see, after someone you love dies, watching someone come into the world to live just hurts too much."

Thomas closes his eyes, but he does not do so to sleep. He rests his head on his pillow, but he is not tired.

Nancy takes her cue. "Well, I don't need to trouble you with my loss." She quickly gathers herself and walks away.

"Do you remember?" Thomas asks quietly.

Nancy is frozen. They had said it would be impossible for him to speak this soon.

"Remember what?" she asks fearfully, not turning to face him.

"The name of the last child you helped bring into this world?"

Nancy is stricken. The memory of that day floods her mind. Her skin draws pale. She cannot breath. She turns to Thomas in slow motion.

"His name was...his...it...it was Thomas." Her knees give way. She catches herself before falling to the floor. "Just like you, just like my son...Can it be?" Nancy braces herself against the wall. "You were the last child I delivered, aren't you?" she asks in a broken voice.

Thomas opens his eyes and lifts his head to face her. "Be not afraid. The days of fear and pain are over," he says kindly. "A new day is here. It's time to be glad in it."

To speak a blessing over someone's life is not hard at all.

You put your lips together and remind everyone every time that they will always pick themselves up after they fall.

You tell them their dreams are more than fairy tales, that when action is put to their passion upon their desires, they will sail.

This is why we must always try to create life instead of strife with our words, so together we will always succeed and never fail.

—Thomas James

Dwell Not on Mistakes You Have Made

Dr. Striphe rushes down the hall. His white lab coat flaps in the air behind him as he weaves in and out of the many he passes. "Coming through, coming through," he says, nearly crashing into them all. He is distracted. Uneasiness has settled about him. Known for his quick wit and childish sense of humor, this is a side few ever see.

"Can I borrow this?" Colin snatches a wheelchair parked next to the nurses' station. He pops a wheelie and hurries toward Thomas's room. After turning the corner, two police officers stop him from entering Thomas's wing.

"Identification," the larger of the two asks while his partner takes out a sign-in sheet.

"Here you go." Colin hands him his badge impatiently.

The officer inspects it carefully and hands it to his partner. Colin signs in and is given a nod of approval.

"Have a good day, gentlemen." He bursts through the double doors, using the wheelchair as a battering ram.

Colin enters the coma wing to a different scene completely. There is no hurrying about, no questions from anxious reporters, no arguments from patients that the noise in the hall is too loud.

His pace slows. How calm things are in this area of the hospital. How few people found.

Allan, the massive security guard, sits alone in the hall outside Thomas's room.

"Morning," Colin says with a voice that echoes down the hall.

Allan's face lights up. He is as sweet as he is gigantic. He closes his muscle magazine, folds it, and places it under his armpit. He stands to greet the approaching doctor. "Morning, Doctor," Allan says with a smile.

At six foot, six inches tall with 295 pounds of pure muscle filling out his enormous frame, his smile is welcome to Dr. Striphe indeed.

"Colin…A-Train, the name is Colin. Only my patients call me Doctor."

Allan chuckles. "Who told you to call me A-Train?"

"Are you kidding me? Who hasn't followed your football career? They said you were so fast and hit so hard, when you sacked someone it was as if they were run down by a locomotive. You were a legend in this town."

The smile fades from Allan's face. "Yeah, I guess I was."

Colin hit a nerve; he knows it. "You still are, Allan. No football injury is going to erase those records you put up on the boards."

"Thanks." Allan stiffens his upper lip and grabs the log to sign him in. "How long are you planning to see him today?"

"About an hour or so." Colin looks out the window and stretches. "I've got some tests to run. Then after that, maybe I will go outside. It is nice today. Maybe we'll have lunch on the roof and visit the garden. I haven't done that in ages."

"You should take Thomas with you." A-Train finishes and snaps the log shut.

"Excuse me?"

"He's been stuck inside this hospital for the last six years. Maybe you should take him up to the garden with you. I'm sure he'd like the fresh air."

Colin snorts a laugh, as if being told a great joke.

"Why is that funny?" Allan's jaw clenches. Allan is not amused.

"Have you been outside? Haven't you seen those people?"

Allan does not understand.

"A-Train, why do you think this floor is locked down? Thomas is a celebrity now. There are reporters scouring this place to get a picture or a statement. And that boy is in no state to deal with any of that. Not to mention all the crazies out there who think he is a sign that the end is near, or some messenger for the future, or whatever other nonsense they believe. Thomas is not safe until this circus lets up. And I most certainly am not going to put him in harm's way."

Allan locks eyes with Colin. "And what if he is a messenger, then what?"

"Come on, A-Train, you're smarter than that."

Allan rolls his eyes in disappointment and hands Colin back his badge. "Maybe there's more to him than you think."

"Look, there is nothing special about that kid besides the fact that he is extremely lucky. He's just today's headline. You think people will care about what that poor kid has to say in a year or two? Besides, we don't even know if he'll ever be able to speak to begin with."

"But Nancy said—"

"Nancy? Oh yeah, Nancy, that's right. She said Thomas talked to her yesterday, right? Thomas told her not to fear, that we should be happy or something. New moon or sun is rising? The Age of Aquarius. Happy, happy, joy, joy. Something like that?" Colin fumbles hypocritically.

"Nancy said Thomas told her not to be scared, that a new day is here, and that we should be glad in it," A-Train says with authority.

"Allan, I don't mean to...you know...burst your bubble or anything, but Nancy also said she was visited by an angel. The lady is sweet, she's a great nurse, but she's a bit too heavenly minded for her own good, if you know what I mean."

"Then how come Thomas woke up exactly like Nancy said he would?"

Colin looks at Allan without an answer to give. His eyes roll to the window to find one. He knows Allan is right. Thomas did wake up exactly as Nancy said he would. And there is still no explaining the strange results found on the scans of his brain. But there has to be an explanation; there always is. Miracles are something Colin gave up on long ago. No twenty-year-old ex-football star is going to make him think any different.

"Lucky guess, Allan. Now if you'll excuse me." He grabs hold of the wheelchair handles and readies himself to enter.

A-Train sits down without giving him another look. He opens his magazine and buries himself in it.

"Well, good talking to you, Allan…I think," Colin says sarcastically as he passes him.

More pressing matters await Colin than finding out what has Allan in such a huff. The success of his new therapy depends on the myriad of tests he has to run on Thomas today.

He enters the room hastily. He does not take the time to notice the wonderful stillness in the air as Nancy had. He does not even close the door behind him.

The light coming in from Thomas's window blinds him. He shades his eyes with his hand, leaves the wheelchair at the end of Thomas's bed, and makes his way over to shut the curtains like a blind man.

"Bright in here," Colin states. "I hope you don't mind, it was a late night last night." Colin closes the curtains and turns to his patient. Thomas is sitting up in his bed. He is relaxed, yet his deep blue eyes are intense as he stares at the doctor.

"Well, I have to tell you, Thomas, you look good. You look really good." Colin grabs his chart and sits on the chair next to him. "A couple of months, the right diet and exercise, and who knows, you may even look better than me." Colin laughs uncomfortably at his own joke.

He feels Thomas's eyes on him. He tries to ignore it, but there is something strange about his gaze. It is not the look of a young man with worry. Not the look of a patient concerned with what the doctor has to say. Thomas stares as Colin speaks as an adult would when a child does or says something foolish because it knows no better.

"Well, your blood work looks great." Colin puts the chart down. "Let's take a look at you." Colin stands. He lifts Thomas's shirt. The bones protrude from under his skin. He looks like he is finally free from a concentration camp.

"Well, you don't look that bad." He lets the shirt fall. "It is nothing a bunch of milk shakes and french fries won't cure."

Dr. Striphe blows hot air into his hands and begins rubbing them together, using friction for warmth. "My hands shouldn't be too cold. I just want to see what kind of mobility you have. So I'm going to take your hand and check to see, okay?" Colin reaches slowly for him. The instant his fingers meet Thomas's skin, he recoils as if burnt on a hot stove.

"Wow! What was that?" Never has he felt static electricity like this before. He inspects his hand curiously. His arm still tingles from it.

"You gave me a shock there, Tommy. Have you been walking around with your socks on the carpet again, young man?" He makes light of the situation and reaches cautiously for Thomas's hand again. Upon grabbing it, he notices the hairs on his arms standing erect. "Well, they told me you have an electric personality, but this is ridiculous."

He ignores the phenomenon and begins moving Thomas's left arm up and down, checking his range of motion. "Okay, good. Let's try the other side now." Colin reaches over Thomas to get to his right hand. Before he does so, Thomas snatches the doctor's arm. He pushes back the cuff of his coat, revealing a large horizontal scar beneath Colin's wrist, one he has hidden for years.

Colin angrily pulls his hand back. He covers the wound of his past and grits his teeth. "It was a hunting accident," Colin explains. "If you're thinking it's something else, it's not."

Thomas closes his eyes sadly.

Colin is in shock. The boy is stronger than he imagined. He wonders why Thomas would do such a thing. The boy is more alert than he lets on.

"Why lie?" Thomas says in a soft but powerful voice.

If Colin's jaw could reach the floor, it would. Not only is Thomas speaking, but he knows Colin is not telling the truth about that four-inch scar.

"Excuse me? Wow! You can speak. Wait, did…did you just call me a liar?"

"I asked why you would lie." Thomas opens his eyes widely. His brow furrows and his head bows sadly.

"I have no reason to lie to you, Tommy. You don't mind if I call you Tommy, do you?" A change in topic is just what the doctor orders.

"Is there ever a reason to lie?" Thomas asks softly, forcing him to make eye contact.

Colin walks over to the companion chair nervously. "Excuse me?" He sits and plays possum.

"You told me you have no reason to lie to me, and I asked if there was ever a reason to lie."

Colin is confused. Thomas's words make Colin feel like the child, not the doctor. "I don't know what to tell you, Tommy." Colin shrugs ignorantly.

"Tell me the truth." Thomas says it so plainly, as if the truth is something that is so freely and often shared between people today.

The truth could compromise Colin as a physician. He thinks. The truth would be crossing the line. Can he be honest? No, like most today, he is more comfortable with the lies he tells than the very thing that is honest and true.

"Maybe when we get to know each other better, we can have nice, long, deep talks like this. But in the meantime"—Colin jumps to his feet dramatically and plays the fool—"let's get you in this sexy ride over here." He points to the green wheelchair and walks to it.

"You know me already, Colin."

"Excuse me?" He clears his throat. "And I'm 'Doctor' to my patients."

"You said when we know each other better, we'll talk. But you know me. You just don't remember."

"Trust me, Thomas. We have never met. And I have to warn you about sniffing those latex gloves. It'll get you nowhere fast." Irritated, Colin positions the wheelchair at the edge of Thomas's bed. "What do you say we take a spin around the block, say hi to a couple of pretty nurses, and then run you down for some tests to start your therapy?"

Thomas does not answer him. He simply nods his head in agreement.

"All right, let's swing your legs out." He positions Thomas for the wheelchair. "Now, I'm going to lift you up gently, and then I'm going to throw you down real hard in this here chair. You ready?"

Thomas looks out the window as Colin wraps his arms around his torso. "I'd like to go outside if that's possible."

"Today's not the day for that." Colin grunts as he lifts him. He places Thomas in the wheelchair and crouches down to position his feet on the footrests. Before he can do so, Thomas moves them on his own. He places his feet easily where they need to be.

Colin is confounded. How can Thomas have the strength to move that way after six years? It may not be impossible, but it is highly unlikely. "You're doing better than I thought." He says the only thing he can.

"And better even than that." Thomas smiles mysteriously.

Colin tries ignoring the young man's words and the fact that he already can move his feet on his own. He focuses on getting the results back from the tests he is about to run. He begins to wheel him out of the room.

Thomas slams the wheelchair lock in place, stopping the two abruptly.

"Hey! Don't do that. I almost dumped you."

"Why is today not the day to go outside, Colin?"

"I think I liked you better when you didn't talk." Colin unlocks the wheel and moves the two into the hall.

Thomas sits quietly. He looks to Allan as they pass him, and he smiles.

Allan stands up in awe. It is the first time he lays eyes on Thomas, but after seeing him, he feels as if somehow he has seen him before.

"It's good to see you, Thomas," A-train says as if a celebrity is passing.

Thomas grabs the wheel lock and stops the two from rolling again.

"You have to stop doing that, Tommy!" Colin shows his growing frustration.

Thomas acknowledges the daily devotional book sitting on top of Allan's muscle magazine. He leans in toward him. "Would you like to visit me later, Allan?"

"How do you know my name?"

"I have ears that can hear." Thomas grins.

"Yeah, and the fact that you're wearing your name tag, A-Train. But besides all that…" Colin interjects under his breath.

Ignoring Dr. Striphe's words, Thomas extends his hand for Allan to grab. "You're here to protect me. Thank you."

Allan reaches for his hand nervously. When their hands meet, his face lights up like a child on Christmas morning. "Yes, yes, well…the pleasure's mine, Mr. James." A-Train continues to shake Thomas's hand happily, not wanting to let go.

"Okay then, A-Train, we got to be going now," Dr. Striphe hints strongly.

"We'll talk later," Thomas assures, shaking his hand.

"Sure…sure…if that's okay?" Allan answers in a daze.

Colin breaks their hands apart and quickly hurries Thomas down the hall. He has but an hour, and time is wasting.

A-Train stands on his toes and yells, "I told you he could talk, Doc!"

"Yeah, yeah...whatever, A-Train." Colin grimaces and looks at the back of Thomas's head. "You have a very strange effect on people, Tommy."

"You'll see greater things than this, Colin."

"It's Doctor, Tommy. Call me Doctor."

The two reach the elevator.

"Where are we going, Colin?" Thomas asks, ignoring the doctor's request.

Colin rolls his eyes. "No respect, kids today...We're going to the first floor, Thomas," he says sarcastically.

Thomas slowly stretches his hand forward and presses the button. His arm is steady in doing so. The button lights up, and the elevator doors open to the sound of a chime. There is no wait.

"Thank you," Colin answers with surprise. For someone who has been immobile for six years, Thomas's recovery is like nothing he has ever seen.

The two enter the elevator. The doors close, and Colin notices Thomas is looking at him in the reflection of the mirrored doors. He nervously shifts his weight from side to side, wishing the elevator would hurry already.

"I had a dream last night," Thomas says calmly.

"Oh yeah, what was it about?"

"Two brothers and a large tree," he says, closing his eyes sadly.

"What was that?" Colin's heart pounds heavily in his chest.

"They dared each other to climb higher than the next. When the older reached the top, the younger grabbed hold of the branch, keeping him safe, and the two fell forty feet to the ground."

Colin storms over to the elevator panel. He presses the red emergency button in place. The elevator stops dramatically. The bell rattles as Colin positions himself in front of Thomas. His face is drawn red. "What the hell are you talking about?" he demands.

"The older reached out for the younger to save him from the fall. When the two hit the rocky ground, the older was crushed by the younger, and his body went limp."

"What are you talking about?" Colin grabs the armrests of Thomas's wheelchair in a threatening manner. He shakes the chair to stop him.

"The younger believed it was his fault. And his guilt was great," Thomas continues, ignoring Colin's anger.

"Stop it!" Colin slaps the wall. "Who did you talk to?"

"So great was his guilt that either he would kill himself or find a way to make his brother well." Thomas opens his eyes and directs them to Colin's wrist.

"Who told you about my brother?" Colin asks with a fire growing inside him.

"Everything happens for a reason. And it is all for the good of man."

The color in Colin's face drains from a sinking fear. "Who told you about my brother?"

"Is that what happened to your wrist?" Thomas asks calmly and reaches to release the emergency stop button.

At a loss, Colin relaxes against the wall of the elevator. His eyes are red with grief. He tries to think about the tests he must run on Thomas. But he can't now that the floodgates to his painful past are open. Few, if any, knew about his brother and their accident. Few, if any, knew that his guilt drove him to help those with paralysis and to find a cure. It is why he created the EPS machine, and it is why he became an orthopedic surgeon; it is his purpose, his life.

How can Thomas know this? What fear grips Colin that he almost stands paralyzed himself? Perhaps there *is* more to this young man. Perhaps he is a messenger after all.

"I could use some fresh air. How about you?" Colin says, pressing the button marked Roof with a trembling hand. "The tests can wait."

He swallows back his fear and rolls his shoulders to ready himself for what may come as the two ascend in silence to the garden above.

If I have hope, I have no reason to fear
If I love, many draw near
If I forgive, I will never again hate
If I accept people as they are, there's no need to debate
If I am kind, it helps others to smile
If I am positive, I can always go that extra mile
If I am patient, I never again have to wait
If I am giving, all that I have, I appreciate
If I am open to new ideas, there is no end to what I can know
If I have faith, there is no telling where I will go
If I am content, I have everything I ever wanted in life
If I take the "IF" out of all these things, I have finally seen the light!

—Thomas James

All That Seems Wrong Isn't

Dr. Felicia Adams watches the perpetual motion of counter-balanced dolphins swing back and forth on her desk. Degrees and awards from Harvard, Columbia, and other prestigious schools of medicine fill her walls.

Her head rests between her hands over the desk. The clicking sound of the dolphins swinging back and forth is all she hears. Her defeated look tells a tale of a woman who worries all is about to go wrong.

Between her elbows, beneath her head, is Thomas's file. On top of the file is a letter from the board of directors resting face-down. For ten minutes she sits this way, waiting for the courage to read it. For ten minutes, she worries what this memo will say.

If the board allows Dr. Manus to evaluate Thomas, Felicia knows it will not be long before he exaggerates the facts and makes a play to place Thomas under his full care. Then Felicia will not be able to do anything for him. Manus has many supporters in the hospital. It does not matter how unorthodox his techniques are; many cannot see past his vain exterior.

Felicia has heard stories of abuse, tales of perversion, and worse. With no evidence, no charges are mounted. Regardless, there is something devious about that man; Felicia can feel it in her very soul. This is why she has not been able to bring herself to read this simple letter. Fear.

As the dolphins' movement ends, so does Felicia's patience.
"This is ridiculous!" she says angrily.
She flips the memo over and reads.

Dr. Adams,

Please be advised that I, along with Leah James, the legal guardian of Thomas James, feel that it is necessary for the patient to be evaluated by Dr. Vince Manus at your earliest convenience. We are all concerned for the young man's emotional state, and instead of delaying this evaluation until you feel it is necessary, as chief of neurology, I must insist you cooperate fully with Dr. Manus and his staff. If you have any questions or concerns, please contact my secretary, and I will be glad to field them.

Francis Natal, MD
Chief of Neurology
Bethel Memorial Hospital

Her fears are correct. Manus has gotten his way.

"You have *got* to be kidding me!" She pushes the letter from her desk.

Her head begins to throb. The pain was there before, but now it becomes intense. She rubs her temples.

Manus has won the first round. He will document whether he believes Thomas is competent enough to move on without further therapy. She knows his evaluation will not be an honest one. A published study of the now-famous Thomas James can garner Manus millions in research grants. It will make him a household name. This is what he covets the most.

"What am I going to do?" she asks, slouching into her chair as if defeated.

A knock sounds at the door. She snaps to attention and quickly fixes her appearance. She straightens her jacket, wipes away any trace of tears, and gathers her composure.

"Come in," she calls out, refusing to show defeat.

The door opens slowly. Colin peeks his head in from behind it.

Felicia sees him and begins to cry.

Immediately, he enters the room. "Hey, you okay?" Colin says with compassion in his eyes. He closes and locks the door behind him.

Felicia covers her face with tissues and chokes back her tears.

Colin prances over to her, trying to cheer her up. He sits in the chair on the opposite side of her desk and raises his best doctor's eyebrow. "Allergies making you cry?" he asks in a deep voice.

Felicia laughs. "Yes, I'm allergic to stupidity." She points to the memo on the floor.

Colin picks it up and reads. Felicia folds her arms and waits with a sour look on her face. "Can you believe that?" she asks candidly.

He stands to his feet. "That's ridiculous."

"You're telling me."

"How many lawsuits does Manus's hospital have to have before they say, 'Hey, maybe we should get rid of that Dr. Frankenstein-loving Antichrist of a doctor we have there'?"

"At least Frankenstein's intentions were good."

Colin holds the memo out in front of her. "Rip it up." He shakes the memo up and down. "Rip it up good. Think of Dr. Maniac while you're doing it."

"What?" Felicia takes the memo in hand and looks at him curiously.

"I said rip it, tear it up, into millions of little pieces."

"Why would I do that?"

"It'll make you feel better." Colin sits down and wraps his hands behind his head. He props his feet on her desk.

"Get your nasty feet off my desk." She knocks them to the floor. "And I'm not going to rip it up, Colin. I'm not two years old."

"Come on, lady. I know there's a tiger deep down inside you dying to get out." He leans forward, flirting.

"I just don't understand how they could make such a bone-head decision. As if Manus even cares about the child's mental state. The man only cares about one thing, money. That greedy, rotten, self-centered..." Her anger builds like water boiling over.

"Rip it up!" Colin screams.

Felicia cannot take it anymore. Like an animal, she tears into the letter and shreds it, littering the ground like a dusting of snow.

"Now we're talking," Colin says, admiring his handiwork.

She throws the remains into the air, allowing some of it to fall into her hair. She collapses into her chair and puffs out her upper lip. "What should I do, Colin?" Her question is simple.

Colin's answer is not. His fingers tap nervously on her desk, waiting to find the right words.

She looks at him curiously and wonders just what is going through his head.

"You should have a press conference," he says candidly.

Felicia becomes rigid. Brought to the edge of her chair by his words, she slaps both hands on the finely polished maple desktop with a loud thud. "What?" she screams.

The request is strange. Colin knows this. He places all kidding aside and gets to the heart of the matter. "Thomas wants a press conference. I don't know why he does. But that doesn't matter. I think we should do it."

Felicia slowly rises to her feet. Her hair dangles in front of her face. "Are you out of your mind?"

"Once the public sees he's competent, it won't matter if Manus says he's not. The public will not stand for having the world's sweetheart locked up in some dungeon called a psychiatric hospital. Use the press to our advantage before Manus's evaluation gets the poor kid committed."

Felicia looks at Colin as if he has ten heads. She squeezes her eyelids tight around her eyes and shakes her head in confusion. "He is in no shape for that."

"Thomas says he has something important to say." Colin picks nervously at the loose string hanging from his jacket, as a child would while waiting for a mother's approval.

"And what could he possibly have to say that is important, Colin?" She places one hand on her hip and points the other in his face.

"Don't talk to me like I'm two." Colin takes a deep breath and walks over to the window. He rests his hand on the wall and allows his head to sink to his armpit. How can he tell Felicia of the conversation he had with this boy? How could she believe what he barely believes himself?

"Well?" she demands. "What is so important that he has to say?"

"Maybe he has more to say than you know."

"What the heck does that mean?" she asks, grabbing Colin by his elbow to turn him around. "What's your angle, Colin? This isn't like you, asking for something on a patient's behalf."

Colin refuses to meet her eyes.

"Did you put him up to this?" Her face grows tight.

Colin will not back down. "Now why on earth would I do that?"

"You tell me."

"You haven't talked to him, Felicia, I have. The boy is fine. I would not say so if I didn't think he was. Trust me."

Her mouth is dry from nerves. Her head pounds from stress. "Trust you?"

Colin sees her frustration. He moves in close to console her.

She shoves him back. "He's been in a coma for six years. Six years!"

"I understand that. But...there is something different about him. I think you should let the world see that this kid is okay. He is better than okay. I can't explain it, he's, he's just..." Colin finds no words. How can he make sense of something that doesn't even make sense to him? There is just something very different about Thomas. He knows things he shouldn't know. He has insights he shouldn't have. He can't put his finger on what it is, and now he can't even explain this to the woman he cares for the most.

Felicia stares at Colin as if he is speaking in a different tongue. "You're making me nervous, Colin."

He walks her over to her desk. He places his hands gently on her shoulders and looks deeply into her eyes. "Don't you think it's odd that six years of his life are taken from him, and he doesn't care? He doesn't care at all. I mean, has anyone ever reacted that way? He has got, like, this...peace about him. I don't know...I can't...I can't explain it. But he's, he's different...in a good way, I think."

Her eyes widen with fear. "What are you talking about?"

"This may sound crazy, but you know me. I have never met anyone like this kid. He is special, and we have to protect him, like you said. The things he knows...the things he said to me...I don't, I don't know what to make of them." Tears fill Colin's eyes as he remembers.

"What did he tell you?"

"I have to figure some things out before I tell you first, okay?"

Felicia has never seen Colin like this before. He acts as if he has seen a ghost or has come face-to-face with death and lived to tell the tale. She sees the emotion in his eyes and does not want to push him any further. "I don't think a press conference is a good idea, Colin," she says directly and returns to her chair.

The look of disappointment on Colin's face is disturbing. His shoulders slump. He shakes his head as he walks to the door.

"I'm sorry, Colin." Her words do not melt the trouble in his heart. They only push him further away.

He grabs the handle of the door, and without looking back, he says, "What if we were supposed to fall that day?"

"What was that?"

"If my brother and I never fell from that tree, I would have never gone into orthopedics and never designed the EPS." Colin turns to her. His face has never been more severe. "What if we were meant to fall that day?" A tear escapes his eyelid and slides down his cheek. "And it wasn't my fault."

"What are you saying, Colin?" A look of concern grows on Felicia's face.

"I'm saying that maybe everything that seems bad isn't that bad after all. That maybe my brother and I fell from the tree that day so others could learn to walk because of it."

"What does that have to do with Thomas James?"

He takes a deep breath, rolls his head around his shoulders, and composes himself.

Felicia understands Colin has something important to say.

"I've carried that guilt my whole life. I believed I put my own brother in that wheelchair. My every waking moment, I've been burdened by it. Like a weight I never wanted to carry but was forced to." His voice cracks. "And then I meet Thomas...and that weight is gone." Colin opens the door completely to exit. "Talk to him, and you'll see. And you'll know the press conference is the only hope that kid has." He exits, and the door slams shut behind him.

Felicia stands in the midst of the torn paper on the floor. Like the paper, her thoughts are scattered. She knows she needs to do something before Manus gets his way. She just does not know what that will be.

They think they know, and yet with hate in their hands they sow prejudice, greed, fear, shame, and more.

They think they know, but into the land of promise, the blind and the arrogant will never go, because they have forgotten I, the Lord, want love and nothing more.

They think they know, telling others "This is the way you must go" and damning anyone who doesn't. They believe they are God, refusing to leave the land of Nod, because the law of love, to them, simply wasn't.

Sadly, my truth they forgot.

And so, *now they must know,* until they love, if they ask to bask in my glory from above, my answer to them will be, "You may not."

—Thomas James

Nothing Is Ever Lost That Isn't One Day Found

Thomas sits in his wheelchair quietly. He waits patiently in the cold hospital room that is more suitable for police interrogation than a haven for open dialogue. The double-sided mirror set into the wall distracts him. He studies it curiously, wondering who would be spying on him from the other side.

The bare evaluation room walls are painted eggshell white, and the silver-and-black speckled tile floor beneath him gives the room a surgical feel. His evaluation is soon to begin. Thomas closes his eyes and clears his mind to prepare himself for Dr. Vince Manus, the man he dreamed of the night prior.

In his dream, stars fell from heaven and hid their light inside a group of crazed men. They surrounded Thomas as he sat in the center of a dark floor. Saliva poured from their mouths as they whipped him with their shackled tongues. They wagged their fingers at him and stared with blood-soaked eyes. Yet they tormented him in vain. Their skin was leprous, their breath was foul, and they knew only hate, fear, and lust. They all wore dirty bandages that could not completely cover the vile wounds that had taken over their once-perfect frames.

Thomas sat quietly in their midst. They circled him as they laughed and mocked. However, Thomas did not fear them. They feared him. They did not know why. As the night came to an end and the moon no longer held her sway, the crazed men tired. One by one, they fell at Thomas's feet, exhausted.

Patiently, Thomas waited for the last to fall. Silence finally filled the room as the crazed men give up their taunts in exchange for rest. It was then Thomas spoke in a still, small voice.

"Greater is he that is in me than he that is of the world. Greater is he that is in me than he that is in the world," Thomas chanted.

As he spoke, the bandages on the crazed men loosened and fell to the ground. Their wounds healed instantly, and their tongues were freed. Their lunacy became knowledge. Their eyes became clear, and the light of the stars that once fell from heaven now shined bright inside them all.

Thomas pointed to his heart, and with his other hand, he pointed above. He opened his eyes slowly, and fire shot from his sockets. The torch-like flame then wrapped around each of the crazed men's torsos. This fire joined them as one. It burned them all, yet none were hurt by it. Instead, they became clean and began to speak as Thomas spoke. Their voices became his. They now spoke as one.

"Greater is he that is in me than he that is in the world," they repeated until a gunshot ripped through air.

Each to the left of Thomas fell dead instantly, while each to the right stood tall as Thomas stood. They searched for the killer. In an instant, in the twinkling of an eye, they were transported into the day room of a hospital.

Bars fell from the sky, covering every exit. The only door leading out was held by a dark presence. This dark figure dangled a black key before them, but the true key to their freedom was not in this man's hand. Shadow covered the man's face as smoke poured from the barrel of the gun he had just fired.

"Leave us," Thomas whispered, and his voice began to echo through the mouths of those standing with him.

"Leave us, leave us, leave us..." The whispered words continued, and the haunting cadence forced the man's hand to bring the gun to his own temple.

The dark man fought to resist, but the words of the once-crazed men and Thomas were stronger than he was. A shot rang out, and the killer fell to the ground, dead. His black keys fell from his dead hand and turned to gold for Thomas.

The bars that held them melted away, and light shined above. The shadow could no longer hide the killer's true face. It was the face of the man Thomas is about to see. It was the face of Dr. Vince Manus.

This dream was a warning of the man to come. A man that is a devil, a wolf in sheep's clothing.

Thomas does not think of the words he is going to speak. Instead, he thinks of the end of his dream. He remembers the bars melting away. He remembers the light shining bright as his captor gave up the keys to the death that held them all.

Hearing the knob of the large door to the room turning, Thomas opens his eyes. The door drags slowly across the floor, like thick nails across a chalkboard.

Dr. Manus enters with a boastful look on his face. He hangs his dark-brown fedora on the hooks of the wall. He takes off his tweed jacket and lays it across the back of the steel chair facing Thomas.

Thomas stares at him. When will he introduce himself?

From under Manus's arm, he takes out Thomas's medical file. He walks to the corner rudely and thumbs through the file, like a detective calling a thief's bluff. Taking his bifocal glasses out of his wrinkled button-down shirt pocket, he makes his way to the chair again. Clearing his throat, he sits as he places his glasses on his large and crooked nose. Manus taps his fingers from pinkie to forefinger repeatedly on the desk. Thomas waits for him to speak without blinking his eyes.

"Well," Manus says with a loud exhale. "I finally get to meet the legendary Thomas James. How are you?" A sinister smile grows on his face.

Thomas nods his head, acknowledging him, but does not offer the man words.

"I cannot tell you, young man, how happy I am to finally make your acquaintance. I'm Dr. Vince Manus, as you well know, and I am here to help you." He coughs. His voice rattles from the mucus sliding down the back of his throat.

"I must say, Thomas, I am excited to do so. You and I are going to become fast friends. We're going to learn a lot from each other." He pauses for a moment to lick his chapped lips. "So let's get started, shall we?" Manus extends his hand across the metallic table for Thomas to shake, yet Thomas keeps still. He will not give this man his hand yet.

"Oh, I know you're probably tired of all the doctors that keep talking to you. In and out at all hours, saying, 'Take this, take that.' I know how it is. They just want the best for you, Thomas, just like me. Now I don't know about them, but I can tell you this, Thomas, you can trust me...you can trust me." He punctuates his last statement by pressing his swollen index finger into the table until his entire finger grows white.

"I'm not here to draw your blood or give any shots. I am just here to talk, Thomas. Now, we can talk about anything you would like. From sports to, I don't know, girls. You have any pretty girls waiting to visit?" Manus pauses for a response. None is given.

"Well, if not, maybe we'll get you one. What do you say? You're a handsome young man, aren't you?" The lust in Manus's eyes reveals his true intent. "Yes, yes you are, Thomas, a handsome young man."

Thomas does not take his eyes off him. You never do that with a snake unless you want it to bite you.

"I will be square with you. Mainly, I want to talk to you about how you are feeling right now. Are you scared, anxious, or mad? You can trust me, Thomas. I'm only here to help. I'm here for you." Manus plasters on his best smile.

Thomas turns his head toward the mirror in the wall. He points to it. "What's behind that mirror?" he asks calmly.

"So you *can* talk, excellent!" Manus ignores his question. "I had heard you did, but it is good to hear it for myself."

"What's behind the mirror?" Thomas repeats quietly. His hand is still raised, his finger still pointed.

Manus turns to the mirror. He takes off his glasses as if he has never seen it before. "Nothing, just an empty room," he says frankly.

"Would you mind rolling me in there to see for myself?" Thomas asks.

Realizing Thomas found him out, Manus stands and walks to the mirror.

"I thought you said I could trust you, Doctor. Lies are not the best way to gain another's trust."

"You got me, Thomas." Manus smiles. "You don't really mind, do you?"

"I don't want to be recorded, Doctor. What happens here will stay here and here alone."

Manus clenches his jaw as he knocks on the mirror to alert one of his orderlies in the adjoining observation room to turn the recording camera off.

Thomas folds his hands together on the desk. He continues to stare directly at him.

Manus returns to his chair with a sneer. "You're a smart young man, I'll give you that. I do apologize for not being up front with you. It is procedure to tape these meetings for further review later. But if you're uncomfortable with it, we'll keep it off for now." Manus sits down and challenges Thomas by staring back at him. "It wasn't my intention to deceive you. We simply don't want to scare anyone by letting them know 'big brother' is watching." He chuckles, but his attempts of endearment are wasted.

"Why would I be scared?" Thomas leans toward him. He pins Manus under his stare. The doctor can feel his disapproval and uncomfortably looks away.

"No reason." An uncomfortable pause follows. "Do you know how long you've been gone, Thomas?"

"I haven't been gone, Doctor. I have been asleep. But now I'm awake, and all is well." Thomas looks slowly to the left and then to the right, as if he has a secret to tell.

"If you want to call it that," Manus says under his breath and anxiously taps his fingers again.

Thomas leans into Manus and whispers, "Do you know who I am?"

"Yes, yes I do…do you?"

Thomas sits back and allows his eyes to fall on him. "I am who I am," he says in a powerful yet controlled voice.

The veins in Manus's neck thicken. His face grows red. It is easy to see the tension rising in him. "Well, that is good to hear. Do you know how long you have been asleep?" the doctor asks.

"Many, many years, Doctor. Many years," Thomas answers mysteriously.

"Do you feel different? Different than you remember feeling before the accident?"

"Absolutely."

"Why do you think that is?" Manus takes off his glasses and places them on the table.

"Why do you?" Thomas unlocks his folded fingers and places his hands shoulder-width apart from each other on the table.

"I ask the questions, Thomas, not you," Manus says with a chuckle.

"You're asking the wrong ones, Doctor. If you ask the right questions, I will give you the only answer that matters." Thomas taps his fingers on the table once quickly, just as the doctor had done earlier.

Manus exhales in frustration. He places his glasses back on angrily. "Look, Thomas, our time is short, and I really want to make the most of it. So please just answer me honestly."

"I'm not the one who has the problem with honesty." Thomas glances at the mirror on the wall. "I tell the truth."

"Let's talk about your family. What were they like?"

"Who is my family but those who love me and hear me?"

"Well, your mother, your grandmother? Let's talk about them." Manus leans in anxiously.

Thomas smells the stale cigarettes and coffee that clings to Manus's breath as he speaks.

"It must have been devastating to lose everything you held dear right before your very eyes. How did that make you feel?" Manus asks heartlessly.

"Nothing is ever lost that isn't one day found. And when it is found, it is one hundred times more precious than it was when it was lost to begin with. Absence makes the heart grow fonder, you know?" A peculiar smile grows on Thomas's face.

Manus takes out a small pad and paper and begins to write in it. "I'm sorry, Thomas, what…what does that mean? Nothing is ever lost?"

"If I were to tell you what that means, you wouldn't believe me. You'll only hear what you want to hear, and that's why you won't believe me when I tell you the truth."

"Why, Thomas? Is what you have to say so hard to believe?" he asks sarcastically as he documents the conversation. These are the very words Manus believes will convince the board that Thomas needs further study.

"You can't hear my words because they aren't yours. You make your words, and they are not to be trusted. But my words are to be trusted because they are no longer my own," Thomas declares with authority.

"Excuse me, what do you mean? Your words aren't your own?" Manus licks the saliva that forms in the corners of his mouth. His case is being made for him, he believes.

Thomas's eyes become red. A controlled anger begins to build inside him. His words are as fierce as they are pointed. "You're not here for me. If you were here for me, you would know who I am. But you don't know who I am. Nor have you ever known who I am. That is why you cannot hear me, Doctor. That is why you are trying to condemn me." He snaps his teeth together like a lion tearing into raw meat.

Manus looks up from his paper proudly. Thomas is playing right into his hands. "You think I'm going to condemn you, Thomas? I'm here to help you, not hurt you." Manus turns to the mirror and motions for the camera to be turned on again. From the other side, two orderlies oblige his request.

"Keep it off!" Thomas shouts as he leans in further to stare into Manus's dark soul. "What you do now you will regret. And you will suffer greatly for it. You will wish you had heard the words that are spoken today!"

"Is that so?" Manus asks with great sarcasm.

"I am telling you the truth. If you knew who it is that sits before you, you would weep because of all the evil you've done in your life."

Manus grinds his teeth and rolls his eyes. "What are you talking about, Thomas?"

"It will fall from the sky around you, and it will show the truth of who you are. And you will die!"

Thomas snatches Manus's hands as a mongoose would the neck of a cobra. Manus cannot pull his hands away. "Because the light is here, Doctor. The light is here!" Thomas releases his grip. The doctor falls to the floor in a panic. His glasses shatter against the ground. He looks at Thomas with great fear as a fire burns inside his mind.

Memories of what he has done to his patients flash before his eyes. He remembers drugging young patients, male and female alike, and perversely using them. He remembers shocking and beating patients when darker pleasures needed to satisfy his lusts. He remembers all the horrible evils he committed on dozens of helpless victims whose caretakers placed them in his care.

"No! No! No!" he screams as his memories plague him. Now he sees through the eyes of his victims. He feels what they feel—the torment, the abuse, the shame. Manus fights to get away in terror. As if a rat trapped in a cage, his legs kick against the floor.

"No no no! I'm sick!" He rolls over to his knees and begins vomiting. "Help! Help, help me!" he cries in the darkness of his sins.

The two large orderlies from the adjoining room rush to his side. "Are you all right?" one of his men asks while the other lifts him from the ground.

"We're done! We're done! I need…I need…I need air!" His bloodcurdling screams echo in the hall as the men rush him from the room.

The door shuts behind them, and the muffled sounds of Manus crying diminishes the farther they get from the room.

Thomas locks his fingers together and places his folded hands on the table calmly. He closes his eyes and quietly begins to pray.

Moses into the promise land did not lead.

The instruction to trust and to simply speak he did not heed.

And so the land of promise he could not know because to get the waters of life to flow, the heart of man you must never beat.

Only when you depend on Inspiration will Inspiration lend the promise that you seek.

This is why to the Heart of Man, the Shepherd of the Promise Land, will only speak.

His words when heard are as the wind beneath the wings of birds; they are as water to a seed.

And so to get the Waters of Life to flow, faith, trust, love, and compassion is all the Shepherd ever needs.

If only Moses didn't force his will on others, if only to get his way the rock Moses didn't beat.

Perhaps we would all be in the promise land already instead of hearing me to the heart of man begin to speak.

—Thomas James

Everyone Will Know Love

The day's sun-shower leaves a large rainbow in the sky above the hospital's roof garden. A wide variety of trees, flowers, and lush green plants offers refuge to all who visit there.

As Thomas sits in his wheelchair under the garden's only fig tree, Nancy breathes in the morning air next to him and lets out a sigh of relief. "It is a beautiful day," she says with a large sweet smile.

The petals and leaves of the hospital's prize rosebushes glisten from the raindrops making their nest in them. A few bees buzz and hover around the two as if they were flowers themselves. A dozen or so birds feast on the scattered seed of yesterday near the garden's entrance.

With wide eyes, Thomas looks at the rainbow stretching the sky. "It is a beautiful day," he agrees.

Nancy clears her throat and turns to Thomas. "I had a dream about you last night," she says. "We were together in a seven-acre patch of cotton ripe for picking. It was white as far as the eye could see. I stood there with you because I wanted to buy the field. But you wouldn't let me. You told me the field was free, and it wasn't for me alone." Nancy raises her eyebrow. "Now, what do you think that means?"

Thomas continues looking above. Rays of light reflect off the small pond to their left and flicker around him, as if hundreds of sparkling diamonds surround him.

"It means a day of peace is coming," he says confidently.

"I hope I see that day sooner than later." Nancy chuckles as she rocks back and forth comfortably.

"Everyone will, and everyone will know love." He allows his eyes to return to the garden.

Nancy's smile disappears. She sits up straight and forgets to comfortably rock in wonder after his words. *How can it be that all will know peace?* she thinks. There is so little peace in the world today. It seems impossible to believe that all of humanity could truly love each other. How can Nancy believe that such a thing is possible when she herself knows so few people who are kind, gentle, and meek? She believes only a few see such a thing; only few would enter such rest. For everyone else, a horrible endless fate waits.

"You can't mean everyone," she asks seriously.

Thomas closes his eyes, and his head sinks. He exhales. So few can see what he now sees. "The field you saw in your dream is the world. The white cotton represents the hearts of those who have become pure. Everyone will see this day because it is made for them. It is the last day of our ignorance and the first day of our true life."

"I don't understand what you mean, Thomas. Not everyone will choose to be good!"

Thomas groans in his spirit. Pity fills his eyes. "What choice does a pot have in how the potter makes it? What choice does a painting have when the artist creates it?"

Nancy crinkles her forehead in confusion. "What does that have to do with anything?"

"A painting can never understand why the colors are applied the way they are. The pot can never understand why, when imperfections are found, that it has to be smashed and formed again. Like the painting and the pot, we don't see the purpose in our suffering or the changes we face in life."

"You can't tell me that suffering has purpose, Thomas." Nancy looks away and raises her nose in the air. Her mind tells her not to listen to him. But his words cut deep.

"Where would the pearl be without the suffering of the oyster? How much more precious is humility and peace than pearls?"

She stands abruptly.

"Nancy, one day, like all pearls, we too will be gathered together and shown to the world."

Nancy huffs. She will not entertain such philosophy.

"Your suffering is nothing compared to the glory that will be revealed in you later, Nancy. One day you'll see this."

It is a struggle to bottle her emotions. She wants to scream and tell him just how wrong he is. Her life has been a hard one. Many times she questioned why God would allow such things. She lives on after the loss of her son, and her faith, she believes, is stronger. Being told that there is a purpose to suffering is more than she can take.

"I don't believe you! How can anything good come out of so much pain?" she yells.

"Would you rather believe you suffered in vain?"

How can Nancy answer that? Of course, one would prefer to believe that there is a point to the ills of the worlds and the troubles of the heart. However, this makes no sense to her rational mind.

"I don't know what you mean." She says the only thing she can.

"Nancy, do you love more now than you ever have before? Do you not have a greater compassion and patience because of all you've been through?"

Nancy knows he is right. She is kinder and gentler because of all she has suffered. She appreciates life and those around her more; she now knows how fleeting our time here is. But that still doesn't give her the answer she is longing to hear. Why did she have to suffer to learn this?

"Not everything that seems horrible ends that way," Thomas says with a small smile. "If it weren't for the manure, where would the flowers be?"

Nancy is not amused. Like most, she believes she is in control. Like most, she believes man is the cause for the things that affect each one of us. Therefore, when bad things happen, it cannot be because those bad things are for our good.

"I refuse to believe God creates, or allows, the evil in our lives! And I refuse to believe that everyone will find peace. There are bad people in the world, Thomas, and they have to pay for what they've done." Nancy sits again. She folds her arms with authority and refuses Thomas her face.

Thomas reaches his hands out in front of him. He allows the sun to illuminate them. He turns them over and watches as his palm becomes as bright as the sun itself. "Could you ever stop loving your son...even if he did the most horrible of things? Would you ever give up on him because he strayed so far from your hand?"

"Of course not," she says, as if there is no other answer a mother can give.

"Then what makes you believe that a perfect God would not do the same, and more, for his children? Even the most lost."

She inches her head toward him. Her eyes meet his. They are so blue and inviting. His face is so calm and kind. Oh, how Nancy wishes she could have the peace he seems to have.

Thomas rests his hand on top of hers. Her face relaxes.

"Nancy, even a child gets burned on the hot stove before he realizes he should stop touching it. People must find their way, and God is patient."

Nancy feels foolish after hearing him. This wisdom from a child, this faith from one who has lost so much, it is beyond her comprehension. Who is this boy? Why does he speak the way he does, know the things he knows?

"You're only eighteen, but you talk like you're eighty."

Thomas leans in as if to answer the wild thoughts running through her mind. "There is more to me than you know, Nancy... There is more to us all."

Her heart begins to race. It pounds in her chest like the galloping of a hundred steeds. "Who are you?" she asks with eyes too filled with fear to blink.

"I am what I am, nothing more." Thomas takes his hand away from Nancy as the door leading to the roof garden opens with a loud creak.

Out steps Dr. Felicia Adams. The door slams shut with a dull thud behind her, which scares the feeding birds into the sky. Felicia follows the flock with her eyes as they fly up to circle above.

In the center of the flock, she notices a pure white mourning dove. It is different from the rest. Suddenly, it leaves the cycle of flight and descends upon the top branch of the fig tree where Thomas sits. The dove puffs out its feathers to ward off any other birds that may try to take the branch from it.

Felicia is surprised at how calm the bird appears. *How odd,* she thinks. It is a strange sight. Felicia is not used to seeing a wild animal rest so close to a human being. As she approaches, the dove does not move at all. Call it superstition, but she takes this as a good sign. "Hello, Thomas…Nancy," she says quietly, not wanting to frighten the dove away.

"Good morning, Doctor," Nancy says with thoughts that appear to be elsewhere.

"Can you believe that bird? It's beautiful, isn't it?" Felicia points it out, but only Nancy takes the time to look at it.

"Now isn't that something?" Nancy says, rising to her feet and looking for an excuse to leave. "Well, I have to get back. I'll leave you to it." Nancy is distracted as she walks away. She looks back over her shoulder at Thomas. Her peculiar look speaks of the many thoughts now racing through her mind.

"Thanks, Nancy." Felicia takes her place on the small wall. She tries to hide the fact that she notices something is troubling Nancy. But what could this young man have said to prompt such a thing? Felicia looks to Thomas for the answer. He is so composed. Not a care in the world, it seems. How can this be?

"Is everything okay?" she asks as Nancy exits.

Thomas does not answer. Instead, he looks at the white dove perched above him.

"That bird is strange, huh?" She challenges him to speak.

"I've been waiting for you," Thomas says without taking his eyes off the bird.

"You have?" Felicia tries to make eye contact. "Dr. Striphe told me where to find you. Did he tell you I was coming?"

"Do you like it up here, Doctor?" Thomas ignores her question as if her words mean nothing to him.

"Sure." Felicia looks around. She barely notices the many-colored flowers and plants surrounding the two. She does not take the time to admire them at all. "I do. It's very nice."

"Is it?" he asks in an unbelieving voice.

Felicia shrugs him off. She has seen the same garden for the last six years. It has the same bushes, the same plants, the same old trees. Why would she need to take the time to see what she has seen so many times before? Her answer to him is small talk, nothing more. This is not the reason Felicia is here. Manus has recommended Thomas be put in his permanent care. This, this is why she is here. Manus has the board in his back pocket. She needs support, but knows she will not find this among her colleagues. Perhaps a press conference, if he is competent enough, is a good idea after all.

"So how are you feeling, Thomas?" It is her turn to ignore him, it seems. Her knee bounces up and down nervously as she waits for his answer.

The most content of looks fills Thomas's face. He truly admires and appreciates his surroundings. He watches the mist leap from the pool of water beneath the waterfall as if it is the first time he's done so.

"After being in darkness, when you finally wake up to see the light, there is beauty and much of it," he says. "But you have to stop looking at everything else that troubles you to see it."

"Can we please focus on something besides a garden that hasn't changed in the last six years?" she asks heartlessly.

How many times has Felicia been on this roof worrying about things beyond her control? How many times has she come here to relax after a hard shift and only thought on what had troubled her that day? She knows this garden better than anyone does, or so she believes.

In an instant, Thomas's face changes. He looks away from the beauty of the place to stare deep into Felicia's uninterested eyes.

She is drawn to him like a moth to a flame. The nervous shaking of her leg subsides, and a strange calm takes over her.

"Doctor, sometimes people get so focused on things that aren't important that the things that truly matter seem foolish to them."

She blinks her eyes and tries to shake the calm feeling rising in her away. It is his voice. It is so pleasant to her ears. *Why is that?* She relaxes on the stone wall where she sits. It has been ages since she's felt this way. Part of her wants to give in and listen to his words. The other part wants to ignore him. This part is fighting for control.

She clears her throat. "Look, Thomas, this isn't why I came up here to talk with you. It's about this press conference you asked for." Felicia tries to sit in the most professional of ways, but she finds herself relaxing, as if she is in the presence of a longtime friend.

Thomas shifts in his seat and closes his eyes. "People have been tricked into seeing what is wrong instead of what is right. They look for something they will never find. As if money, a different job, or a new lover could ever bring them peace."

Felicia tries to maintain the appearance of control. But it's hard for her to focus on why she originally came to visit Thomas. His words are captivating her. The sound of his voice is as smooth as oil. Her head sinks back slowly. Her hair dangles free behind her. She looks to the clouds in the sky, as a child would on a swing.

"Everyone will stop to see an accident. They will go out of their way to see another's loss and to speak of it. They look to find fault in people, never trusting, never loving, and never looking for what is right. They will talk more about what a person lacks than what a person has to give. They are lost today, Doctor. Lost. They will search high and low for pain, never once seeing all that is right in the world and in their lives. Why is it we rejoice in telling people the bad things and yet get angry when others tell us of the good?" Thomas asks sadly.

She stretches her neck toward him so her ears are closer to his lips. "I don't know, Thomas," she says with bumps rising on her skin as if a cool wind kisses her.

"A laborer and a lawyer die the same day. The lawyer had his health and riches. The laborer was crippled from many years of work and had nothing but a small cot in a barn to call home. When the lawyer was on his deathbed, he said, 'I wish I had something to leave behind, besides a list of criminals I lied for to help set free.' The laborer said, 'Who will care for the field when I am gone?' Which of these men loved the work they were given?"

"The laborer, but what does that have to do with anything?" she asks curiously.

"The lawyer had the picture-perfect life on the outside. He had a large home, family, wealth, and many possessions. But he was always looking for more and was never satisfied. All his blessings were not enough, so he always searched for more. The laborer, on the other hand, had nothing. He had nothing but the field he was given to care for, and he was grateful for it. On the outside, this crippled man looked hopeless. He was poor, always in pain, and had nothing but the ragged clothes on his back. But I tell you, this man is the greater of the two because he found joy and purpose in what he was given. He knew that without him, the field would surely die. He found a point to his life. The lawyer never saw himself this way. The lawyer was lost. And when he died, he regretted his life because he never once took the time to smell the roses or to see the beauty all around him."

Felicia sits up straight. A deep sadness comes over her. "Do you think I'm lost?"

"It depends on how you see the garden."

"What?" Felicia looks around as if there was something she missed.

"In a garden, many things are planted. And whatever you care for thrives. If the garden is ignored and despised, weeds will strangle what has been planted from the beginning, and everything that is good will die. It is not until the gardener comes along that things are restored to the way they were intended to be. Like the garden, whatever is planted and nourished in us will take root and grow. If we believe we are poor and cursed, we shall grow as poor and cursed plants. If we believe we are loved and cared for, then our beauty will shine for all to see. Whatever you think you are in your heart is what you become, Doctor. If you plant fear, you will be scared. If you sow hate, you will be hated. And until those seeds are weeded out by the true seed of love, the garden would be better if it had never been planted to begin with."

Felicia kneels at his feet and rests her hands on the arms of his wheelchair to talk with him. Her position seems like the most natural thing in the world. "You don't talk like any eighteen-year-old I've ever met," she says as she looks up at him curiously. A glow surrounds his head. The sun creates it. From where she kneels, it looks almost like a halo that reaches the heavens.

"People are lost today, Doctor," Thomas says, looking down at her. "And they need someone to lead them back home."

A chill races up Felicia's neck. His last words snap her out of her dreamlike trance. She pulls her hands away from him and leaps to her feet. She dusts herself off and looks at him with worried eyes. He is no longer a comfort to her but rather an offense.

"What do you mean? Do you think that 'someone' is you, Thomas?" she asks angrily.

The dove that had been sitting peacefully above begins to chirp like mad.

"Who do you think you are, Thomas?" *Maybe Manus is right*, she thinks. Maybe he needs more help than she can give him.

The dove flaps its wings violently above her. She looks toward it, but the sun forces her to cover her eyes. The bird is incensed. Its feathers fall to the ground. Some land on Felicia's shoulder. She moves away from Thomas, holding her hands in defense of it. She worries the bird might swoop down and pluck out her eyes.

"What's with that bird?" she yells. Felicia backs away in fear. *Does this bird carry disease? Is it rabid?* Her worries mount as the dove breaks free from the branches of the tree and soars high above the two. Felicia peers through her fingers, refusing to take her eyes off it until she knows it is far from her.

Suddenly, the dove changes direction. In a nosedive toward her, it seems it will attack.

"What the—" She dives to the ground and covers her face with her hands to get out of its way.

The bird barely misses her. Felicia is left on the ground. Her eyes are squeezed together tightly, and her breathing is heavy.

"Are you all right?" Thomas asks calmly with a small smile growing on his face.

She takes the time to realize there is nothing now to fear. She opens her eyes and slowly lifts herself from the ground. Her eyes find Thomas and cannot believe what she sees. The dove now rests on Thomas's hand as if trained to do so.

He takes birdseed from his pocket and places it in the palm of his hand. Ever so gently, the dove begins to eat from it. Felicia gets up and steps toward Thomas and the dove cautiously. Never has she seen such a thing.

"Unbelievable," she whispers as she slowly returns to him.

"If the seed is good, you can't help but eat it," he says mysteriously.

Felicia folds her arms to get back to business. She is between a rock and a hard place. The things Thomas says make her nervous. But if she allows a press conference and he appears sane, than the board will have no cause to send him to Manus.

There is something peculiar about this young man, that there is no denying. He is her patient, and if she cannot protect him from the darkness of that place, no one will.

"Thomas, look, there is a reason I'm here for you." There is a sense of urgency in her words.

Thomas looks up at her. The smile in his eye is gone.

"I'll allow you to speak to the press, if you can tell me why you want to so badly."

The dove takes to the sky again. Thomas's head sinks. He rubs his hands together to get rid of any of the seed that remains.

Felicia looks for the bird, but it is gone. Oddly enough, this makes her sad.

"Give me your hand," Thomas says as he reaches.

"Excuse me?"

"Give me your hand. What are you so scared of?"

Slowly she extends her hand to his. He grabs her wrist gently and turns her hand palm up. He reaches inside his pocket, takes out more birdseed, and places it in her palm.

"Imagine the seed in your hand is the only food the world needs to eat to truly live. It is in your power to keep it from them or to feed them. If you close your hand and keep this food to yourself, no one lives but you." Thomas wraps her fingers over the seed in her palm. He then lets go of her, and she walks backward, holding her hand closed tight, the way Thomas left it.

"But if you open your hand and allow that food to be shared with the starving world, then all will be saved," he says brightly.

"From birdseed?" Her forehead crinkles, making light of what he says.

"What would you do if the seed in your hand could heal the world?"

Felicia looks at her hand. "I would open my hand, Thomas. What do you think?"

"Then do it," he says with a severe stare. "Open your hand, Doctor."

Slowly, she does so. As soon as her fingers are flat and the seed is revealed, the dove returns and lands on her hand to eat.

"Oh my god!" she screams. Felicia does everything she can to keep from falling to the ground. "How? How did you—huh! Do you see this? Oh, it tickles." She laughs, and her eyes grow wide with amazement. The dove continues to feed from her hand, and she enjoys every second of it. "How did…how did you do that, Tommy?"

"Like you, if it was in my power to save those that are hungry, I would."

Felicia takes a deep breath and considers the sincerity of Thomas's words. She looks at the dove in her hand. It immediately stops eating, as if waiting for her answer as well.

"I'll schedule a press conference right away. Just don't...don't say anything crazy, okay?"

Thomas smiles, and Felicia turns her attention again to the gentle dove in her hand. Curiously, his smile fades as if there is something Thomas is not telling her.

We are to put off falsehood and speak truly to our neighbor. In this we all will find great favor.

Let him who would lie, lie no more. Let him who would steal labor to enter into what is real, to work honestly forevermore.

This is the call you must no longer ignore.

For it is not those who commend themselves that are approved, but those the Existing one approves that are ministers of all.

This is why we cry and encourage you to rise from vanity's fall.

—Thomas James

No One Will Miss Him

Leah James wrings her hands nervously as she waits for Dr. Vince Manus in his office. The dimly lit room is dirty. It is an eerie place. Dust lines the bookshelves. They overflow with ancient texts about the mind and ego. In the far corner of the room, a life-sized skeleton hangs from a hook; to her right, a human brain is pickled and proudly floats in a large oval jar for all to see; and next to her feet, a mousetrap sits with week-old cheese.

"Where is he?" she asks as the cobweb-covered grandfather clock ticks away like a haunted knocking at the door.

On the opposite side of the large black desk under a pile of folders, Leah notices a curious envelope. The corner of a strange photo peeks out of it. She leans forward. Her head tilts, and her eyes focus on what appears to be a face of a child.

"What is that?" Her words are to herself. Her thoughts run wild. Her surroundings heighten her sense of fear.

She looks to the door. It is still closed. She listens to hear if anyone is coming. Nothing is heard but the clock.

Sweat beads on her upper lip. She licks it away and moves closer. Her hand reaches across the desk. Cautiously she raises the pile for a better look. Worried she may be caught in this act, she is careful to not expose too much. It doesn't take much to chill her to the very core.

"Oh my god!" she cries and returns to her chair with shaking hands and a pale face.

"Sorry to keep you." Manus enters, and Leah jumps.

"Oh, no, no, no problem," she tries to compose herself. "You scared me."

Manus rounds his desk methodically. Something is different to him. "Well, we can't have that, can we?" He stops to straighten the very pile of folders Leah had disturbed.

She gulps and straightens her blouse to draw attention away from her nerves.

Manus sits and leans back in his worn leather chair. He locks his fingers together and rests them on top of his protruding belly.

"I suppose you're wondering why I invited you here."

"I am," she says with eyes that try to avoid the pile of folders where the disturbing image hides away.

Manus takes his time to answer her. It seems he takes pleasure in making Leah squirm. He sucks through his teeth and finally sits up. "Thomas's doctor has cleared him to speak with the press. Of course, I don't believe this is a good idea."

Leah is angry. She plants her fist firmly on his desk. "He'll speak with the press, but he won't say a word to me?"

Manus smiles. Some of his teeth are rotted away while others are sharp, as if they'd been filed down. "Perhaps he's heard you're entertaining my request to have him committed."

"How would he know that?"

The grandfather clock chimes. The loud gong startles her. It gives her a moment to consider things.

Thomas never truly cared for her. She knows this. She also knows that she doesn't much care for him. However, since the death of his family and after slipping into his coma, Leah has profited greatly from the insurance payouts, the interviews, articles, and multiple appearances she made on his behalf. She knows now that her nephew is awake, the future payouts and residuals will revert back to Thomas if he is capable of caring for himself. Leah has grown accustomed to her lifestyle. What a moral crossroad.

As the sixth gong sounds, her decision is easily made.

"I'm not so sure I'd like to place Thomas in your care just yet. Disability insurance would offer me enough to take care of the boy myself. He'd be better at home with me as some sort of outpatient. Don't you think?"

Manus leans back farther in his chair. *Clever girl,* he thinks. Like most today, Leah has her price, and he is going to name it.

"Of course, I could offer you much more from the research grants I will surely be given, to help you as you prepare your home for the time that I believe Thomas is actually ready for an outpatient regime." He pauses to scratch the dandruff from his matted hair. "It would be a sizably different amount for you to consider."

Leah cannot hide her delight."Well, perhaps it would be best to place him in your care for a time." She sits up straight and reaches as if for a pen. "Where should I sign?" she asks, conveniently forgetting the disturbing pictures she saw.

Manus laughs. He glances over at the pile on his desk and allows his beady eyes to return to hers. "You must love him very much," he says ironically.

"I want the best for him," she says, looking away. Her conscience begins to sting with the decision she makes.

"Unfortunately, we cannot commit him if his doctor thinks he is well enough to speak with the press, can we?"

"But I thought you said—"

Manus takes out his checkbook. He places it on the table and begins to write in it. "Any kind of press is good press for the hospital. And the board isn't about to turn its back on that. But don't worry. Every wrong will be made right." Manus licks his chapped lips, leaving a slimy residue behind. He finishes writing and places his pen back into his pocket. "You leave his doctors to me. And when the time is right, can I count on your good judgment to place the young man in my care?" Manus holds the check in front of her.

"Yes." Leah stands abruptly and snatches the check out of his hand. She gathers her things. "Well, thank you for your time, Doctor."

"Yours as well, Ms. James." Manus stands as she walks to the door. "Oh, and Ms. James?" He takes his glasses off and places them on the desk.

"Yes?" Leah turns to face him.

He rests his left hand on top of the folders she had looked through earlier. "I can assure you, if the press conference does not go well and you decide to place Thomas in my care, the picture you saw of the young man with the horse bit in his mouth is not standard practice for all my patients."

Leah's mouth goes dry. However gruesome this image was to her, what is more frightening is the fact that Manus had not mentioned that the patient was also naked and strapped to a chair. But honestly, Leah doesn't care. The reality is, she never cared about anyone but herself, much less the child she had to pretend to love for these last six years. She will forget what she has seen.

She grabs the handle tightly and exits as quickly as she can. Her greed justifies the place she may soon send her own nephew, if allowed to do so.

The longer we dwell on the faults of others, the longer our peace is smothered.

The longer we replay the pain of yesterday, the harder it is to enjoy today.

The longer we wait to end our debate, a world at war we continue to create.

The longer it takes to appreciate that you can do what you've always dreamed to do, the farther away that dream will stay, instead of being accomplished by you.

When nothing seems to go your way, when you believe you've had the absolute worst day, when it seems people have nothing nice to say, when your blue skies have turned to gray, you must remember times like these won't always stay, because you have entered into a new day where nothing shall be impossible for you.

—Thomas James

Hearts Change

Television crews and reporters from around the world set up their cameras to document the much-awaited Thomas James press conference. At noon the event begins, and the list of questions reporters have is long for the boy who defies medical science by rising from obscurity.

The press conference will be different from most. No time constraints will be enforced and no preparation allowed for the ones being interviewed. Multiple networks will broadcast it live around the world, as well as feeding it across the Internet.

The words Thomas will speak will become headlines the following day on the front page of every reputable newspaper, magazine, and weekly rag. Rumors surface about Thomas's mental state. It leaks that some feel he is delusional and in need of serious psychiatric care. The press welcomes such rumor. The buzz around their camps is that he will be institutionalized soon. They wait like dogs for Thomas to throw them the bone that will confirm such reports.

The concern many once seem to have for the boy has now taken a backseat to a much-greater headline: "The Boy May Be Insane."

If it bleeds, it leads, and Thomas is their sacrificial lamb.

The reporters won't admit it, but they want the gossip to be true. They know that for such a story, the payout will be enormous. A confirmed report of Thomas's insanity will add the necessary spice missing from what some are calling the scoop of the decade.

The tide has turned for the underdog who overcame great odds. Their hearts change. Now may be time for his star to fall. Every reporter in the lobby waits for that moment to come.

Seven chairs are placed behind the large wooden table where Thomas will address the crowd. Neatly pressed white linen covers it. Small name tags are folded crisply and set in place to indicate where the players will sit.

Audio engineers set up bundles of microphones on the table. The hospital staff sets up sixty-six chairs on the floor for reporters and guests. The underpaid staffers nickname this place the pit.

Producers scurry back and forth, bidding for the floor early on. Some tape open and closing segments in preparation for going live at noon, while others rehearse their questions for the cameras.

For the last day and a half, every network has promoted the live event as if the answers to the world's problems would be discussed. They expect huge ratings. Many forget how and why Thomas became as important as he did. But this sleeping giant woke, and at 12:00 p.m., everyone will finally hear what he has to say.

Help me to see it, my Lord, my king.

Help me to believe it so the flowers will no longer cower but on every hill will sing.

Help me to receive it. I have endured while trying to cure this curse of mine. And all alone from this cross, I have continued to cry, "Oh Lord, oh Lord, in this pain I can no longer abide!"

But you knew it was all for the good of those still haunted by the night. You knew I too would choose to suffer, and in so doing become the way, the truth, and the life.

So help me to heal and to yield to your words as if they are mine. Help me to leave footprints in the land that will stand throughout the test of time.

—Thomas James

When a New Day Is Here

If a pin drops outside Thomas's room, all will hear the sound it makes as it bounces off the finely polished floor. A tension is felt not only by those waiting in the hospital lobby for the press conference to begin but by everyone in town. The anticipation is great for this event. It is only moments away. It will be the first time since waking from his coma that the world lays their eyes on the enigmatic Thomas James. Many are only waiting to see if the boy will fall.

No one knows this as well as Thomas himself. He sits alone in his wheelchair, staring out the window. His heart is heavy. He looks outside with sad eyes, as if staring into the very soul of humanity.

There isn't a bird in the sky, for miles it seems. The leaves that adorn the trees do not sway back and forth; there is no wind to make them dance. The bright sun of yesterday now hides behind a gray blanket of clouds lining the heavens. If one were to paint sorrow, it would look as dull and muddy as this day.

"What can I do?" Thomas whispers as he places his hand on his troubled brow.

It wasn't long before he heard of the rumors surrounding him. Not that he is surprised by the whispered words of backbiters and gossip columnists. The world is a fickle place. Thomas is at peace with this. People are the way they are, for better or worse. And Thomas does not care to change the hearts of those who want to remain in such a wicked place. He wants to speak to the hearts of those who crave change. He wants to speak to those who want to be set free.

If many are quick to judge him without understanding, if they are eager to condemn him without hearing the truth, what really can he do?

More people than ever before arrive in Bethel for the press conference. But the reasons are different than they were when the cheers echoed for miles that Thomas was alive.

The days for rejoicing over his recovery are now but a memory. The great love many show each other because of it now has been set aside for debate on whether Thomas is sane or not. The common bond all once found in him is not so common anymore. What they once titled the "Miracle of Thomas James" doesn't seem so miraculous after all.

Thomas closes his eyes for a moment to clear his mind. There is silence until the door to his room opens abruptly.

"You ready for today?" Colin asks, entering like a tornado through a small town.

Thomas straightens himself. How can anyone be ready for what Thomas sees approaching?

Colin picks up Thomas's chart. He hides the uncomfortable feeling he has. His eyes avoid Thomas as he thumbs through the chart, pretending nothing has transpired between the two. "You gained another three pounds. That's great."

Thomas turns his head curiously toward him. The last time they spoke, Thomas's words brought Colin to his knees in gratitude. But now, his heart is hard and his thoughts are far away. It is as if their conversation in the garden never happened at all.

"You're making good progress, Thomas. Who knows, you keep this up, and you'll be walking in no time," Colin says without realizing the weight of his words.

Thomas brings his hands together. He locks his fingers and rests them in his lap. "How long will it be before you believe I can walk, Colin?" he asks plainly.

Colin snaps the chart shut. He swallows the saliva in his mouth and gives his patient a severe stare. "Call me Doctor, Thomas." He places the chart back in place and walks to the sink. "In about a month you should be strong enough to take a few steps with a walker. I'm guessing about five to six months before you're getting around pretty good with a cane."

Colin turns the faucet knobs and places his hands under the spout in the sink. The water spits out angrily, as if work has been done to the pipes and the lines haven't been properly flushed. Colin pulls his hands away before the brown, murky water defiles them. He shuts the faucet off and reaches for the chemical hand sanitizer. He winces as he watches the dirty water drain away.

"That long? Three to four months?" Thomas asks, his face hinting that Thomas knows something Colin does not.

Colin turns to him, still rubbing the sanitizer into his hands. "I'm afraid so, Tommy. There may be significant nerve damage. I'm not going to mix words with you. You may never walk the same, but only time will tell."

Thomas allows his head to sink. His eyes rest on the floor. He shakes his head in disappointment.

Colin sees this. He walks to him, not wanting to but feeling obligated. He rests his hand on the boy's shoulder and gives him an encouraging pat. "I'm sorry, Thomas. It's different with muscle than with the mind. They have memory, but it takes time to coordinate how to use them, if you'll be able to use them at all."

Thomas pushes Colin's hand away gently. He raises his head and looks directly into the doctor's eyes. "What makes you so sure?"

Colin is at a loss. "Experience, Tommy. You have to stand before you can walk. And you may not be able to do that on your own for another month, if that!"

Thomas does not blink. His face does not soften. He seems so strong regardless of how frail and weak he appears. "We must be careful in the things we speak," Thomas says mysteriously. "Like the rudder of a ship, our tongue is small, but it can be the life or death of us and those around us. Our words have greater power than you know." Thomas leans forward in his wheelchair as soft thunder rolls across the sky.

Colin looks out the window. The clouds become the color of soot. "We should get going, Tommy."

"If you say I will not walk and I believe you, how will I ever stand on my own? Our words can be a blessing to those around us, or they can be a curse."

Lightning streaks the sky.

"A storm is coming," Colin says with a fastened stare. "They didn't say it was going to rain today." Colin nervously looks at his watch. "Look, we have to go, Tommy. They are waiting for us."

Thomas slaps his hands together. The loud clap steals Colin's attention away from the storm outside.

"What was that for?" he asks angrily.

"After all I have told you, you still can't see."

"See what?" Colin has had enough. He storms over to the door, opens it, and slams his foot down on the lock to keep it open for their exit. "You want to know what I see?" he asks impatiently. Like a dimmer turning down the intensity of the light, the room becomes dark from the unexpected storm. "What I think is all that religious mumbo jumbo you spout is making people, like me, very uncomfortable. Or making people, like Allan, very gullible. Who, by the way, is waiting outside your door with the belief that he is destined to protect you at the press conference."

"Allan will protect me today," Thomas says, directing his eyes to the hall. "You can't see what I see, but one day you will."

"Sure, whatever you say, just like you're going to walk soon." Colin's words are as sharp as any knife. He does not consider what he says before he speaks. Ruled by his emotions, he hasn't learned yet to be ruled by love.

Thomas knows why Colin is angry, why he has lost all faith in him. A promise was made to Colin about his brother by Thomas, a promise that has not yet come to pass. This is the source of his anger. This is the reason for his sudden change of heart.

"If we hope for what we see not, then we do with patience wait for it, Colin," Thomas says sadly. He places his hands on the armrests and sits quietly.

"What are you talking about?" Colin stamps his foot and refuses to blink.

"You've condemned me to this chair because you have no faith your brother will rise from his."

Colin slumps. Thomas cut right to the chase. He is right. This is the reason Colin said the very words he said. He wanted to rid himself of the pain caused by his lack of faith. He knew no other way to do this than to hurt another by trying to steal theirs. Thomas had shown Colin what was in his heart. Colin is ashamed of it.

"Look, I'm sorry," Colin says, trying to hide behind proud words. "But that's the truth, and if you're not careful in the things you say to the press today, walking is going to be the least of your concerns. Take my advice, when you're down there today, thank the reporters for their concern, thank your doctors and lawyers and whoever else for the great work they've done, and be done with it. Save the spooky spiritual talk for those dumb enough to believe it, okay?"

Pitiful tears well up in Thomas's eyes. "Your words cannot keep me in this chair."

Colin ignores him and walks behind the wheelchair. He grabs its handles and pushes, but the wheelchair will not move. It is as if the wheels are cemented to the floor. Colin strains against it to no avail. "What the—"

Thomas grabs his armrests tight and presses down. He slowly rises from his seat.

"What...what...what are you doing? Be...be careful!" Colin stutters and rushes to the front of the wheelchair to catch Thomas if he falls.

The thunder roars overhead. Veins of lightning streak the now-black sky.

Thomas stands tall without any support at all. He pushes his wheelchair behind him seamlessly. "But the words I speak will help others to walk again!" Thomas declares.

Lightning strikes the hospital's protective rods with a sonic boom. The lights flicker, and Thomas's shadow seems fierce from the electrical storm outside.

"Th-th-that's impossible." Colin's mouth goes dry. His legs become jelly.

Thomas lifts his right foot and places it in front of him. This is his first step in six long years.

"My god," Colin fearfully whispers as he lowers himself to the ground.

"When a new day is here, Colin, the world must know it." Thomas extends his hand to help Colin back to his feet. "I'm ready. Are you?"

Help me, my Lord and my King, for I feel short on power and influence as this temporal thing.

I feel alone, with no place to call home, on this journey, you see?

Lips close but hearts far, how much longer will they ignore this beautiful feeling? Please increase my reach with your light inside me.

For who among them truly walks in the light? Who knows good from evil, wrong from right?

So give me the strength, oh Lord, to continue to fight this good fight.

Not by my will but by thine, O Everlasting Spirit that am I.

Do not forsake your sons and daughters to the horrors of the night.

Do not leave this world the way it is. Use me, oh Lord, to reshape misery into bliss. So that they will all love and forgive, so paradise isn't something we will forever miss. Let my words when heard become your loving kiss, so to you all will sing,

"Help me to see my dream come true, help me, My Lord and My King!"

—Thomas James

It Will Be Shouted from the Rooftops

The reporters' cameras flash like the finale of a fireworks display as Allan wheels Thomas into the hospital lobby. Allan shields his eyes from the blinding lights as he slowly pushes Thomas to the press table. Thomas is curiously unaffected by their flash photography.

The reputable journals, conspiracy magazines, rumor rags, news crews, and even reporters from religious periodicals show their force. There are only sixty-six spots for the press in the pit, but hundreds more wait outside for the event to begin.

The press table is set. Thomas's doctors and members of the board are seated. Thomas is placed in the center of it all.

Dr. Felicia Adams pats Thomas on his knee. She feigns a nervous smile next to him. *It will be okay*, she says with her eyes. Thomas nods in agreement, but he feels something is not right.

Allan takes a few awkward steps in retreat. This crowd frightens him. He does not know why. He waits nervously in the corner behind the group as television lights are focused and those in attendance jump to their feet.

"Thomas!"

"Thomas, over here!" various reporters scream, waving their hands high in the air.

Thomas squints as he lowers his eyes to find them below in the pit.

"Thomas James, look this way!"

They shout over each other. Some shoving and name-calling begins. Security takes position on either side of the press table. The presence of security is meant to maintain order, but no one seems to care. It is obvious there will be no order until Thomas speaks.

Felicia takes a deep nervous breath. She cautiously leans toward the bundle of microphones in front of her. "Please, everyone, take your seat," she asks with a voice that cracks.

The reporters ignore her and continue their petition for Thomas's attention.

"Where have you been, Thomas?" one screams.

"Are the rumors true?" another yells.

The crowd is anxious and unsettled. Without sleep or even a shower for days, their emotions run hot. This press conference will be the climax of their long days spent trying to figure out what makes this boy so special and why the entire world wants to know more about him.

As if in slow motion, the crowd seems to move before Thomas. They scream their questions like barking, rabid dogs. Their bloodshot eyes, sweat-stained shirts, unshaved faces, and rude behavior show an aggression that otherwise should not exist. Thomas wonders what has riled them so.

His answer is given the moment he alone notices a foul odor creep into the room. This smell is familiar and unnatural. As the press shouts, he feels a dark presence. One Thomas knows quite well. The cause of the stench and the reason for their unrest.

His heart begins to race and his palms sweat. Could this be the monstrous phantom who stole his family six years ago? Is it the beast that gathered in the smoke of the flames that killed those he loved the most? Has the foul creature returned to finish what he tried doing so long ago?

The unwelcome sensation of fear grips Thomas. His teeth chatter, and his hands nervously shake. Where is the peace he knows so well?

Thomas catches his breath and tightens his eyes. He alone sees a dark mist form on the floor of the lobby. He watches in horror as this black haze grows in size while engulfing the area, like a thick fog clinging to a dark shore.

The reporters in the pit are ignorant of its influence over them. It covers their feet like splattered black mud on a boot. But like ignorant sheep, they are not aware of what is driving them into a frenzy.

The evil has waited six years to destroy him. Now the demons hiding in this dark cloud will use those in the pit to silence Thomas before he is given a chance to speak.

The foul haze rises to their kneecaps. The reporters become incensed.

"Lord, help us," Thomas whispers.

Felicia nervously tries to calm the crowd. "Can we please have order before we begin?"

Her words are not only ignored, they are criticized.

"We want answers!" the angry reporters yell.

A chill sweeps the area, like a gust of wintry wind. Thomas is numb because of it. He alone sees his breath fog before him. This evil chills the room for him alone. It may as well be winter at the height of spring.

"Help us, Father," Thomas whispers again. His mouth turns to cotton.

With so many like-minded spirits in one room, their power is great. No one can stop them. Their screams thunder around Thomas as he notices hundreds of tormented faces taking shape inside the dark cloud.

Felicia stands angrily. "There is no point in everyone shouting. Just sit down, raise your hand, and you will be called." She finishes and takes her seat in a huff.

The crowd roars defiantly. "Let the boy speak!"

The black demons cackle inside the cloud as they caress the legs of those standing in the pit. They wrap around their hosts as a snake would its prey. No one is aware of the darkness tempting the group of sixty-six to follow their perverse ways. They give in to the demon cloud, and cursing follows.

"We didn't come to hear from you!" one reporter mocks.

"You're the one who needs to shut up!" another shouts as she gives Felicia the finger.

Felicia covers the microphones. She looks to the other members of the board. "Why are they acting like this?" She cannot hide her strangling fear.

Thomas's ears begin to ring as he alone hears the twisted thoughts of those possessed in the pit. The wicked spirits place hate and prejudice into the reporters' hearts. They grow angry because of it.

Thomas grinds his teeth as he tries to silence their thoughts. *The boy's crazy. Look, he is insane. The rumors are true. Lunatic. Nutcase. Sick.*

He closes his eyes and begins to pray. "The Lord is my Shepherd, I shall not want. I shall fear no evil, for thou art with me. I shall fear no evil, for thou art with me."

In the back corner of the lobby, Colin enters behind the restless crowd. His heart jumps into his throat as he arrives on the scene. He stands on his tiptoes for a better look. "What in the name of God?" Colin says nervously.

Jim Williams, a short reporter, bumps into him. Jim also is taken by the growing madness of the crowd. "What's got their panties in a bunch?" he asks with a slack jaw, not one to hold his tongue. Jim's scruffy looks and lazy thick beard hide the talent of a bright journalist who sold his career for cheap, sensationalized headlines. As the lead reporter for the *Sentinel*, the town's only conspiracy theory magazine, he is the subject of great ridicule. With feature stories about vampires, government cover-ups, aliens, and the world's largest baby, no one takes him as seriously as they should.

"This isn't normal, is it?" Colin asks, never taking his worried eyes off the crowd.

"This? No. I've never seen anything like this," Jim answers, shaking his heavy head. "What did the kid say?"

"He didn't say anything yet."

"You're serious?" Jim reaches into his pocket for a stick of gum. He places the gum in his mouth and throws the wrapper in the air in front of the doctor's face. "Nice talking to you, Doc." He shoves his way toward the front.

"Twenty seconds to live!" a producer screams behind a large partition keeping her from harm's way. "Everyone settle down. Or I *will* pull the plug on this thing!" the producer screams.

An unexpected hush comes over the crowd. All take their seat but one.

It is Dr. Manus. He enters the room with a swagger. He has a disgusted but content look on his face. He makes his way to an empty chair in the front row. In taking his seat, he winks at Thomas and licks his lips.

Beneath Manus is the darkest part of the demon cloud. It spirals around him wildly and runs up and down his inner thighs, as if the black haze is part of Manus itself.

The producer runs to the front of the table and signals that time is up. The press conference will begin.

Felicia gathers herself and takes a deep breath.

"In ten, nine, eight, seven, six, five, four, three…" The producer counts the rest on her hand and ducks out of sight. She cues Felicia to speak by pointing at her.

"I'd like to thank you all for coming. On behalf of Bethel Memorial Hospital and our staff, we welcome you. Now I would like to open the floor up to any questions you may have first about Thomas and his recovery. Then we will allow questions to be directed to Thomas himself."

The crowd erupts as the demons prompt.

"We don't have questions for you!"

"We have questions for the boy!"

"Is it true your doctors think you're insane?" a woman holding a small notepad in hand cries out.

"Thomas, what are your doctors hiding?" an elderly reporter shouts.

"Are the rumors true?" another asks, elbowing for a better position on the floor.

Thomas swallows nervously. Felicia's frantic bouncing of her knee vibrates the entire table.

"Everyone, please wait till you're called," Felicia asks with a shy voice.

The audience jumps to their feet again. They are beside themselves. This time they attack each other.

"Sit down!" one reporter scolds another for standing in front of him.

The other turns to answer the fat man with a snarl. "Mind your business!"

The arguing is contagious. Security moves in. With one hand on their clubs and the other on their guns, they threaten that if things don't cease, force will be used.

Thomas watches the madness escalate hopelessly from his seat. He knows those in the pit have no control. They are puppets now, ruled by the vanity of the demons' thoughts.

"Everyone calm down!" security insists. "Calm down!" they threaten, yet none listen. The sixty-six snarl and mock the guards. They thumb their noses at them and wag their tongues. "No one can tell us what to do!"

"Shut it down!" the head security guard demands.

In a moment, the live television feed will be cut. The press conference as well as its broadcast will be over. Thomas's time is short to act.

The dark cloud spins violently on the floor. The men and women possessed by them act as animals fighting for scrap.

Allan rushes to Thomas's aid as two reporters rush toward the press table. Security tackles them. But a handful of others follow suit.

"We want answers!" they cry, pushing against the secure perimeter.

"End it now!" the head guard insists.

Thomas closes his eyes. He reaches for the microphones on the table. He slides them close, rolls his head, takes a deep breath, and speaks. "The spirit of the Lord is upon me!" Thomas shouts.

The madness stops instantly. The reporters stand in a daze. Security lowers their batons as everyone waits for his next words.

"He has anointed me to preach the gospel to the poor. He hath sent me to heal the brokenhearted, to preach deliverance to the captives, and recovering of sight to the blind. To set at liberty those that are bruised and to preach the acceptable year of the Lord."

A deep silence follows as the sixty-six reporters and those in attendance process his words.

"No, no, what are you doing, kid?" Colin worries. "Stick to the plan, stick to the plan!" he says to himself, knowing Thomas will not.

The sound of locusts chirping fills Thomas's ears. The demons will listen to his words no more.

"What does that mean, the spirit of the Lord is upon you?" a reporter from the *Tribune* asks in the most devilish of ways.

"It means who I am makes a way for others to see," Thomas replies confidently.

"Talk normal, Tommy," Felicia says under her breath. She grips his leg and squeezes. She knows he will be judged by his words. His words are not like those the sixty-six are used to.

The crowd looks at each other as if in on the same joke. The black demon haze rises to their chests to provoke them further, if possible. They laugh and taunt him. The rumors are true about Thomas, they believe.

Dr. Manus smiles; his eyes are black as pitch. Soon nothing will stand between his orders to have Thomas committed to his care.

"The kid is insane!" the reporters declare.

Thomas slams his fist into the table. "I'm not crazy as some of you claim!" he yells, and the crowd laughs louder. "The things of this world are insane. You kill children because of inconvenience. Promote lust for profit. Homes are torn apart. Suffering is ignored. You imprison the sick and free the criminal. The hungry go unfed, the cold without shelter, and the only truth there is, you pervert and call a lie. Everything that is good you destroy. Everything that is pure you corrupt, and everything that tells you to turn from your wicked ways you ignore. You are the ones that are lost!" Thomas demands. "You are the ones that are insane!" he finishes, slamming his hand into the table again.

Their laughing stops to facilitate rage. The demons make sure of this.

"That's enough for today!" Felicia motions for Allan to take him away.

"Just who do you think you are?" the reporter from the *Tribune* demands and spits on the ground.

Allan grabs hold of Thomas's wheelchair. Thomas grabs hold of the table so he cannot be moved away.

"The whole creation has been waiting for this day," Thomas declares. "Joel spoke of us. It is in his book. That day is here. It will be shouted from the rooftops!"

"What are you saying, Tommy? Joel? Who is Joel?" Colin exits sadly. There is nothing to be gained by watching Thomas fall harder than he already has.

"The kid thinks he is Jesus Christ," a member of the religious press cries, throwing her notepad and pen at Thomas in the front.

The demons encourage the other reporters to follow suit. They curse as they throw anything and everything they can find at him, as if stoning Thomas for committing an unforgivable sin.

The members of the board run for cover. Felicia, Thomas, and Allan are left alone to dodge their fiery darts.

"This press conference is over!" Felicia yells, holding her hand in front of her face. "Allan, get him out of here!"

The cameras continue to roll as the crowd pushes forward. Security fights against the sixty-six in the crowd, but the demon haze urges the mob on.

"Everyone back!" Security shouts.

No one listens.

"Get him out of here!" Felicia screams again.

Allan tugs at Thomas's wheelchair with all his might, but he cannot pull Thomas away.

Tears fill Thomas's eyes as he watches the darkness steal the souls from those who once loved him.

"What is going on here?" Jim Williams fearfully asks himself, taking the lens cover off his camera. He weaves in and out of the angry crowd. He gets to the front of the lobby and positions himself between two large pillars. Not only will this protect against what is thrown, but it gives him the best camera angle for the madness taking place in the lobby.

The tormented faces of the demons hiding in the dark cloud turn their stare to Thomas. Together they scream and immediately rush into their hosts as if commanded to do so. They are absorbed into the hearts of those in the pit, but their bloodcurdling shriek is like a trumpet blast in Thomas's head alone.

Thomas's hands cover his ears, but he can no longer silence the deafening sound of defeat. He rubs his eyes to rid his mind of the sight. He envisions the reporters' skin tearing, their eyes clouding over. They are blind and angry. Their tongues are black as pitch. Their skin is covered with leprous sores. Now that the demons are inside them, there is no quenching their appetite for Thomas's destruction.

Pandemonium breaks loose. They tear their press badges from their chests to throw them to the ground. They rant like mad and lunge at the table, screaming for Thomas's head.

Thomas lets go of the table. Allan pulls him away moments before a chair is thrown. The chair bounces off the table and crashes into Felicia's head. She falls immediately to the ground.

"Wait!" Thomas demands. Allan stops.

Felicia is unconscious. Blood pours from a huge gash on her head. Thomas bends down to reach her as security swing their clubs to keep the sixty-six at bay.

The television broadcast continues nonetheless. Chairs are thrown, tables are overturned, and fights break out. They scratch and claw to reach Thomas, ignorant of the evil that moves them to do so. Hundreds of millions watch in amazement around the world.

"This is insane!" Jim says to himself, snapping pictures of the gruesome scene. He turns to Felicia and Thomas. Jim raises his camera and focuses on her bleeding wound.

"Blasphemer, blasphemer!" they yell. Finally security is trampled underfoot.

Through his viewfinder, Jim sees Thomas reaching for Felicia on the floor. "What is he doing?" he asks, zooming in.

Thomas closes his eyes and drags his two forefingers gently across her open wound.

Jim snaps picture after picture, catching all of it. "Oh my god," Jim says to himself with a quivering lip. He lowers his camera as a chill races on his neck. He moves in closer to Felicia and Thomas and raises the camera again. Feet away from the two, Jim gasps as he documents Thomas wiping her blood away. It is now as if there was never a wound to begin with. Felicia is miraculously healed.

"It can't be. It can't be." Jim snaps picture after picture. The gaping wound is gone. "How?"

The table separating Thomas from the mob is overturned. Jim reacts. He rushes to Felicia. Thomas and Jim lock eyes just long enough for Thomas to acknowledge him curiously. Jim pulls Felicia away from the scene as the crowd presses in.

Thomas looks into the mob's eyes as they climb over the table to get him. They are black, empty, and cold.

"Hang on!" Allan screams as he opens the emergency exit and quickly shoves Thomas through it.

The two escape moments before the mob reaches the door.

Be a leader, a follower never be.

Don't allow yourself to become victim of that "herd mentality."

If you surround yourself with negative people, their stinking, destructive thinking you will soon know.

You must think for yourself, or you will believe whatever nonsense another person sows.

Faith comes by hearing, this statement is true.

People's opinions, gossip, and complaint, if not shut out, will not only taint, but will soon become a part of you.

So guard your heart and be careful with what you allow into your ears; test the spirits to see if they are rooted in love or if they are rooted in fear.

If you want to know joy, hope, and peace in your life, the next time that "herd" comes near, make sure you steer clear because a lie has no place with the truth.

—Thomas James

Those Who Hate the Most Must Be Loved the Most

The heavy metal door slams shut and locks. Allan hurries Thomas down the hall as the enraged crowd bangs on the door from the other side. All control is lost in the lobby. The crowd's muffled screams chill Allan to the very core as he rushes Thomas to safety.

"Are you okay?" Allan asks, wiping a good deal of sweat from his nervous brow.

"I am. Are you?"

"I don't know. What…what happened there?"

Thomas takes hold of Allan's trembling hand. "It's going to be okay," Thomas says confidently. "If it wasn't for the storms, towns and homes would never be rebuilt."

Allan's growing worry turns to anger. He pulls his hand away. "What does that mean? Why do you say stuff like that? That's the reason they hate you. Can't you see? Stop acting like you're special!"

"Where are we going?" Thomas asks plainly. He ignores Allan's questions as he is pushed faster down the dimly lit corridor.

"To the underground garage. There's an elevator there. It will get us back to your room without the press."

"Thank you, Allan."

It is Allan's turn to not respond. Instead, he tries to ignore the feelings he has growing inside. Fear and confusion grip him. Now that everyone seems to be turning against Thomas, Allan questions whether he was blind to think the young man was special at all. If Thomas had the truth the way Allan once suspected he might, then why would everyone hate him for it? *How could I be such a fool?* Allan thinks as he shakes his head with a huff.

"There was a time men thought the world was flat," Thomas says as if answering the worry in Allan's mind. "They feared that if they sailed too far or explored long enough, they would find the world's edge and fall from it. And once someone said different, the world hated them for it."

Allan continues to hold his tongue. Thomas's words hold Allan's thoughts captive as the two turn another corner.

"No one wanted to hear the truth. No one wanted to believe that they were deceived. In fact, like today, many fought to keep the truth from being heard. Because the lie allows them to live wrong, as if they are right. But the world is nevertheless round, Allan. It doesn't matter how many declare it to be flat. Truth is truth. And once the truth is spoken, it will not return without destroying the very thing that isn't true to begin with."

"We're almost there," Allan grunts. He picks up his pace once again while pretending to ignore what Thomas is saying.

"Does saying 'the world is flat' make it any less of a lie because everyone agrees it's true?"

Allan scratches his head. *What is Thomas trying to say?*

"If the whole world were to say the sky is green, would that keep you from appreciating how blue it really is? It isn't up to me to get you to believe in the things I say. But the words I speak, like a seed planted in rich soil, they will grow inside you until you understand that…they are true." Thomas exhales sadly as they once again navigate another turn.

Allan opens a door marked Garage and pushes Thomas over the threshold. The door creaks behind them eerily as it slowly shuts. The lights flicker as they descend down the ramp into the dark parking lot. Few cars park here. Leaking pipes leave dank puddles in the cracked pavement for many to step in. The stale air makes it uncomfortable to breathe.

"Why should I believe anything you say?" Allan asks and accidentally steps in one of the dark puddles. "Darn it!"

"Four men were given four pieces of a desert map to lead them to water. Each piece had a different direction. Each man had his own piece. The first said, 'My map is the way, we will start in this direction.' Another said, 'No, I am sure mine is the way. We must go the way my map says.' And like the first two, the last two argued as well. So four men set out in four different directions. They wandered apart for days. The sun beat down on them, cooking their flesh from above, and one by one they fell. They all died alone, Allan. They never found that well or the life-giving water. But what these men didn't know was had they placed all four pieces of the map together, then together they would have found that living water and had much of it to drink, instead of each dying of thirst alone in the desert."

Suddenly, a look of concern takes over Thomas's face. His breathing becomes rapid. He looks over his left shoulder as if worried the two are followed.

"What's wrong?"

Thomas looks nervously into the shadows surrounding them. He sees nothing, but something is not right. As they approach the elevator, his lips quivers. Allan doesn't understand why.

"Don't worry, Thomas. No one will find us here."

"You can't hide from your purpose, Allan." Thomas clenches his fists tight and allows his knee to nervously shake.

"Well, you said I was going to protect you. I've done that already, so we should be good."

"You haven't protected me yet, Allan, but you will."

Allan presses the elevator button. His skin begins to crawl.

Thomas closes his eyes and takes a long, cleansing breath. Something is about to happen. Thomas knows this with every fiber of his being.

The elevator door chimes. A whispered voice is heard. "I've been waiting a long time for this."

Allan turns to see who it is. From the shadows, he is hit with a steel pipe. It splits his head open, immediately knocking him unconscious. He falls to the ground with a loud thud.

Thomas turns his chair around. He raises his eyes slowly as the steel pipe is dropped at the attacker's side. The high-pitched clang of it bouncing off the cement echoes in the parking garage.

The dirty-looking young man wheezes as he struggles to breathe after his attack. His clothes haven't been washed in months. He slowly curls his black-stained fingers. His ripped jeans are more brown than blue from the grime covering them.

"Remember me?" the foul man asks. His face hides away inside the shadow created by the dark hood of the tattered gray sweatshirt. Although his face is not seen, his red bloodshot eyes appear like two rubies from the pit of hell.

A single tear falls from Thomas's right eye. "I do remember you."

The foul man reaches for his hood and pulls it from his head. His nostrils flare as he arrogantly displays his gaunt dirty face for Thomas to see. He scratches his thin beard. The track marks on his arms give away his drug addiction.

"Don't do this, John," Thomas asks, allowing more sympathetic tears to fall.

"So you do remember me." John walks toward Thomas with a limp. He leans down and takes hold of the wheelchair. His stench bites the inside of Thomas's nose.

John is a far cry from what he once was. John, the great bully of Bethel Junior High, is now a weak drug-addicted dying young man. Yet his fear and pain still drive him to hate and abuse those he does not understand.

"You should've stayed dead, James!" John yells and flips Thomas's wheelchair over. Thomas crashes to the ground but does not scream or cry.

John twitches and laughs as Thomas sits up and turns to face him.

"You're the reason I'm like this!" John yells. He bends down, snorts, and spits directly in Thomas's face.

Thomas wipes the wet green mucus from his eyelids. His compassionate eyes find the emptiness in John's stare.

John's face shakes with anger. His rage builds inside him. "You're the reason I lost everything!" he screams as he pulls up his sleeves to reveal more scars from his past. "This is your fault!"

John slaps Thomas in the face with all his might. "Because of you, they took me away. They put me in that crazy house, that hell! They said I was the one that put you in that coma. They blamed me. They said I smashed your head against that mirror and into the ground because of what everyone saw me do to you at the parade. They blamed me for your accident. And they sent me to hell for it."

John slaps Thomas again, harder this time. His hand stings as he pulls it away from the side of Thomas's face. Blood slides down Thomas's cheek and into the corner of his mouth. Thomas wipes it away as he straightens himself.

John is taken aback. *How is this kid still conscious?* "So you still think you're tough...and the world thought you were such a big deal. But I knew better. I knew there was nothing special about you. And now they know just like me that you're still nothing but a lying loser!"

John reaches into the back pocket of his filthy pants. He takes out a box cutter. He holds it in the air and waves it in front of his cocky face. He slowly extends the rusty blade. "They I said I tried killing you once. I was everybody's bad guy. I was every parent's nightmare come true. But now I don't think anyone will care if I really kill you this time!" John smiles widely, revealing decaying brown teeth.

There is a change in Thomas's face. His look of pity is replaced by a severe stare. He braces himself against the wall and slowly rises to his feet. He lifts his right hand and extends his forefinger at John. "You are the cause of your own suffering," Thomas declares. "You hurt others, and now you are hurt. If you had love for me, you would know love in return. But you can't love anyone or anything if you hate everything that is you!"

"The hell with you!" John screams. In his fury, he slices the palm of his own hand open from one end to the other with the box cutter blade. "I'm going to take you out!" John holds his bloody left hand in front of his face. He licks the blood and swishes it back and forth in his mouth. "You're going to die, and this time it is me who does it."

The word is familiar to Thomas. It is the same word John wrote on his locker six years ago. He still wants Thomas to die. Not much has changed in the young man's heart since then. All his pain and hardship taught John nothing. He never learned that we reap what we sow. He never learned that the trials in life are meant to drive us away from hate. That what we endure is meant to humble us. John never turned from his wicked ways. This is why his life got worse.

As John extends the blade completely, he tightens his fingers around the box cutter handle and readies himself to plunge it deep into Thomas's gut.

"When you hurt others, John, you are only hurting yourself," Thomas says. He closes his eyes and allows his arms to relax at his side. Thomas will not fear the animal standing before him. He will not back down from the monster trying to destroy him. Instead, he will willingly lay his life down if need be.

"I hate you! I hate you! I hate you!" John screams. Thomas does not move as his attacker lunges forward. Just before the blade reaches him, John is brutally tackled and launched off his feet by Allan.

Allan and John soar above the ground and come crashing down many feet from Thomas. Allan drives the battered young man into the cement basement floor with his shoulder. Crackling pops like the crunching of a can are heard as John's rib cage collapses from the impact.

Allan rises to his feet. His face is covered in blood.

John gags. Chunky blackened blood spews from his mouth.

Allan wipes the blood from his eyes. The steel pipe had dug deep. His chest heaves in anger, and his eyes are beet red from the blood vessels that burst.

John wheezes through his collapsed lung. He cannot catch his breath. "Please...please don't...please don't," he whimpers fearfully as Allan stands tall above him.

Allan rolls his shoulders back. The buttons on his shirt do all they can to hold his uniform from ripping at the seams. He raises his fist high in the air and then brings it down slowly to the side of his face. His knuckles crack as he tightens his fist, preparing it to crush the side of John's face. His feet stamp the ground like a bull waiting to charge as John weeps with hands raised as a coward would.

"Please don't...I'm sorry...I'm so sorry!"

"Sorry isn't good enough!" Allan cocks his arm back into position.

"No, Allan," Thomas demands.

Allan immediately stops. He drops his fist to his side.

"It's enough," Thomas says calmly. "It's enough."

Allan turns to him as if to say, *The guy tried killing you and me.*

Thomas's sad eyes pitifully rest on John. John cries uncontrollably on the floor. His life had been nothing but pain. No one had shown him that there is a better way.

"Those that hate the most must be loved the most, Allan. John is our brother. He just doesn't know it yet." Thomas takes a cautious step toward his overturned wheelchair. He wobbles in doing so. Allan rushes to his side to steady him.

"No, Allan. That man needs your help, not me."

Allan is confused. How can it be that Thomas cares more for the safety of the man who hates him than he does for himself?

Thomas lifts his wheelchair. As he sits in it, a white glow surrounds him.

Allan shields his eyes as the light grows brighter and warmer. He shakes his head and squeezes his eyes tight. "What the..."

"Thank you for protecting me, Allan," Thomas says with a smile.

Allan falls to his knees. "Who are you?" he asks in a weak voice.

Thomas's eyes meet his. "I am the same as you, Allan. You just cannot see." Thomas wheels himself over to the elevator.

Allan is in awe. He closes his eyes, confused, and shakes his head again to get his bearings. When he opens his eyes again, the white glow is gone.

Thomas turns his head to face him. "Our friend needs your help, Allan," Thomas says calmly. He presses the elevator button to go up once again.

Allan slowly stands, motivated by his words. He walks over to John in a daze. John trembles as Allan bends down and cradles the frail man in his arms. "It's going to be okay," Allan assures as he picks John up and carries him to the elevator.

"Thank you," John says in a pained but grateful voice.

Thomas smiles to himself as Allan enters the elevator and takes his place next to him. The door closes, and they are lifted away.

Words when heard are like seeds within you and me.

Some words when heard can become chains, while others can set a person free.

If someone told you from birth you have no worth and you believed, a worthless, sad, pitiful life you would most likely receive.

If society brainwashes you into thinking you must be a certain way, then the possibility of what else you can become will be put to death that day.

Words when heard can tear friends and family apart, and that's just the start.

However, words when heard can do so much more; they are indeed mightier than the sword.

Words can heal and inspire, bring truth to a liar; they can lift up and set a person free.

Words can allow a person to let go of all of their fear and give them the freedom to just simply be.

So be careful with your words because they are as seeds within you and me.

—Thomas James

The Lost Cannot See Clearly

The light from Colin's computer screen spreads across his dark home office. It is 3:00 a.m. Colin hunches over his keyboard with heavy eyes. For hours he's sat with nothing but the monitor's faint blue glow in his face.

His eyes squint as he scrolls down the computer screen. The joints in his index finger ache from the perpetual use of his mouse. He clicks on various Internet sites dealing with coma research and paralysis. What Colin looks for eludes him. But he is compelled to continue on nonetheless.

Spending hours that pass in moments, he searches diligently for anything that will give him insight into Thomas's abnormal test results and recovery. Nothing is as mysterious to him as the way Thomas acts. His words seem foreign to Colin.

He is not the first to wonder why the boy says the things he says, how he knows what he seems to know. And there is nothing more concerning to a doctor than a patient who seems to have no fear.

"Ugh, this is ridiculous!" he declares as he throws his hands up in the air. "What am I looking for?" He pushes himself away from his computer and stares at the screen. The words Thomas spoke at the press conference run through his mind, as do the actions of the sixty-six in the pit.

Colin knows it won't be long before Dr. Manus makes his play to have the boy committed. If Colin doesn't find an explanation to Thomas's behavior, he won't be able to continue his research, and most importantly, he won't be able to protect the young man from that dark place.

What it is about Thomas that got under the crowd's skin is beyond him. How can an eighteen-year-old coma survivor be the cause of so much turmoil? What did he say that was so wrong?

His words at first were so welcome to those who heard him. So many claimed the young man was special; they said he was a miracle. And just like Colin, many wondered if Thomas found something in the darkness of his coma. What he found, if anything at all, no one knows. Was it peace? Was it the meaning of life? Did Thomas find God?

As an atheist, it is curious Colin wonders about this at all. Not exactly the actions of someone who has never been a man of faith.

Colin prides himself on being a devoted man of science. He deals in things that are seen, not things that cannot be. How can Colin believe in God? Much less the God Thomas so easily spoke about in the garden the day they met.

Earlier in the Week

"God is love, Doctor," Thomas said with a twinkle in his eyes. "He is patient, kind, gentle, meek, strong, and free. God is truth. He is the truth hidden in us all."

"Thomas, I'm not here to talk about some God with you, okay?"

"And yet here we are." Thomas faces the wind. He allows it to tickle his cheeks. He smiled as he closed his eyes and breathed it all in.

"Well, I don't really believe in God."

"Funny thing about thinking your life is your own," Thomas said confidently. "If you fail, it's entirely your fault." Thomas turned to Colin and searched his eyes. "But knowing life is beyond our control, well, that is freedom indeed."

Colin shrugged. "What, no free will? Come on, Thomas. We make choices every day."

"Every choice is influenced by everything else. What makes you so sure you're the only one in control?" Thomas grabbed a small pebble from the ground and tossed it into the small fountain beside him. "What choice do the ripples in the water have when a stone is thrown?"

"That's physics, not God, Thomas." Colin huffed and shook his head in denial. "So what, God led us here to talk about this? Is that what you're saying?"

Thomas looked into the sky. The sun shined directly on his face. "I'm saying, how much better would things be if everyone knew that where they are right now in their lives, for better or for worse, is exactly where they were meant to be?"

The question was a hard one for Colin. He had never felt settled in life. Never believed he was good enough or had done enough.

"But where we are now and where we have been is not where we will always be...We aren't our past. We aren't our mistakes or our wicked deeds. We are the moment. The past doesn't exist, and the future is not here. Yet the whole world seems to live for both. And no one is content."

Thomas threw another pebble into the small fountain. The water rippled again from it. "The ripples change with every stone thrown, but they still don't have a choice."

Nervously Colin walked away from Thomas to get his bearings. He hadn't told Thomas the true reason for his lack of faith.

Twenty Years Prior

It was the hottest summer in history when Colin and his brother fell from the tree. There hadn't been rain in forty long days, and the heavens refused to shade the dried ground with their clouds.

The small mining town wasn't known for much beside its poverty and religious beliefs, not that Colin was raised to think of himself as either.

His mother, who many considered a devote atheist, raised her children to love others and to put their faith in what their heart told them was right instead of what religion commanded. She had her reasons, and her lack of religious faith was well noted among those who dwelt there.

Despite the town's growing poverty and the drought that virtually wiped out all of their crops, the four churches, which many called the Four Points, on Prosperity Road in downtown Babylon were thriving.

Colin's mother believed these churches and their leadership exploited the struggling residents by promising that if the townsfolk gave everything they could to God, one day God would give them back one hundred times more.

She watched the churches grow fat as the town grew thin. She saw her brothers and sisters suffering, struggling, and crying out to God as to why their homes were lost and their businesses sold.

But the Four Points told the mourners they needed to have faith. They told the residents to give beyond what they could afford. They commanded them to show God that they meant business. So the town did, and things got worse.

Colin's mother asked the churches to donate some of their funds to help alleviate the struggling community. But the Four Points refused. They said it was more important for the church to have money to continue spreading their good news abroad.

In anger, she protested. She refused to believe that God could be bought or sold. She tried organizing the town against the four churches, to boycott attendance until the fat church leaders would help the way they claimed God would.

The religious leaders condemned her. They warned the community that the devil was using her to keep people from being blessed. They said that if any listened to her ranting, they would be thrown from the congregation, never welcome again, and would most surely find themselves in hell one day.

Colin's mother made a choice after that; if God was like those who claimed his name, she didn't want her or her family to have anything to do with him.

And as Colin walked aimlessly by the Four Points after hearing of his brother's paralysis, the weight of the young boy's guilt was too much for the child to bear. The agony of not being able to make things right hung like a noose around his neck.

Colin stopped and fell to his knees. "It's my fault! It's all my fault! I'm sorry. I'm so sorry, Jeffrey!" he cried in front of the tallest church in the points.

"It's not your fault, son," the overweight pastor said as he pulled young Colin to his feet.

Colin looked up at the bloated man with the eastern seaboard in his eyes. "You don't understand. I'm the reason my brother can't walk."

"You're the Striphe boy, right?" the pastor asked in his thick Southern accent.

"Yes, sir." Colin sniffled.

"It's not your fault, son."

Those were the words Colin needed to hear the most. And for a moment, his tears stopped. "You promise?"

"It's your momma's fault," the fat preacher said heartlessly. "God is punishing your brother for what Momma has been doing to our church."

"What?" Colin's heart sank into his stomach.

"That's what happens to heathens. God don't like when you don't go to the Lord and you touch the hand of his anointed. So since your family don't walk his walk, looks like God is gonna keep your brother from walking for the rest of his life, don't it?"

The fat man patted the top of Colin's head and left the boy to his thoughts.

Earlier This Week

Colin grimaced at the memory of that day as he looked down into the filled hospital parking lot. "It would take more than a talk with you to change my mind about this, Thomas."

"You don't believe because of everything that happened to you. But what choice did you really have? If the blind lead the blind, won't they both end up in the ditch?" Thomas asked.

Colin shook his head and tried to ignore his words.

"I'm telling you the truth, Colin. Your brother will walk again."

"What?" Colin turned to Thomas as the color of his face drained away.

"Your brother will walk again, and you will believe. Then you will know it was all for the good."

Present

The words Thomas spoke to Colin on the roof garden that day stick with him. As hard as they are for him to believe, he wishes they could be true. But how is that possible?

He pulls himself back to his computer for one last search before calling it a night. The memory of what Thomas said at the press conference comes to him. "What did he say to the press? It is in his book. Wait a minute, that's it! Joel! Thomas said Joel spoke of us. Who is Joel? What does he mean it is in his book?"

Colin types the words "book of Joel" into his Internet search engine. Twenty-eight thousand hits appear on his screen.

"Man, this Joel guy was something else, huh? Let's see here, the guy's a prophet, Old Testament, and, wait a minute, here it is. The book of Joel." Colin clicks on the website, and the small book appears on the screen. Colin presses the print button. His printer begins to buzz and shake and hum as the small book is copied for him.

The phone rings. Colin jumps from his seat. He staggers over to the phone and picks up the receiver. "Hello? Jeff, is that you?" A look of worry takes over his face. "Wait, wait, wait a minute. Slow down, brother. What happened?"

Colin listens to his brother explain on the other end.

"I'll be right there." Colin drops the phone. He runs to the table in a panic, grabs his keys, and rushes out of his home as the printer finishes its job.

If gratitude is not the attitude that you hold dear, a conscience you will have that will never feel clear.

If you are never content and you allow jealousy and regret to rent space in your mind, you will forever be a clock watcher who feels as if they are running out of time.

But if you are kind and you always seem to find people who simply need to be lifted up, then there will never be an end to the depth of what you can accomplish and the overflowing of your cup.

—Thomas James

IT CAN'T BE

The pungent smell of developing chemicals fills the air in the makeshift darkroom of Jim Williams's apartment. The room glows red as Jim methodically places eight-by-ten photos into large developing bins. He taps at the pictures with wooden tongs, flips and turns them, and waits. As a seasoned photographer, it is a routine procedure. But his excitement and anticipation at this moment is unlike anything he has known before.

The photos he develops will be different from the hundreds he has doctored in the past. There will be no need to add to them. No reason to make these images out to be something they are not. These photos are special. Most importantly, they are legitimate.

Once the world sees how Thomas healed Felicia's head wound with a simple swipe of his finger at the press conference, Jim will be taken seriously again.

There is no denying what he captured on film just twelve hours ago. Regardless of what he has been called in the past, this so-called hack has the real deal developing in three separate bins before him. He has proof for what he has fabricated so many times before. There is hard evidence that the supernatural exists. It has been the one thing Jim's searched for his entire life. It is also the very thing he gave up believing in when nothing was found.

As a journalist, Jim lost his way after losing his faith. Turning instead to cheap parlor tricks with his camera and unreliable sources, he lost sight of his calling in life.

But now things have changed. Now Jim can raise his head high and call himself a journalist once again.

He takes the picture of Felicia Adams unconscious on the press conference floor from the developing tray. He carefully hangs the picture on the clothing line above him to dry. He leans into it and smiles wide as he inspects her gaping wound. The image is clear. There will be no denying this injury. Her cut is deep, and it is clearly recognized. Blood puddles around her head; her hair soaks in it. The shot is perfectly framed, the composition is dramatic, and with his camera's time stamp, these before-and-after pictures will be irrefutable.

Jim reaches for the second picture with butterflies in his stomach. His hands shake as he hangs it to dry with the others. This picture shows Thomas running his fingers over the gash in Felicia's head.

Once again, Jim's framing is impeccable. *These are the shots Pulitzers are made of*, he thinks as he places the last picture into the developing tray.

This image will be his pièce de résistance. It is the photo he's been waiting for. The picture that, when developed, will make up for every white lie he has told, erase every untrue story he has reported, and make right every hoax he and his magazine has pulled.

He watches the film as it slowly develops before him.

"Let's see it…let's see it!" he says, staring as the close-up of Felicia's head being healed becomes clear.

His eyes widen. He slowly licks his lips. "Amazing," he says with eyes that forget to blink.

There is not a scratch on Felicia's head after Thomas touches her. Her face is serene, not a care in the world. This is a dramatic difference from the image Jim hung just moments ago. Upon close inspection, Jim wonders if the boy healed more than just her wound. If he were to title this picture, he would call it "Peace."

Could Thomas have healed her very soul when he touched her? Is this why Felicia now looks like an angel in the photograph as opposed to the victim she was? All these questions, and more, race through his mind.

However inspiring this photograph is, it isn't enough to keep the very human feeling of greed from rising inside his heart. The money Jim will make from these photographs will be more than he has ever known. Perhaps the miracle isn't what makes his smile after all. Proof of the supernatural isn't as important as fame.

Jim folds his arms and steps back to admire the historic photos hanging on his dry line. "I'm going to be rich," he chuckles. A sudden explosion of light blinds him. "What the—" He screams and falls to his knees. The burst of light comes from nowhere, tenfold brighter than staring directly at the sun.

Jim presses his palms against his eye sockets. It feels like his eyeballs are slit with the sharp corners of paper. He tries to open his eyes, but the pain is too great. He reaches for the table to get to his feet and mistakes a developing tray for its lip. He flips the bin over. The chemicals splash against him and the floor.

"No!" Jim cries. But it is not the pain or the mess around him that drives him to do so. It is not even his lack of sight.

The pictures—they are all that matter to Jim now. His eyes will heal and the mess can be cleaned, but if the pictures are ruined, no one will believe the story he has to tell.

Jim crawls on the floor and finds the sink. He picks himself up by it. He runs the water and begins to splash his eyes and face. The cold liquid stings at first, but soon the pain all but disappears.

Jim straightens himself. He reaches for the brown hand towel hanging on a large rusty nail in the wall. He blots his face with the towel until he is dry, takes a deep breath, and opens his eyes.

His sight is restored. He blinks five times and squints. The room glows red still.

Where did that light come from? he wonders as he turns slowly to make sure his pictures are safe.

"No! No! No! No!" Jim screams, running over to the photographs.

Each picture has been corrupted. A starburst now stands where the proof of the miraculous was. Each picture degrades before his eyes. It is as if Jim had focused his camera on the hot sun. Quickly, he inspects the negatives. Like the photos, they too are corrupt.

"It can't be!" he cries, ripping the pictures from the line. His much-needed evidence is gone. As are his dreams of fame and wealth.

Is there anything we can imagine that cannot come to pass?
Is there anyone too far gone that love cannot bring back?
Is there any height we cannot climb, any depth we cannot descend?
Can we not live a full life, or choose to put it to an end?
Whatever therefore we think, we find and become.
What we believe can either defeat us or helps us overcome.
So remember, the power of life and death is in your mind and in your tongue.

—Thomas James

SILENCED

The dew on the grass dries quickly from the heat of the morning sun. The Bethel Memorial Hospital parking lot fills with protesters. A company of angry men and women hold signs of contempt where once they held vigil for the recovery of Thomas James.

The hospital is severely criticized for allowing Thomas to speak. The water coolers around the world are abuzz with what happened at the press conference. Pictures of the madness in the pit plaster the covers of every newspaper and magazine. Many say Thomas is to blame.

The incident at the press conference has been played and replayed on almost every major network for the past sixteen hours. Reporters come out in force but are not allowed within one hundred feet of the building.

Threats on Thomas's and his doctors' lives continue to pour in after the live feed is cut. The news of a possible transfer for Thomas to another hospital creates more concern for those paid to keep order. Riot police stand guard outside the hospital while security sections off the lobby and places its staff on high alert. Many believe Thomas's transfer is when these threats will be carried out.

Outside, in the center of the crowd, the priest who presided over Thomas's mother and grandmother's funeral six years ago stands on a makeshift platform. His assistant hands him a megaphone. He raises the loudspeaker to his lips as the crowd gathers around him.

"Some have passed this boy off as lunatic. Others have gone so far as to say he is an alien or a ghost."

The crowd laughs as the priest speaks.

"These outrageous stories are giving Thomas James a bigger name than ever before. And is this what we really want? The world's eyes are on the people of Bethel today. And there may be more to this young man than many think."

Dozens of cameras focus on the priest. The crowd lowers their signs and turns a curious ear to the large man.

"For six years Thomas was in his coma. In the sixth month, on the sixth day, he miraculously rose. Six, six, six—the number of the beast."

The crowd gasps. But the priest knows there are many who will need more convincing. "I know many may not believe the words I am about to speak. But there was a time when many did not believe Thomas would live again, and yet he is alive!"

The priest scans the crowd with his bloodshot eyes. He is taken by an onlooker who seems different from the rest. It is an old man, the same old man who spoke with Nancy many weeks ago, the same old man who helped Thomas to his feet at the parade. The priest looks away from the man to continue.

"There is prophesy in the book of Revelation, and it speaks of a man, a beast, rising out of the sea. A devil! An Antichrist whose fatal head wound is miraculously healed. It claims that this monster would declare he is God to the world. And it just so happens that yesterday, the so-called miracle, Thomas James, spoke to the entire world the very prophesy of our Lord and Savior...as if they are his words to speak!"

A silence falls upon the crowd. The priest's prophetic words begin to make sense to the pilgrims who once came to Thomas because of hope and now come because of hate. They nod their heads in strange agreement, yet the old man watching does not.

"The sea this beast rose from was his coma! The fatal head wound that heals is the very injury that put Thomas in the coma to begin with! We have already given this boy a public platform, and look at what he said. We have all heard the stories of how he can read minds and heal the sick, how his recovery and test results are unlike anything this world has ever seen. We need to pray. We need to seek God for an answer. We need to make sure that this boy is never again allowed to say the things he has said before it is too late for us all!"

The crowd erupts in agreement.

As the priest wipes the oily sweat from his brow, the old man makes his way toward him. The priest uncomfortably watches as the crowd parts for the old man without being asked to move. He effortlessly walks toward him, as if gliding and not walking at all. The closer he gets to the front, the faster the priest's heart races. The old man's eyes are darker than night.

The priest tries to ignore his stare. An eerie feeling rises up his neck. He raises the megaphone to his lips again. "The Bible says the devil can come as an angel of light. We must not be deceived...we must...we must..."

The priest struggles to finish, but a tickle in his throat keeps him from doing so. He coughs and motions to his assistant to get him a glass of water. The tickle gets worse, as if his throat is closing. The priest drops the megaphone at his side and places his hands around his neck. He looks around for help and tries to cry out for it, but he cannot.

He sees the old man standing directly in front of him. The old man's stare is cold. He shows no emotion. "An angel of light, you say?" the old man whispers.

The terrified priest falls backward from his platform.

The excited crowd panics. They rush toward the fallen priest as the old man calmly walks away.

The priest's face turns blue. He grabs at his collar and rips it from his pressed black shirt.

"Someone, get help! He can't breathe, he can't breathe!" his assistant screams.

The old man's eyes are sad. He shakes his head as he walks away from them.

The crowd surrounding the priest is frantic.

The old man calmly raises his hand and snaps his finger. The sound of it echoes around the priest, and instantly the air returns to his lungs.

The priest inhales, and the color returns to his face. He takes a few more breaths with fear in his eyes.

"Are you okay?" his assistant asks, raising the priest to a seated position.

The priest does not know what to say.

Seize the moment, this moment, and every moment, for the moment is yours.

Why weigh yourself down with tears and frowns, believing life to be nothing more than a chore.

It's your moment, this moment and every moment, and it is a moment you must no longer ignore.

You are a creator, trapped in the prison that has become of this world of yours.

You spend your time never allowing yourself to unwind and have forgotten the point was to explore.

This is your moment, this moment, and every moment, so pick yourself up off the floor.

Rip yourself away from the glue that been holding you; rise up, oh God, and live for more!

—Thomas James

Nothing Shall Stand in Its Way

As maintenance crews plaster holes in the walls and clean the mess from the chaos of the press conference, the board of directors meets privately to discuss image control. They sit around the large oak table in conference room A. Their eyes avoid each other as they wait for Dr. Felicia Adams.

A knock at the door pulls their attention. Dr. Natal stops the tapping of his foot and straightens himself in his chair. He gives a confirming look to the rest of the board sitting with him. Some swallow nervously. Others shake their heads and wring their hands.

"Come on in, Felicia," Dr. Natal says with a stiff upper lip.

The large carved oak door slowly opens. Felicia enters from behind it. She knows why this meeting is called. After all the criticism, the board is looking for a scapegoat. It seems trivial to her, however important it may be to them.

Things have changed for Felicia since the press conference. She's spent hours in her home wondering how the wound in her head magically disappeared. That chair hit her harder than anything has hit her before. She felt the warmth of her blood pouring down her face before she lost consciousness. It was her blood she washed out of her hair in the shower, and yet not a scratch is found.

Perhaps there is more to Thomas as he himself mysteriously told her in the garden that day. Before meeting him, Felicia was living her life as if it were black-and-white. There was no life to her days, each blurred into the next. But now, as crazy as it seems, there is the possibility of meaning—the taste of hope. Now Felicia has color to her life…and much of it.

"Have a seat, Felicia." Dr. Natal motions to the empty leather chair before her.

The chair is positioned at the opposite end of the table from where he and the board members sit.

"What is this? The inquisition?" she asks sarcastically. Felicia grabs the back of the chair and slowly pulls it out. She scans the faces of those in attendance. *Not a good sign*, she thinks.

Not one has the courage to look her in the eye. The very people who had laughed and cried with her now seem foreign to her. No longer her peers at all, now they seem to be her adversaries. How can so much change because of one young man?

"Good morning, Frank, Stephanie, George," she says in an attempt to engage them. Their lack of response does not surprise her.

Dr. Natal clears his throat and inches toward the envelope in front of him. "You know why you're here, so I'll dispense with the formalities and get to the point." Natal opens the large manila folder and takes out a small stack of papers. He places them on the table, reaches into his coat pocket, and takes out a pen. Natal rests the pen on the stack of papers and slides the packet of information toward her, as a shuffleboard player would a puck.

Felicia catches them before they hit the floor. She takes the papers in hand and studies them.

"I'm sorry about this, Felicia. I know you have been through a lot already. But this is something that needs to be nipped in the bud right now."

The rest of the board remains silent as she thumbs through the pile with a growing look of disgust on her face. "What is this, Frank?"

"It's your apology to the hospital and commitment papers for Thomas James."

Felicia throws her hands into the air. "First of all, I'm not apologizing for anything. And secondly, I won't sign off on his commitment."

Natal nervously adjusts his tie and locks his fat fingers together in front of him. "You will if you want what is best for this hospital and your career."

His threat is clear.

"And why would I do that? Because the press didn't like what an eighteen-year-old boy who just came off a coma had to say?"

"You are a competent doctor, Felicia. But what you allowed to happen yesterday is unacceptable."

"What *I* allowed to happen?" she asks rhetorically. "I was the last person to agree with this press conference. All of you demanded I get in line. 'It's good press for the hospital,' you said. 'Just think of the publicity.' You don't remember saying that? 'It will put Bethel Memorial on the map,' you proudly declared. Those were your words, Frank, not mine."

"You should have used better judgment, Felicia. You should have said this boy was not competent!"

"What did he say that would lead you to believe otherwise?"

"He said he was Jesus, for crying out loud. The boy is insane!" Dr. Natal slams his hand onto the table.

"He did not! All he said was that the world is a messed-up place. I agree. Does that make me crazy?"

"That boy is sick, and if you cannot see that, perhaps you are. And if that's true, then you're not the physician we all thought you were," Dr. Natal says coldly.

"He is an eighteen-year-old boy with one of the largest hearts I have ever seen. He talks differently, sure. But he loves people, and people here love him. You don't know him, Frank! If you did, you would know what I am saying is true. There is nothing wrong with that child."

"The boy is beyond our help."

"I've had enough!" Felicia stands and folds her arms. Her eyes are like daggers to those on the opposite end of the table.

"Dr. Manus made it clear that the boy needed his help, and that is what this hospital is going to do—unless of course, you think we should pray for him and leave the rest in God's hands?" Natal arrogantly leans forward in his chair.

"Oh please. You don't care about him. You don't want what is best for him. You only care about your precious image."

"You ignored his diagnosis and allowed egg to be thrown on the face of this hospital because you have a problem with Dr. Manus personally," Natal says calmly as he stands from his chair to wave an angry finger at Felicia. "So now we want you to clean the egg up. Make this right and sign the papers."

"You want me to step down? Fine, I'll step down. But I am not signing any of those papers." She slides the stack of papers back toward him and walks toward the door.

"Wait right there!" Natal gathers the papers and waves them at her.

She takes a deep breath as she slowly takes her hand off the knob on the door. She turns to him slowly. She wants to slap the smug look off his face. "What?"

"You better sign these right now. Last chance."

Felicia's hands shake at her side, and her face becomes red. "And if I don't?" she asks nervously, already knowing the answer.

Everyone at the table uncomfortably squirms in their chairs. Without hesitation, Dr. Natal clenches his jaw and gives his firm answer. "Then I guess we will have to rethink your position here at the hospital."

"You're serious?"

"Do you really want to find out how serious I can be, Doctor?"

"Well, how about that." Felicia pauses, trying to catch the eye of any of her supposed friends and supporters sitting at the table. "My friends, isn't this ironic?"

They all stare at their hands, leaving Felicia out to dry. In disagreement, she shakes her head and takes another deep breath. "Well, I'm kind of between a rock and a hard place, I guess."

"Just sign the papers and take the rest of the day off. No one wants to hurt you. We all love and appreciate you here. We just want you to make the right decision, that's all." His candy-coated words are bitter to her.

"Well, I sure am glad I'm loved and appreciated by you all." She takes the pen in her hand again. "If I'm hard-pressed to make a decision right now, then here it is!"

Felicia snaps the pen in two and throws it at Dr. Natal. The ink from the broken pen splatters across the table and lands on his crisp white shirt and hands.

"This is just great!" Natal yells, looking at the mess on him. His blood boils as the members of the board quietly chuckle to themselves.

"Oh, I'm real sorry about that, Frank. I didn't expect that to happen. Then again, I didn't expect to be forced from my position today. I guess today is full of surprises, huh?"

"You are out of line, Felicia!" Natal screams, cleaning his tie and shirt with a kerchief and drinking water.

"*I'm* out of line?" She places her hands on the desk and leans in. "You demand that I sign commitment papers for a boy who is in his right mind, and *I'm* out of line? All of you sitting here are out of line!"

Frank mimics her by placing his hands on the table and leaning in as well. The two square off. The eyes of the board follow the confrontation like a tennis match. "I'm not asking anymore. I am telling you, if you don't sign these papers, so help me."

"What are you going to do, Frank? Fire me?"

"I'm waiting," Natal says firmly while the stains set in his shirt.

"Then you'll be waiting till hell freezes over because that's about how long it will take me to sign that nonsense. Thomas isn't crazy, and I will not have him committed. He is my patient, not yours. I make that decision, not you! Understand?"

An uncomfortable silence follows her words. A cocky grin grows on Frank's face. "Well, I guess you've made your decision then." He returns to unsuccessfully cleaning the black ink spotting his pudgy digits.

"I'm done talking to you, Frank. I won't sign this nonsense." She turns around quickly, grabs the door handle firmly, and turns it. But before she can exit, she is stopped.

"Before you leave, you should know. We never needed you to sign anything. Thomas is no longer your patient, and your opinion doesn't matter." Dr. Natal gathers the scattered papers together. He returns them to the now ink-stained manila folder.

Felicia releases the handle and walks back over to the table. "What do you mean he is no longer my patient? You can't decide that. He is eighteen years old. He's an adult."

Natal slams the lid of his briefcase. His eyes arrogantly roll up to meet Felicia's. "Dr. Manus, the boy's aunt, and this board are in agreement. We don't need his consent, and we most surely do not need yours. Good day."

"You can't do this!"

"It is in the boy's best interest to be released from your care and to be placed in a facility that is more adept with handling his condition."

"Where are you sending him, Frank?" She waits, but no answer is given. "Where are you sending him?" she screams.

"He's being transferred midafternoon to Legirion Psychiatric. Dr. Manus will be following up with him on-site personally."

"Legirion Psychiatric, are you out of your mind? Eighty percent of the patients there are violent."

"He will have a private room and will be kept under close surveillance. Now you may leave." He points to the door with a Nazi salute.

"Please don't do this to him, Frank." Felicia looks around. Her eyes plead with the other members. "Look, I'll even quit, just don't send him there."

"Felicia, we'll call you when we need you. Thank you for your time." Natal pulls out another file and places it in front of him. "I would like everyone to take out the expenditures from last month."

It is as if Felicia disappears. They ignore her as she stands alone, wondering how she could have been as blind as to never notice how heartless these men and women could be.

"You haven't heard the end of this, Frank!" Felicia storms out of the room. She exits with a fire in her. She slams the door behind her. Her actions gain the attention of a pregnant Latino woman and her husband trying to find their way through the hospital.

"Sorry." Her head sinks. She notices that the woman is in labor. "The emergency room is at the end of the hall." She points them in the right direction.

"Thank you, and God bless you," the husband says as he leads his wife there with a smile.

"God bless you too," Felicia replies, thinking of how strange these words sound coming from her own mouth. She takes a deep breath and straightens her suit jacket by pulling it down tightly beneath her waist. She quickly fixes her hair and lifts her head high. No one will ever see her sweat again.

What do I do now? She is worried. *What am I going to do?*

She tries thinking of a way out of her trouble as she walks to the elevator. She grinds her teeth, realizing that short of kidnapping Thomas, she can do nothing legal to reverse what Manus and the board put in motion.

Reaching the elevator, she presses the button with the pressure of tears behind her eyes. She no longer feels comfortable in her own skin. Like a snail without its shell, she is vulnerable and weak. Her job was everything to her, and now that it may be gone, who will Felicia be?

The elevator bell rings, and the doors open. She enters, not knowing where to go. The elevator doors close her in. She stares at her sad reflection. "All will be well, huh?" She laughs, thinking of Thomas's words as her eyes swim in tears. How can all be well when everything seems to be so horribly wrong? Felicia presses the button leading to the garden. It is the only place she believes she will find the answers she is looking for.

For every person, there are two voices in their head.

One that leads to life and peace, and another that leads to doubt and death.

A double-minded man is unstable in all his ways.

Sadly, we've been conditioned to believe all the negative things we hear, think, and say.

However, we need not suffer a double mind another day.

—Thomas James

Oh Lord, What a Day It Is

A startled Nurse Lauren spits out her tea as Nancy approaches.

"Hey, what…what are you doing here?" she asks Nancy like a child with her hand caught in the cookie jar.

Nancy is confused. She stops and places her hands on her hips. This young blonde coworker is always rude to her. She is always quick with a snide comment or a roll of her eyes, but her attitude this morning is different. "I'm working, what do you mean? What am I doing here?"

Lauren brushes the question off with a shrug and cleans the mess on the desk as if she didn't hear her.

Something isn't right. Nancy knows this. Lauren isn't one to keep a secret, and there is definitely something she is hiding. It is written all over her face.

"I asked you something, Lauren. What do you mean what am I doing here?"

"Nothing. I guess…I didn't know you were working, that's all." Lauren takes a handful of paper towels and sops up her spilt tea.

"That's all?" Nancy taps her right foot, like a teacher would to a first grader who refuses to tell the truth. "How come I don't believe you?"

Annoyed, Lauren's face becomes flush as she throws the dirty towels into the small trash can next to the desk. She turns to face Nancy with a huff. "Look, I'm confused, okay. Don't make a big deal out of it!" Lauren sits and aimlessly shuffles through papers. She has had enough of Nancy's inquisition for one day.

"What aren't you telling me, young lady? I'm in no mood for games. Is this about Thomas?" Nancy's stomach fills with nervous butterflies as she waits for an answer. She hopes the rumors of Thomas's transfer are nothing more than rumor itself. But she has no illusions.

"I'm not a child, Nancy!"

Surprised by her attitude, Nancy takes a moment to look around. Everything is the same, but it all feels different. People stare at her, as if they know something she does not.

"What in the devil is going on here?" Nancy stamps her foot and points to the window. "The parking lot is filled with angry people screaming and yelling. It took me twenty minutes to get through security at the front door. And now everyone here is looking at me sideways, and you're telling me you don't know?"

"That's what I'm telling you." Lauren rolls her eyes.

With an angry shake of her head, Nancy reaches for Lauren and pinches her.

"Hey!" Lauren straightens up.

"Young lady, I don't have time for this. I know there's something you're not telling me, so out with it!"

Lauren huffs and angrily pushes herself from the desk. She rubs the back of her arm where Nancy's nails had dug into her. With a careless flip of her hair, she confronts Nancy. Tired of always being talked to like a child, now is her chance to finally put the veteran in her place.

"Fine," Lauren says with an arrogant smile. "I was told this morning that they moved you to another floor."

"Another floor?" Nancy's knees get weak. She grabs the desk for support.

This floor is all Nancy has known for the last eighteen years. The patients here each hold a special place in her heart. How can she leave this place? How can she leave them? They are the only family she has.

"Sorry," Lauren says, trying to hide her sarcastic smile. She returns to her seat without truly meaning what she says. Like many her age today, she cares more about herself and her wants and needs than those around her. Nancy means nothing to Lauren. She never has.

The light in the hall seems to dim for the veteran nurse as she stands sadly, not knowing what to do next. Her arms drop to her sides. Her chest grows heavy.

"I have worked on this floor for eighteen years," Nancy says with tears of unbelief. "How can they move me without having the decency to talk to me first?"

"Ask them yourself," Lauren picks up the phone and holds it out callously.

The last time a phone was handed to Nancy in such a way, she learned something she wished she could forget. She stares at the receiver but cannot find the strength to reach for it. In this moment, she remembers the worst day of her life.

Eighteen Years Ago

Nancy rushed down the emergency room hall. She tied the bottom of a surgical mask around her neck and let it hang below her chin.

"Nancy!" an ER nurse called desperately behind her. "You have an important call." The nurse held the receiver in the air. Her face showed concern.

Nancy turned. "Take a message. An unconscious young mother was caught in the storm. They're bringing her to delivery now." Nancy put on her latex gloves and started to walk away again.

"It's about your son!" the nurse yelled and raised the receiver higher in the air.

Nancy stopped. Her heart sank. She looked at the phone in the nurse's hand. For a moment, she didn't know what to do.

"They say it's important," the ER nurse said.

Nancy closed her eyes and reached for the gold cross dangling from her neck. She rushed to the phone, took a deep breath, snatched it out of the nurse's hand, and placed it to her ear. "This is Nancy Hearst."

As Nancy listened to the caller on the other end, her eyes grew wide. She released the gold cross from her fingers and leaned back against the white wall. Her lip quivered. She shook her head in unbelief. "An accident? No, no, it can't be my Tommy."

The ER nurse behind her bit her nails as she watched sadly.

"Not my Tommy!" Nancy demands and allowed the phone to drop. It fell to the ground and bounced off the floor. Nancy's face was blank.

The ER nurse placed her hand on Nancy's shoulder to comfort her. "Are you going to be okay?"

Nancy slowly turned to face her. Her eyes were red with grief. "It's my Tommy, they say...they say he's dead."

The ER nurse gasped as Nancy walked away, trying to ignore the news. She raised her surgical mask and tied it back in place. She tried to convince herself that she didn't have time to deal with it.

"Where are you going, Nancy?"

Nancy tightened her fists and picked up her pace. "There's a young mother who needs me." Nancy continued to walk away from the nurse and toward the delivery room. She stopped at its double-door entrance. She let out a painful sigh and burst into the room. The patient and team had not yet arrived. Nancy was alone. In that moment, the realization hit her. "My boy...my Tommy...not my Tommy," she whimpered. Her hands trembled at her side. Her child was dead, and now she had to bring someone else's into this world. She looked up and shook her head. "How could you let this happen, Lord?"

A loud thud outside the room stole her focus. She looked to the door in shock.

"Make way!" someone shouted as an emergency room team crashed through the delivery room doors.

Nancy snapped out of it. She took a deep breath and stood tall. She could not let

anyone see her the way she was.

The group stared at Nancy. "Where do you want her?" one nurse asked.

"Right here." Nancy pointed. "OB is on the way." She grabbed a freshly laundered sheet from the warmer.

They rushed the patient into position.

This is the last time, Nancy thought as she reached for the unconscious pregnant girl.

Present

The memory of that day haunts her still. It was a week before Nancy gathered the courage to identify the body of her dead son. He was all she cared for in the world. That is why she tried to ignore the news. That is why instead of leaving the hospital and dealing with the tragedy, she chose to help a young mother named Sophia James.

It is not a coincidence to Nancy that in those moments after her son was declared dead, she helped bring another Thomas into the world.

How poetic it is that the same child she delivered was given the same name as the one she would soon lay to rest. How peculiar it is that twelve years after the death of her son, in the coma wing, she would begin caring for the very same Thomas she brought into the world. How tragic it is that after eighteen years, a single phone conversation may determine if, like her son, Thomas will be taken from her as well.

"Are you going to call or what?" Lauren asks impatiently.

"Give me that phone." Nancy grabs the receiver with courage. She dials her supervisor and waits as the phone rings. "Oh Lord, what a day this is." Her supervisor answers. "This is Nancy. Lauren tells me I no longer work on this floor. Is that true?"

Nancy does not speak as her supervisor gives her the lengthy explanation on the other end of the phone. She unbuttons the top of her blouse and begins to fan herself. Her face grows flush with emotions.

"Did I do something wrong?" Nancy fights to hold herself together. "I've been working on this floor for years. I love this floor. Isn't there something you can do?" she begs. "How can you say that to me? I have an impeccable record!"

Lauren takes sick pleasure in the drama unfolding before her.

"Listen. I have patients that depend on me here. I'm not trying to be disrespectful, but…I can't go there! I haven't worked in obstetrics in years. I can't…I can't help deliver babies anymore. That's why I left. My son, Thomas, he died. I can't do it anymore."

Time stops for Nancy as her fate seems to seal.

"All right, fine," she says weakly and slowly returns the phone to Lauren.

Lauren takes it from her and hangs it up without acknowledging Nancy's distress.

"I'm moving to another floor. You were right," she says in a daze.

"I told you so." Lauren twirls the ends of her blonde hair.

"They are moving Thomas too," Nancy admits, straightening herself.

"Good!" Lauren makes her disgust toward Thomas clear.

Nancy turns her back on Lauren and heads for Thomas's room. As she walks, her shoes click against the white tile floor. The hollow sounds of her footsteps echo in the hall as the glimmer of hope usually in Nancy's eyes fade away. She reaches for her gold crucifix and takes it off from around her neck. The gold chain and cross are no longer a comfort to her.

You cannot count on anyone or anything to make you happy.

You cannot count on anyone or anything to make you feel secure.

You are all you have in this world truly, so be at peace with how things are, and stop thinking to be happy you need more.

Be at peace, be at peace, be at peace, my friend, for disappointment lies behind expectation's door.

When Enemies Betray You with a Kiss

Police move barricades away for a black Lincoln Town Car and a Legirion Psychiatric transport vehicle to enter the hospital parking lot. The automobiles part a sea of onlookers. Reporters sprint toward the vehicles without regard for those standing in their way.

The vehicles stop next to the lobby entrance of the hospital. Security guards rush to the Town Car. They force the paparazzi to back away to allow the occupants of the vehicles to exit without incident.

The Town Car door opens. Dr. Vince Manus steps out dramatically. Cameras flash as reporters greet him with a barrage of questions. Manus runs his fingers through his matted hair, spilling dandruff onto the shoulders of his worn tweed jacket. His dark blue shirt and gray tie don't match his brown pants, and he looks like he hasn't bathed in a week. Yet Manus holds himself like Adonis would if standing in one of his gardens.

Security holds a perimeter around him as the reporters scream for the doctor's attention.

"Dr. Manus, is it true Thomas James is now under your care?" a thin reporter from the *Tribune* asks while another reporter tries to pull him back.

Manus rolls his head and fiddles with his tie as he steps forward to answer. "Yes, it is true my staff and I are continuing

Thomas's care at Legirion Psychiatric. We are very hopeful that with the right medication and therapy, Thomas may one day be able to exist without our care."

As Manus soaks up the attention like a child starved for it, two large orderlies dressed completely in white exit the transport vehicle behind him. Reporters ignore the two as they meet each other at the back of the vehicle.

Weighing in over two hundred pounds each, their presence alone would make anyone think twice about crossing them. The larger of the two, Justice, a nickname given to him by friends, has bleached blond hair, which he wears cropped tightly against his head. His right eye is partially closed from an accident blinding him years ago. The eye is clouded over, and a three-inch scar runs horizontally across it. His skin is fair. His other dark brown eye seems out of place because of his pale complexion. On his right forearm there is a large tattoo of a knife piercing a bloody heart. The words *Born to Kill* are tattooed beneath it. His thick mustache and patch of hair on his chin only add to his menacing appearance.

The other orderly, Lance, is not nearly as intimidating to look at. With jet-black hair and olive skin, his Italian roots are easily noticed. His face is smooth and cleanly shaved. A twinkle shimmers in his eyes because of his obvious excitement.

"I'll be right back." Lance walks away to hear what Dr. Manus has to say.

Justice shakes his head angrily. He spits to the ground in Manus's direction, folds his arms, and leans against the back doors of the van. He will have nothing to do with Manus's circus.

Lance stretches his neck and stands on his toes for a better look over the crowd as Manus speaks.

"I evaluated Thomas early this week. I made my recommendations clear. It was obvious to me the boy was delusional as well as paranoid. My suggestions to have him put in my care immediately were overlooked by Thomas's former doctor, who felt the diagnosis was premature. However, after his episode in front of many of you, it is clear to this hospital, as well as Thomas's family, that the boy is very sick indeed. We are going to make sure that he is well taken care of. I will be happy to give any of you updates on his condition as the days progress. You can contact my office to schedule any interviews as well." Dr. Manus smiles for the cameras and reveals his coffee- and nicotine-stained teeth.

As Manus basks in all his glory, Jim Williams fights his way to the front. The pit bull reporter from the *Sentinel* is skilled in such a feat. His short stature makes it easy for him to weave in and out of those standing in front of him. This is one story he will not miss. With recorder held above his head, Jim finally takes his place in the front row. He is just feet away from Manus.

"Doctor, Jim Williams here. Is it true that during your evaluation of Thomas James, you became very ill and screamed to leave the room in fear? What were you so scared of?" Jim holds his recorder as close to Manus as he can.

Manus's cheek begins to twitch. He tries to avoid the question by taking off his glasses to rub them with a kerchief. "That is the most ridiculous thing I have ever heard, next question please."

Jim smiles sarcastically. He won't give up that easily. "I have my sources, Dr. Manus. And these sources also tell me there is more to Thomas James than you and this hospital are letting on. Rumors of reading people's minds, elevated brain activity, and even…" Jim looks around awkwardly. He knows this last statement will come from what he himself saw with his own eyes. "And even healing—miraculous healing, Doctor, like in Jesus's day. So what are you and this hospital trying to cover up?"

Heads in the crowd turn toward the reporter. It is as if Jim himself was the Bigfoot he had reported two weeks earlier being seen in Lyons Belt.

No one has ever taken Jim serious as a journalist, not even his own editor in chief. This day proves to be no different. Jim is a bottom-feeder. His is a sleaze who never double-checks a lead or verifies a source. The only investigative journalism Jim Williams concerned himself with over the last few years is thumbing through magazine stands to get ideas for his own pathetic articles.

But now, things have changed. Now he believes. Now he speaks the truth. "I asked you a question, Doctor. Are you covering something up or what?" Jim persists.

"Oh, that's right." Manus snaps his finger and then shakes it in Jim's direction. "You're that reporter from the *Sentinel.* Quite a reputable journal, isn't it?" Manus scans the crowd for supporters with a sinister grin on his face. Many are found. "Let me see how I can answer your question without making you feel like I'm covering up some grand conspiracy."

The crowd laughs.

"You see—Jim, is it?—I practice medicine. I work with hard facts, data, studies, and true science. So let me make myself very clear right now for your sake. Thomas James is a sick young man, and up till this point, the battery of tests that he has been through, unfortunately for you and your magazine, has proven that he is not an alien, a ghost, or even Nessie." Manus cackles, prompting the rest of the reporters to join in louder than before.

"Right, right, real funny." Jim's hand begins to shake as they play him for the fool. For the first time in many years, Jim wants the real story. They mock him for it.

"No, Jim, what is comical to me is your belief that you're actually a reporter." Manus grabs his belly as he laugh hysterically.

"We'll be talking again real soon, Dr. Manus. You can be sure of that," Jim threatens as he turns off his tape recorder.

"Next question please." Manus tries to contain his laughter.

"There is more to that kid then you're letting on, and I'm going to find out what it is! Count on it!" Jim yells as the other reporters fight for Manus's ear.

As Jim makes his retreat, he thinks to himself that everyone has a closet filled with bones. He smiles deviously as he thinks where Dr. Manus's will be found.

Away from the crowd, Justice screams to get his partner's attention. "Lance, let's go!" He opens the back of the transport van and slams the door in place, notifying Lance that Justice is in no mood for games today.

"I'm coming already, chill," Lance fires back as he returns to his partner with eyes still focused on Manus and the crowd.

"Well, hurry up, it's not like we have all day." Justice opens a medical bag. He searches its contents. "We're good here." He zips the bag up. "Heads up, slacker!" Justice throws the bag at Lance with enough force to knock him back a few feet.

Lance barely catches it. "Easy there, Hercules. What's your deal today?"

Justice turns and angrily looks into his partner's eyes. "What's up with me? What's up with you?"

"What do you mean?"

"'What do I mean?'" Justice parrots.

"You gonna keep repeating me? Or are you going to answer me?" Lance brushes past him to get the wheelchair out of the back of the van.

Justice raises his eyebrow and replies, "You want to know what I mean?"

"That's why I asked!"

Justice turns his head and looks at the hospital. A smile grows on his face. "Didn't you used to work here?"

Lance's stomach drops. He shakes his head and gets annoyed. "Yeah, like eighteen years ago. Why?"

"Just wanted to know how you went from being an EMT here to wrestling whack-a-doos and cleaning up their urine there. I know it wasn't the pay, youngster."

Lance stares at the emergency room entrance. He remembers his last night working there.

Eighteen Years Ago

Ironically, it was his first night as an EMT. As a rookie, he was nervous to begin with. The young pregnant woman stumbled into the ER and grabbed his arm. It burned and left a glowing imprint on him that he could never forget.

Lance told his supervisors what happened. No one believed him. They said he wasn't ready for the stress of the emergency room. Lance did not disagree. How could he ever go back to that place after what happened?

When the pregnant woman grabbed his arm, she did more than temporarily scar his skin. In that moment, Lance saw his future. As she grabbed his arm tight, Lance saw himself grabbing a handgun and raising it to his forehead. He felt his finger squeezing the trigger slowly. He heard the blast it made. He felt the bullet bury itself deep into his skull.

Lance saw and felt his own suicide when she grabbed him. How could he ever be the same after that night?

He tried to rid himself of the prophetic vision. He tried to convince himself that it was his imagination and nothing more. But deep down, he believed it was the way he was going to die.

A short stay at Legirion Psychiatric paved the way for his new career.

Present

"Are you going to answer me or stare like a sad puppy at the ER all day?"

Lance turns to him impatiently. "It just didn't work out, that's all. But now, look at me." Lance smiles wide. "Now I'm going to be closer to Thomas James than any one of those reporters. How about them apples?"

Justice takes out his pack of Salem cigarettes from his right front shirt pocket. He turns them upside down and packs the cigarettes by banging the package into his left palm. "There's nothing special about that kid, believe me." Justice looks to the crowd surrounding Manus with a look of disgust.

"Are you kidding me? Nothing special?" Lance pulls the wheelchair out of the van quickly and lets it slam to the ground. He opens the restraints on the armrests and leg rests, readying it for their pickup.

"That's what I said. What are you, deaf?"

Lance shakes his head with a chuckle. "Justice, the whole world is talking about this kid…and he's nothing special?" Lance motions to the crowd. "There are, like, hundreds of people in this parking lot alone, just waiting to get a glimpse of him. What are you, blind?"

Justice shoves his cigarettes angrily back into his pocket and clenches his jaw. He shoots a look to Lance to let him know he's crossed the line.

"I didn't mean it like that, you big baby! I mean, there's got to be something about this kid that has the whole world up in arms, don't you think? I'm just excited to see if there is or not. That's all."

"Why?"

"Do I need a reason?"

"The kid thinks he's God, for crying out loud. He's got issues. Believe me, big ones." Justice clenches his jaw again.

"First of all, he never said he was God. And second of all, how do you know?"

"I just do." Justice looks over to the crowd and spits on the ground in their direction. "How much longer is this chooch going to take questions? It's not like we don't got anything to do today."

"Well, maybe you're wrong," Lance says uncomfortably. "I've never heard anyone eighteen years old talk like that. And what about how Manus freaked after meeting with Thomas that day?"

Justice kicks the back of the wheelchair. It races toward Lance, hitting him in the leg.

"Hey! What was that for?"

"Maybe you should be putting yourself in that chair."

"Look, Justice, I'm serious, man. You're not even curious why Manus acted the way he did after interviewing him?"

"No, I'm not!" he says firmly and turns away.

"Even after Manus wretched all over your pants? That wasn't normal, dude."

"He had a panic attack, for crying out loud." Justice fumbles for his cigarettes.

"Must have been some panic attack," Lance says sarcastically.

Justice takes a cigarette out of the pack and flips it into his mouth sharply. "We pick up guys that think they're Jesus all the time. What makes this one so different, Lance?" He snaps a match across his heel, lights his cigarette, and takes a long drag. He exaggerates this with a pained look on his face.

"You really want to know why?"

Justice turns to him with a frustrated look. He exhales smoke into Lance's face. "Yes, Lance. I want to know why."

"All right, I'll tell you, but you have to promise to keep it between us. Okay?"

"Fine!"

"Pinkie swear?" Lance holds out his pinkie.

Justice grabs it and twists. He takes pleasure in the pain it inflicts.

"Ow, let go!"

Justice releases his finger with a grunt. "Man up, will you? You're an embarrassment."

Lance sucks the knuckle, wrestling with the thought of how he can tell his partner his reason.

"Just tell me what you have to tell me already…Unless you want me to get you a boo-boo baby bear ice bag for that pinkie of yours."

Lance looks to the left and right to make sure what he is about to say cannot be heard by anyone else. "It was about him. I dreamed about Thomas last night. It kind of freaked me out. Okay?"

"You had a dream? Oh, you have got to be kidding me. You had a dream? This is why you're acting like this? This is the big thing you had to tell me?"

"You see, this is why I didn't want to tell you, you big jerk! It just freaked me out, okay? It was a really weird dream. I mean, it wasn't like any dream I've ever had before. It didn't even feel like a dream."

"Look, reality check, Lance, he's been committed. The kid is a Fig Newton. He's got a messed-up life, a messed-up family, and now he is a messed-up kid. Okay? I know you've been searching for the meaning of life and all, but this kid doesn't have the answers you're looking for. Believe me. I know more about him than you think. Trust me, the kid is nuts. Just like his mother."

"Wait, wait a minute. You know his mother?"

Justice lunges for Lance and grabs his shirt in a bunch. "Do me a favor and get a hold of yourself. The kid is no different than any other nutjob we deal with, you got that? He's just a celebrity right now, but soon his fifteen minutes will be up, and he'll be eating chalk off the floor like the rest of them. You understand?"

"You want to know what my dream was about or what?" Lance pushes his hand away.

"Fine." Justice lets go and takes a step back.

"I fell asleep watching the replay of the press conference on the couch last night, and then I had that dream. It was weird, man. I was walking down one of the hallways in the basement of our facility when I hear this kid calling me from the other end. He says, 'I will forgive them because they know not what they do.' Again and again he says, 'I will forgive them because they know not what they do.' The closer I get, the louder he gets. 'I will forgive them because they know not what they do.' Then all of a sudden, he gets silent. He stares at me and shakes his head, like he's disappointed in me. I ask him, 'Who are you, and what did I do wrong?' He smiles slightly and then points to my head with his two fingers and says, 'I forgive you. Be whole.' And then I woke up. It was freaking weird."

Justice is uninterested. "Let's go." He takes one last drag of his cigarette and flips it away toward Manus and the crowd.

Lance laughs to himself. "You're unbelievable. Is it your time of the month again? Is that it? Is your little friend here? Is that why you're acting like someone put a bee in your boxers? You want me to get you some Midol? Will that help with the cramps?"

Justice turns his stare from Manus to Lance again. "You want to know what the problem is?" He shakes the tip of his thumb over his right shoulder at the crowd behind him. "That's the problem, Lance. Bunch of people claiming they stand for truth. Pretending they want to know about something they could care less about, as long as it makes them money. A week ago, this kid was a miracle to them, and now they call him insane? He's bigger news now that people hate him than he was when they claimed to love him. What does that tell you, Lance? Huh? What does that tell you?"

"I don't know what to say, Justice." Lance is taken aback. He has never seen his partner this way.

"Then you got these religious folks who say Thomas was healed by God one minute, but then they change their minds and say the kid is the devil brought back from the pit itself to corrupt us all. I mean, look at them." Justice points toward the signs held in the crowd by the religious community condemning Thomas as a heretic. "Hypocrites!" Justice yells at the top of his lungs. With a disheartening look, Justice turns again to Lance and continues. "Truth is, nobody knows who this kid is. And I'm tired of everyone making such a big deal over him. If they really knew who he was, they wouldn't even be here!" Justice kicks the wheelchair. It flips over on its side.

"Okay, man, okay," Lance says in a calm voice as he bends over to pick the wheelchair up.

Justice shrugs him off and heads for the back of the transport van to grab another medical bag. After grabbing it, he stands up straight and stares Lance down. "I'll tell you this, if Thomas gives me any trouble, I will dope that kid up so much he won't even know how to spell God, let alone talk about him." Justice takes three needles filled with tranquilizer out of the bag and places them in his upper right shirt pocket behind his cigarettes. "Now, let's go get this kid for ourselves. The sooner he's locked up, the sooner the vultures can look for someone else to call Messiah and then crucify." Justice storms off.

Lance is shocked. "Okay." Lance hides his concern as he follows Justice into the hospital. He in unaware of the storm clouds gathering above.

The sun rose above the garden today, the birds are singing, and the children are at play. I sit alone with a sad look on my face; how I wish my life was different in this place.

I am the smallest of small and the slowest of slow; I never get ahead, and this everyone knows. I have no friends, no family, and no purpose, it seems; they point, they stare, and some even scream. Oh, how I wish someone could tell me what my life means.

I am not a worm, but I'm almost always on the ground. I haven't traveled far, but I know there is more to this world than I have found.

Then I saw something to take me away from that sad place. It was a butterfly floating with such beauty and grace. Not a care in the world, not a worry in sight, the color of its wings—rubies, pearl, and jade—seemed to dance in the light.

That could never be me because with the butterfly, everything in the world seemed right.

It was high and I was low. It was beautiful, and I, no one wanted to know.

What is the point of life if where the butterfly went, I could never go?

Then it happened, in that very day. I became tired, so in my bed did I lay.

My heart pounded, and in my chest there was great pain. Could this be it? I wondered. Is this the end of my days?

It can't be! I worried. With my life, all I've done was complain. Everything got quiet, and all I could do was pray.

If I can't be like the butterfly, God, at least let me live to learn to love myself one more day.

I woke up in a prison of death, in a place tighter than any rope tied tight. I could not move, I could not be heard, but I refused to give up without a fight.

I tossed and turned to reclaim what was once mine. "My life matters!" I screamed. "I'm going to do it right this time. I don't care how I look, I don't care what I do. I know who I am on the inside, that much is true. I am kind, I am patient, I am friend to anyone in need. Please just give me the strength to succeed!" Then it happened, I finally broke free. But now, there was something very different about me.

I went to crawl, but I began to fly. I looked at the garden below me, and all I could do was cry. I never thought it was possible, but who I wanted to be, I always was on the inside. Who knew a lowly caterpillar would someday become a beautiful butterfly?

—Thomas James

Don't Worry, My Little Butterfly

Thomas sits peacefully on his bed. How he can do this is beyond those in the room with him. The place he is going to is foul and dark. It is more like a prison than a hospital. Named after the small province located on the border of Bethel, Legirion Psychiatric proves the old adage true—you'd have to be insane to go there.

Thomas has no choice, other than deciding how he spends his time waiting for his captors to take him. He chooses to be at peace.

Nancy closes the blinds to the window of the hospital room. She turns to Thomas with a look of great concern on her face. "They're coming now," she says with a voice that cracks.

Allan fidgets in the companion chair next to her. He is distracted and upset. "Who is coming?" Allan asks nervously.

Nancy ignores his question. She rests her hand on Thomas's knee to comfort him. "They have a chair with restraints, Tommy. Now, don't you give them a reason to use those, understand?"

"Who is coming?" Allan asks again. "And what do they need restraints for?"

Nancy takes her hand away from Thomas to grab Allan's sweaty palm. "Two orderlies from Legirion are coming."

Allan breaks her embrace and stands angrily. "What? Why didn't you tell me they were taking him there?"

"I didn't tell you because I didn't want you to worry. Now, everything is going to be fine. So there is no need to get upset. Isn't that right, Tommy?"

Nancy looks to Thomas for support, but none is given. He closes his eyes and takes a deep breath through his nostrils. His reaction worries her. This is unlike the young man.

"It will be all right, I promise." Nancy makes light of the situation. Her face tells a different tale, and Allan is not persuaded.

He storms over to the window and pries apart the aluminum blinds. He looks down at the parking lot and grimaces as he watches Manus walk away from the crowd like a rock star would his fans.

Nancy leans in and rests her hand again on Thomas's knee. "You just do as they say. You hear me? You do that, and everything will be fine."

Thomas's eyes snap open. He shakes his head slowly in disagreement. "No, Nancy. First, everything must go horribly wrong before it becomes right again."

Nancy is numb. She pulls away from him slowly. She does not understand these words. How can she? There is so much she doesn't understand already. As she stares deep into Thomas's gorgeous blue eyes, she remembers the moment he was born. She also remembers the pain of losing her son that day. Tears fill her eyes as the realization hits her; once again a child she cares for will be taken from her. There is nothing she can do.

"What's wrong, Nancy?" Thomas says sweetly. "Don't you know it is always darkest right before the morning sun?"

Allan walks over to the two. He is brooding. "Let's just take him out of here. We can bring him to my house. No one will look for him there."

Nancy stands. She wipes the remnant of tears from the tops of her cheeks. "No, Allan, there are police at every exit and entrance. There's nothing we can do." She walks away from Thomas, defeated. The image of her dead son fills her sight. She has had dark days before, but never has she felt so lost.

"When things are taken from us, they are taken for us," Thomas says, looking directly at Allan.

Allan's smooth forehead wrinkles in confusion. He processes Thomas's words and grows uneasy because of them. "What about my dad?" Allan asks. "Why did he have to die?"

Nancy turns around. "Allan, honey—"

"No, Nancy. He can't say things like that without explaining himself. My father was a good man, and he suffered when he died. And he never gave up on God. So why did God give up on him?"

Nancy walks to Allan and rubs his shoulders gently to console him.

"Your father was a good man, Allan. That is true. He was also a great teacher," Thomas says with a smile.

"How do you know that?" Allan reaches for Nancy's hand with a tingling in his fingertips.

"I knew your father," Thomas says, remembering the day he embraced Mr. Brooks's withered hand. "He was one of my favorites."

Allan takes his hand away from Nancy and steps toward Thomas. "He was your favorite what?"

"He was my teacher when I was younger, Allan." Thomas swings his legs out to face him, readying himself to stand.

"I don't understand."

"No, Allan. What you don't understand is why bad things happen to good people. Like you, your father, like Nancy…and me." Thomas plants his feet firmly on the floor and pushes himself up from his mattress.

Allan gives him room to stand.

"Be careful, Tommy," Nancy says, reaching for him, in fear that he may fall. But Thomas stands tall. He takes her hand, but it is not for her support.

"One day you'll see why everything has to happen the way it happens. And you'll be grateful for it."

Confusion paints Allan's face.

Thomas takes Allan's hand as well. He smiles angelically and shakes his head as a proud parent does when their child pleases them.

"What has to be…has to be. Have faith. All will be well."

Thomas knows he must be taken from them. He knows of the awful place where he will go. He knew the instant he woke from his long sleep that this day would come. It's just part of another chapter that has to be read so all will know to stand tall in the face of adversity. But he cannot tell his friends. This is something they must come to understand on their own.

"I don't want you to worry when I'm gone," Thomas says in a cheerful voice. "And I don't want you to take any thought for yourselves while you're waiting for me to be with you again."

What is he talking about? Allan wonders.

"I will be with you again, Allan," Thomas promises. "And when I am, you will know who it was that was with you from the very beginning. Truth is, we can never be apart because who I am is with you always. Even those who don't know me one day will."

"What? What do you mean?" Allan lets go of Thomas's and Nancy's hands.

"Allan, you don't understand now. But one day you will. And in that day, you will know that as I am, so are you in this world. And you will cry no more because"—Thomas looks above and closes his eyes to finish—"because… you'll be free."

Their faces are blank. His words are so hard to comprehend. It would be easier for them to understand if he were to say that night was day and that day was night than to hear the truth of who they may be.

"Why do you talk like that, Thomas? Can't you see that's why they are taking you to that place?" Nancy wrings her hands in front of her waist.

Thomas returns his eyes slowly to hers. She tries to look away but cannot. His gaze draws her in and won't release her.

"Hard times must follow those who are chosen. I'm telling you this now so you'll remember when it happens to you. Our sufferings are but the testing of our faith. There is a point to it. You just can't see it now. But take comfort in this—your trials, though they may be many, will seem as nothing when you realize the truth of who we all are. That day is coming soon."

Nancy slaps Thomas's face. "Stop this!" she screams. Allan turns to her. She stamps her feet to the ground. "I won't listen to these words anymore! Can't you see this is the reason they're taking you from me?"

Thomas walks to the window. He turns his back to Nancy, but he is not upset.

"I'm talking to you, Thomas!" Nancy demands he listen.

Thomas grabs the small chain keeping the blinds shut and pulls them open. Sunlight floods the room. Thomas turns to face Nancy and Allan slowly, his countenance growing bright before them. His eyes find Nancy's eyes. "Don't worry, my little butterfly. You won't always feel like a little worm," Thomas says calmly. He sits in the chair against the window sill facing the door.

The blood drains from Nancy's face. Her legs are weak. "What...what did you just say?"

Thomas doesn't answer her. He locks his fingers together and rests his hands on his lap.

"You called me little butterfly. My father called me that." Nancy takes a few cautious steps toward Thomas. He doesn't take his eyes off hers as she does so. "My father used to say that to me, Tommy. 'Don't worry, my little butterfly. You won't always feel like a little worm.' He used those exact words. I never told anyone that...How did you know?"

Thomas does not answer.

The closer she moves toward him, the more compassionate his eyes become. She crouches down in front of him. "How did you know that, Thomas?" she asks fearfully. "Who are you, child? Who are you really?"

"I am who I am, little butterfly. Close your eyes and see." Gently, Thomas presses his thumb to the top of her hand. Nancy's eyes close immediately, as if his thumb triggers it to happen. In the darkness beneath Nancy's eyelids, the image of a fiery golden man arrayed with the brilliance of a thousand lights appears before her. A perfect golden crown is upon his head. Nancy's reflection is inside it.

"Holy Jesus!" She screams in terror with eyes now wide-open. She pulls her hand from his and falls to the ground.

Allan reaches for her. "What did you do to her?" he yells as Nancy begins to weep. Her lip quivers. Her hands shake. But her eyes stay focused on Thomas the entire time.

The door to the room opens with a loud bang as it bounces off the wall. Justice and Lance enter from behind it.

Allan jumps to his feet and stands tall between the men and Thomas. He holds a halted hand high in the air to keep the men from coming any closer. "This room is off-limits," he says, knowing he is outnumbered but without fear of his odds.

Justice turns and gives Lance a readying look. "Easy there, big man. We're just here to take Thomas to his new home for a while. That's all." He makes a tight fist at his side away from Allan's view.

Lance takes his place in between the two as peacemaker. He raises Thomas's signed commitment papers. "These are his papers." Lance reads Allan's badge. "Allan, is it?"

Allan nods without trust.

"Dr. Manus, Dr. Natal, and Thomas's aunt signed them. We're not here to give anyone any trouble. We're just here for Thomas."

Lance rises on his tiptoes and looks over Allan's large right shoulder. He sees Thomas sitting quietly in the chair behind him.

"Hello, Thomas. I'm Lance, this is Justice, and we're here to take you to your new facility."

Thomas tilts his head curiously as Allan tries blocking Lance's view.

"Why don't you give us a minute so we can say good-bye, and then you can take him?" Allan asks with a snarl.

Justice pushes Lance aside. "Why don't you say good-bye now and get out of our way so we can do our job?" Justice stands toe to toe with the young security guard. He tightens his other fist. "You can always just stand there and let me move you."

"Now wait, let's just take a second here, guys." Lance holds his hand up and makes the peace sign, making light of the situation. "We all have our jobs to do. No one wants any trouble."

Justice puckers his lips and kisses Allan good-bye in the air, attempting to provoke him further.

Allan does not take the bait. "Let's go, Nancy." Allan turns to her and finds she is too overcome with emotion to do so. "Nancy?"

Tears run down her face. She ignores Allan and stands to her feet as if possessed to do so. She stumbles over to Thomas and falls to her knees. She bends over, reaches for his feet, and begins to kiss the top of them. "I am so sorry," she whispers in a daze.

Allan and Lance look at each other in shock.

"What did she say?" Justice asks angrily.

Thomas reaches down and lifts her chin. He wipes the tears away from her puffy eyes. "There is nothing to be sorry for, little butterfly."

Allan grabs Nancy under her arm to lift her to her feet. "I'm going to take her home," he says, pulling her away from Thomas.

"Is she going to be okay?" Lance asks, wondering what provoked her to act this way.

Allan spits at his feet and says, "As if you care."

Nancy stops for a moment to look into the orderlies' eyes. "He's not who you think. He's not who you think at all. Oh Lord, he's not who you think." Nancy's mumbled words are as frightening to the orderlies as they are thought provoking. If Thomas is not who they think he is, then who is he?

"Take care of him. Or I'll take care of both of you," Allan threatens as he leads Nancy out of the room.

"Yeah, whatever, sweetheart," Justice grumbles and turns to face the patient he must transport.

Thomas does not blink. His body does not move. He sits still, as if waiting for what is to come next.

Justice shakes his head. He is annoyed. "You see what I mean? Did you hear that lady? You see what this kid is doing to people?"

Thomas focuses his stare on Justice alone. His eyes fill with pity.

Justice can't believe the frail teenager is brave enough to do such a thing. He smirks and clenches his jaw. He steps toward him. He rubs his knuckles in the palm of his hand. "I'm not like the little cult you got around you, kid. So don't you eyeball me."

Thomas refuses to look away. He knows Justice is an angry man. But he also knows that beneath anger and hate is a heart, a heart that only love can heal.

"I said, don't you eyeball me! What are you, deaf as well as dumb?"

"Take it easy, Justice," Lance cautions calmly.

Like a threatened snake, Justice snaps his head around to Lance. "Lock the door."

"What? Why? Wait a minute, there aren't any locks on these doors."

"Figure it out!" Justice screams.

Worried what might happen if he doesn't do what Justice commands, Lance puts his back against the door firmly so no one can enter.

Justice walks over to Thomas with a sinister glare in his eyes. His nostrils flare as rage builds inside him. On the floor beneath Justice, Thomas alone can see that the dark haze has returned. Possessing Justice seems a much easier task than the sixty-six it controlled before him. There is no escaping its torment.

"You think you know what you're doing, but you don't," Thomas says, adding fuel to the fire growing inside the orderly.

"Oh no, you're wrong about that, Thomas. I know you. I know you very well. You're Jesus Christ, right?" Justice says sarcastically.

"You say that I am. But you don't know who I am." His words provoke the dark spirits around Justice. The demon cloud quickly enters Justice. Thomas alone sees his right eye turn the color of coal because of it. Ripples appear on his face as if worms crawl beneath his skin. Lost to the darkness, he is no longer a man but an adversary. He is an enemy who wants Thomas dead.

"You know, back in the day, they stoned false prophets for talking like you." Justice takes off the latex glove from his right hand and places it in his back pocket. "Well, I guess this will have to do in the meantime." He backhands Thomas with all his might.

"Justice, stop!" Lance yells as his partner grabs Thomas from his chair and throws him into the wheelchair with restraints. "What the hell are you doing?"

Justice begins strapping Thomas in. He does not care that he makes the restraints too tight. In fact, he tries to cut off his circulation to punish him more.

"You little liar! You got them fooled, but I know you!"

Lance is frozen, too scared to act.

Thomas raises his eyes to the man punishing him. "You don't know me, Joseph."

"What did you call me?" Justice asks angrily. Thomas alone sees black blood shooting through the veins under the skin of his neck, leading to his temples above. The dark force is in complete control. "What did you call me?" Justice screams.

Thomas studies the black mucus covering his teeth, which now appear to be sharpened like daggers.

"I asked you a question!" Justice demands. He is oblivious of the demons' manipulation. "How did you know my real name?" he screams with a voice different from his own. "Answer me!" he commands, painting Thomas's cheek with another hard slap.

"Enough!" Lance grabs Justice by the collar and pulls him back. "What's wrong with you?"

Justice shoves Lance away with the strength of two men. "Stay out of this!"

Lance falls to the ground. Justice reaches inside his pocket and takes out the needles filled with tranquillizer. "This is for what your mother did to me six years ago!" He bites the protective plastic top of the needle off and spits it in Thomas's face. "Say good night, Tommy boy." Justice jabs the needle into Thomas's shoulder and empties the full contents of it without thinking.

"What are you doing?" Lance lunges for Justice and tackles him to the floor.

Immediately, the black force possessing him evaporates into the air. The demons release Justice from their grip. His senses return.

As Thomas's eyes begin to close, Justice realizes what he has done. "Oh no, what did I do?" He backs away in shock.

Lance shakes him. "He wasn't fighting you! He was calm! Why did you do that?"

Justice pushes Lance off him. His chest heaves as he gets to his feet. "I don't know…I don't know."

"You don't know?" Lance shoves him.

Justice looks at the needle in his hand. He turns his head and looks over at Thomas. Drool leaks from his mouth. Thomas is unconscious, but his right eye has yet to completely close. Justice allows his head to sink as he walks over to the biohazard garbage. "You never asked how I knew the kid, Lance," he says, disappointed in what he'd done. He opens the container and throws the used needle inside it.

"What?"

"My eye." Justice points to his scarred eye. "I had great career, benefits, and a great retirement plan. I was doing what I loved until the night I saved this so-called messiah and got attacked by his mother." Justice places Thomas's feet gently on the footrests and straps his legs in.

"What are you talking about?"

"You think I like working in a freaking nuthouse? I hate it…I hate everything about it. My life sucks because of what this kid and his mother did to me."

"What? What did she do?"

"She blinded me. She scratched my freaking eye out while I was trying to save her. I lost my fiancée, my job, my future—all because this kid, who acts like he's God, didn't have the sense to leave a burning building on his own."

"But what you just did…it's…wrong." Lance glances at the door, nervous as if someone might enter.

Justice walks over to his partner and backs him against a wall. "This never happened. You understand?" he threatens.

Lance shakes his head undecidedly.

"That's what partners are for, Lance. We look out for each other."

"I don't know, Justice. What if you do it again, man? He's just some dumb kid, that's all. He's just some dumb, confused kid. What his mother did has nothing to do with him."

"Look, I lost it, I know that. I'm sorry. It won't happen again. I don't know what happened…but you can't tell anyone, Lance. You can't, man. This job, as much as I hate it, is all I have," Justice says. "Don't take that from me too." He turns and exits the room with a heavy heart.

Lance stands alone. Deep down, he knows Justice is a good man. But he had no idea what his partner was capable of. He looks over at Thomas. "Don't worry, Thomas, that won't happen again," he says, taking his place behind him. As he places his hands on the handles to wheel Thomas out of the room, he is distracted by his patient's mumbling.

"What was that?" Lance asks. Again he hears Thomas mumble, but he cannot make out what is said. Lance leans in to him. He places his ear next to Thomas's lips.

Slowly Thomas whispers, "I…will…forgive them…because… they know not…what they do." Thomas's body goes limp.

Goose bumps rise on Lance's neck and arms. His stomach falls. *Who is this kid?* he questions in great terror as he remembers the very same words Thomas spoke to him in his dream.

It's time for the excuses in our lives to be gone.
For the time to truly live our lives has begun.
It's time for the rising of the sun.
No longer alone, no longer blind, deaf, or dumb.
It's time to finally have some fun.
Who, oh who, will choose to win instead of lose?
Who, oh who, will race toward blue skies instead of gray?
It's time to do this, I must say.
For you are the reason for everything that comes your way.
The time is now, no more ifs, ands, buts, or hows, for excuses to be gone; it's time to live as children at play.

—Thomas James

The Day of the Lord Is Here

Felicia sits on the stone wall surrounding the garden on the roof. As she weeps, she clasps her hands tightly around her damp handkerchief. She watches her tears drop from her chin and splatter to the ground as she wonders what she will do next. Her life is not what it once was. Everything has changed in such a short period of time.

She believes herself to be a good person. For the first time, she feels like life has dealt her a bad hand. What has she done wrong? How could God do this to her? *If there truly is a God*, she wonders. Felicia always wants the best for her patients, and she wants no different for Thomas. For this, she is punished. For doing right, she is mocked. For standing up for what she believes in, she is torn down.

"Why?" she cries, wiping tears with her handkerchief. The reins of her life have slipped out her hands. "What am I going to do now?" she asks, looking into the sky for an answer.

Rays of sunlight pierce the clouds like a laser through cotton. They shine on her as a spotlight would a stage actor. Felicia shields her eyes from the unexpected light and, for a moment, forgets her dilemma.

Days ago, a mourning dove ate from her hand in this very spot. Oh how she wishes that dove would return to do so again.

But there are no birds in the sky today. And if there were, she has no seed in her hands to feed them with.

"Felicia!" Colin roars as he enters the roof.

She is startled from her seat.

The two make eye contact. Colin runs to her. Felicia notices a small pile of papers in his hands.

Thank God he's here, she thinks as she fixes herself to look the best she can.

"I've been looking everywhere for you," Colin says, fumbling through his papers.

"I…I just needed some time alone," Felicia says, not yet finding the courage to tell him that she has lost her position at the hospital.

"I didn't sleep last night, not a wink. I was up all night working on this." Colin points to the papers. Preoccupied with what he has in his hands, he does not bother to notice how upset Felicia is.

"And what is it?"

Colin looks at her nervously. He isn't sure if he should tell her or not.

"Come on, Colin. What is it?"

Colin pauses. He looks into her eyes and grimaces. "Have you been crying?"

"You ran out here to tell me something, Colin. So tell me." Felicia folds her arms and taps her foot. If he won't ask if she is okay, then she won't tell him. "What is so important that you didn't sleep all night?"

Colin holds the papers loosely in front of him. He shrugs his shoulders and exhales his worry. "It's, uh…it's…it's the book of Joel. I downloaded it from the Net—"

"The what?"

"The book of Joel, it's from the Bible?"

"The Bible?" Felicia throws her hands into the air and storms away. She looks to the parking lot below and shakes her head angrily. "I can't believe this."

Colin follows. "I know it sounds nuts, Felicia, but you have to listen to this."

Felicia turns around, a woman scorned. "I lost my job, Colin!"

"You what?"

"I lost my job. The board is forcing me to resign after I stuck up for Thomas, for God knows why. They are going to fire me, Colin, and you come here saying you were up all night reading the Bible?" Felicia tries to bottle her emotions. "What is going on with everyone today? None of this makes any sense."

She turns her back on him and looks again at the parking lot below. He was supposed to be her voice of reason. She wants to hear him say that everything would be fine and they'll get those jerks, but those aren't the words leaping from Colin's tongue. The man who quoted Nietzsche and proclaimed that God was myth is now spending his night reading the Bible? Searching for answers as to why Thomas is the way he is?

"This makes no sense, Colin," she says as the psychiatric transport vehicle pulls away from the hospital.

Colin's head sinks. "They're taking him now."

Angry protestors scream after the van. They pelt it with eggs and rotten fruit. Felicia looks away from the madness and takes Colin by the hand. "I need you to be rational right now. I need you," she begs.

Colin treads lightly. He knows Felicia may not be ready to hear what he has to say. Colin can barely believe it himself. But how can he deny the feeling he has inside him? How can he turn on the mystery unfolding right before his eyes? Colin knows what he is about to tell Felicia sounds ridiculous, but that is only because she doesn't know what he now knows—because she hasn't seen what he has seen.

"I need you, okay?" Felicia's eyes are watery. Her stress level is high.

"At the press conference, Tommy said Joel spoke of us, and there was something about that name that…I don't know, just made me want to find out just what the heck Joel had to say."

Felicia pushes Colin's hands away. "Are you listening to yourself? You sound like a nut!"

"You don't understand, Felicia. Just...just give me a chance to explain."

"I don't understand?" she yells in absolute anger. "I lost my job for this kid, and I don't understand?"

Colin stares at her reluctantly. "Are you through?"

She paces back and forth. It is clear Felicia is not.

"You know what? I don't care if you're through with your little pity party or not!"

She turns to him in disbelief. "How dare you!"

"My brother can walk," Colin states matter-of-factly.

His words don't take effect immediately.

"How dare you talk to me like—" Felicia's face drops. "What did you just say?"

"My brother, he can walk. It's like he never had a problem walking in his life."

"Wait a minute, wait a minute...That's...that's impossible."

"Yes, that's what I thought too when Thomas told me he would walk again."

"Thomas said what?"

"No, let me rephrase that. He didn't say it, he promised it. He promised me my brother would walk again, and that it was all for the good."

"And can he?" Felicia tingles all over from the strange and unbelievable news Colin gives her.

"Yes, he can."

"It can't be!"

"He called me and said he was starting to have feeling again in his legs, feet, and toes. I told him they were just phantom pains. He told me it was different. He couldn't stop crying, he was so happy."

"But that's...that's impossible Colin."

"That's what I thought too. I thought he was just, I don't know, hallucinating or something. So I rushed over there."

"And?" she asks with her heart beating fast in her chest.

"It's true."

Felicia retreats. She is scared. She refuses to believe what he says is true. "No, it can't be. It's impossible!" she yells, and tears once again fall from her eyes.

"This has to do with Thomas," he declares, pointing at the papers in his hand. "There is more to that kid than we thought. I know there is." Colin walks toward her as she continues to back away.

"Enough! Enough about Thomas. I don't want to hear about him anymore."

Colin puts the papers in front of him and reads, "'Blow you the trumpet in Zion. Sound the alarm in my holy mountain. Let everyone tremble, for the day of the Lord is near.'"

"Stop this, Colin! I don't want to hear any more!"

Colin continues on, "'A great people, an army like there's never been, a fire burns before them and behind them a flame burns. Before them is the Garden of Eden and behind them a desert wasteland.'"

"What are you saying, Colin?" Felicia demands, hitting him on the top of his chest.

"Thomas said he was one of the first. He said he was the one that would declare the day. What if that day is here? What if Thomas is part of this army?"

"An army? What army? This makes no sense." The roof spirals around her. Felicia's legs become weak.

"God's army…'the sons of God.' There is a passage in the Bible that says all of creation has been waiting for the manifestation of the sons of God. What if Thomas is one of them? What if everything he said is true?"

"One of what, Colin?" she demands, pulling at her hair with shaking hands. "Enough! Just stop it, Colin! Stop it! I don't want to hear any more about God or anything else. I don't want to hear about this anymore."

Colin does not know what to do next.

Felicia wails in front of him. It is hard for her to catch her breath to speak. "I want my life back...I want it back the way it was. I want my life back, Colin."

He reaches out and pulls her close to him.

She fights to be free from his embrace. "Let me go! I want out!" She bangs on his chest until she tires. Giving up, she rests her head on his shoulder and allows herself to cry.

Colin looks up as Felicia closes her eyes. A white mourning dove circles above them. "It's going to be fine. All will be well, you'll see," Colin says with hope in his eyes for the first time in years.

I am Jacob, yes, I must confess, Jacob is me.

I was tricked into working for Laban for many years, you see.

When I was there, prosperity was in the air, and yet I declared the knowledge of the Lord was not found anywhere; this is why I ultimately had to leave.

But not before taking with me the ***speckled***, the ***spotted***, of all the ***goats*** and all the ***sheep***.

—Thomas James

I Know Who You Are

The air is foul in this damp, dark room of Legirion Psychiatric. This room is worse than a prison cell. Not like a place for healing and rest at all.

Thomas's eyes flutter open as he slowly comes to. He is disoriented. The stench in the room bites his nostrils. He grimaces. His head hurts. His mouth is dry, and his tongue is swollen. The tranquillizer had done more than put him to sleep. He is still groggy even after waking from it.

Thomas tries to bring his hands to his throbbing head, but he cannot. The straps on the table cut into his wrists, keeping him restrained.

He forces his eyes to open completely. He shakes his head to focus on his surroundings. Everything is a blur. The obscene amount of sedative given to him makes it is hard for him to get his bearings. He lifts his head as high as he can and looks toward his feet. His legs are restrained as well. He cannot move his feet at all. From this, there is no escaping.

His fingers inspect the table he is strapped to. It is as cold as it is hard. More like a slab at the morgue than a bed.

Thomas turns his head to the right. The walls are covered with writing. His eyes squint to make out what is written. There is profanity everywhere he looks. Words of hate, words of torment, words filled with pain, everywhere. He blinks his eyes to shake more of the fog from his head to inspect them further. The blurry words come into focus, and the horror of how these words got there is revealed.

These words are not written in pen or marker; they were scratched into the cement walls with a metal shard or something else. The more Thomas focuses his stare, the more imperfections he finds. Scratches from human nails are the most prevalent. They line the walls with bloodstains deep in their crevices.

Whoever stays in this room, it seems, tries scratching and clawing their way out.

As Thomas looks closer at these scratches, he envisions the many children before him tearing at these walls in tears. Bleeding fingers, broken nails—nothing disturbs Thomas more than their broken spirits. He feels their pain and hopelessness as if it is his own. It weighs on his heart like a thousand stones.

"What is this place, Lord?" Thomas asks.

It is not a place of healing. It is not a place for the sick and infirmed. It is a hell, a prison. It is death.

Above Thomas flickers a single lightbulb. It swings back and forth slowly from the draft that funnels in through the dirty vent above it.

Thomas turns his head to face the only window. No light enters in from it. It is protected by worn steel bars. Another vision fills Thomas's sight. He sees multiple people, ranging in age from teen to adulthood, screaming and yanking at these very bars. Some bang their heads into the bars again and again. All who grab at them realize there is no escape.

Legirion is a sad and ugly place. For many, it is the end of the road.

"What am I to do?" Thomas asks, swallowing the lump of dread gathering in his throat. He closes his eyes to regain his peace. The unwelcome feeling of fear begins to strangle every bit of it away. Thomas tries to block it out, but only succeeds in hearing the voices of those out in the hall and in the adjoining rooms. Some laugh as madmen, while others mumble incoherently and scream out in pain. And the cries, the cries of women in mourning are the saddest of them all. These sounds build in Thomas's head until he can take them no more.

"Father, help me," he whispers.

With all his might, Thomas tries breaking free from the leather straps that hold him in the center of this dismal place. But he is their prisoner now. His strength alone will never be enough.

The jangling of keys is heard outside his door. The lock to Thomas's room opens with a loud snap. The door creaks as it slides into the room slowly. Thomas turns his head toward it fearfully. It is Lance. He enters the room with his head hanging low. He fumbles to get the stuck key out of the door lock.

Lance takes a deep breath as Dr. Manus enters the room next. He has a smug look of contentment on his face. Outside the room in the hall behind them, Justice waits silently. The sting of regret keeps him from entering.

Manus circles Thomas like a shark waiting to devour a wounded fish. Thomas lies helpless before him. His heart pounds in his chest.

"Leave us," Manus says, waving Lance off as he would a bothersome fly.

Lance yanks at the key a final time, and it returns to him. As he exits, he gives Thomas a look that shows him his concern. But Thomas needs more than a concerned look if he is ever to be free again. Lance hands the keys to Justice. The two watch Manus from the hall.

"Give us some privacy," Manus commands.

The door shuts. Manus and Thomas are closed in together.

Manus licks his lips and rolls his head back and forth to loosen his neck. As it cracks, Thomas's bottom lip begins to quiver. It is clear Manus takes great pleasure in the bonds he has Thomas placed in. The look on his face is almost orgasmic.

Manus closes his eyes, takes a long deep breath, and exhales. "Oh, what fun you and I are going to have," he says and opens his eyes dramatically. Manus walks to the window. He looks at the dust lining its ledge. He drags his finger across it slowly. It leaves a sharp line in its center. He lifts his dirty finger to eye level and inspects it. "I am sorry we had to put you in one of the old rooms, but it seems there is very little room in our facility these days. So many people who need our help..."

Thomas yanks at his restraints angrily.

"Oh, and I am so very sorry about the restraints. They are for your own good, of course." Manus approaches Thomas. He pulls the arm restraints tighter.

Thomas whimpers from the pain. His hands and fingers become white with his circulation cut from them.

"When you're not so hostile, we'll get these restraints off," Manus says, grabbing the leg restraints to tighten them as well. "You have my word." He smiles savagely and pulls the leg restraints until he can pull no more.

Thomas begins to cry. The pain is so great.

Lust grows in Manus's eyes. "Not so brave anymore, are we?" Manus leans in to study Thomas's face. He wipes away some of Thomas's tears. "I never noticed just how good-looking you are. You are a handsome young man, Thomas. But a young man that is nonetheless...sick!" Saliva follows his last word, landing on Thomas's face.

Thomas continues to say nothing. It isn't that he refuses to speak to the man mocking him. It is that he cannot speak at all. His words are strangled by a dark fear.

Something is different about Manus. It is not like the first time the two met. There is something new, something foreign and dark, something powerful.

Manus begins perversely combing Thomas's hair back as a mother would her child. It makes Thomas's skin crawl.

"So do you like it here?" Manus asks with a cackle as he motions to the foul room like a tour guide from hell.

Thomas stares into Manus's mouth. Manus's brown teeth repulse him. His foul breath makes him wince.

"You start group tomorrow, Thomas. We're going to introduce you to some of your peers."

Thomas's eyes meet his with anxiety.

"Oh now, don't you worry about them. Some are violent, that is true, but I am sure they are anxious to meet you." Manus continues to gently rub the side of Thomas's face. "You may even know some of them, Thomas. I believe two or three here are about your age. Wouldn't that be something?"

Manus inches his face toward Thomas's as if he was going to kiss him. "Let's take a closer look at you." He quickly snatches Thomas by his cheeks with his left hand. He squeezes Thomas's face like a python around its prey. As Manus turns his head from side to side, Thomas's teeth grate together.

"Do you remember our last encounter?" Manus asks, and his nostrils flare.

What is it about this man that scares me so, Lord? Thomas worries.

Manus quickly snaps Thomas's head toward the left and speaks quietly in his right ear. "I don't know what you did to me in that hospital room. I don't know how it is you know my…my hidden corners, if you will. But if you ever tell anyone what you think you know about me, I promise you—the worst thing I have ever done before you will pale in comparison to what I will most assuredly do to you."

Manus's hand shakes as he squeezes Thomas's cheeks together as tightly as he can. Blood drips out of the corner of Thomas's mouth as the inside wall of his cheek is ripped apart by his own teeth.

The door to the room opens suddenly.

"Is everything okay in here, Doctor?" Lance asks, knowing everything is not.

Manus stops what he is doing. He shakes his head and fixes his jacket, making his annoyance known. "Everything is fine," he says and notices the blood leaking from the corner of Thomas's mouth. Quickly, he uses his index finger as a tissue and wipes the blood away. "I'll be there in just one moment."

Lance slowly steps out of the room. He leaves a crack in the door so he can hear what is going on inside as he waits for the doctor.

Manus looks at Thomas's blood on his fingertip. He puts this finger in his mouth and licks it clean. The blood swirls Manus's teeth.

Knowing he is being spied on from the hall, Manus returns to Thomas quietly. "Welcome to my hospital, Thomas James," he says with words that are no longer his own.

Thomas looks deep into Manus's eyes and sees the evil that possesses him. It is the source of Manus's strength and power. They are not the eyes of men. No, they are the eyes of the monstrous demon that has terrified Thomas from his youth. The foul beast has returned, incarnated in Manus's flesh, to finish what he began six years ago. The death of Thomas's mother and grandmother, the theft of his youth—none of it is enough to quench its appetite for destruction. It is Thomas the foul beast wants dead.

"I know who you are," Thomas says in a strained voice.

Manus straightens. He walks over to the door to exit.

"I know who you are," Thomas repeats.

Manus grabs the door handle. He does not open the door yet. Instead, he turns his head toward Thomas, farther than what his neck should allow. His eyes are blacker than coal. "And I you, Thomas...and I you." His shadow grows behind him on the door and wall. It forms the great dragon that haunted Thomas's childhood dreams. The shadowed dragon screams. Thomas alone hears. Soon all Thomas feels is the wetness seeping through his pants because of the fear it inspires.

"Sweet dreams, Thomas James," Manus says and slams the door, taking the shadowed creature with him.

Thomas is alone.

"Lord, help me, help me, help me, help me, help me..." Thomas mumbles as if he is losing his mind.

All things were given to me, for me, and through me everything that is, both misery and bliss, and everything that is not yet, will be.

This is a mystery, you see; it is the mystery of the kingdom that has been hidden within you and me.

You are the reason for your joy and misery, your accomplishments and defeat, your health, your illness, your freedom, and your slavery.

It is time to grow up and allow your peace to show up, so take responsibility.

—Thomas James

YOU ARE FORGIVEN AND LOVED

It is the seventh day since Thomas woke from his sleep of six long years. Like any other day before it, this seventh day starts in darkness. Even if it was a bright sunny morning outside, from inside Legirion you would never know. The windows are painted black so the natural light of the sun can never enter in. The institution relies solely on the light it provides. The environment here is one of complete control. One that Thomas feels the full weight of.

The door to Thomas's room unlocks. As the door opens, the light from the fluorescents in the hall creep in. Lance winces as kicks the doorstop in place. The musty smell of mold and urine is heavy in the air. Like most accustomed to being here, Lance will forget the smell quickly.

"Morning, Thomas," he says uncomfortably as he makes his way toward him.

Thomas turns his head slowly to see Lance. He blinks his eyes, adjusting them to the light from the hall.

Lance shakes his head sadly. He cannot believe the boy has been tied down the entire night. "Unbelievable," he mumbles, noticing the restraints are too tight.

Thomas's hands and feet are blue. The leather straps break the skin in places. Small pools of blood surround his wrists and ankles. The agony Thomas must feel is unimaginable, and yet Thomas never once cried for help.

"Let's loosen these up for you." Lance quickly releases the restraints a few notches.

Blood surges back into Thomas's hands and feet. He moans softly as feeling returns to his extremities.

Noticing the urine and blood staining Thomas's hospital pants and shirt, Lance's eyes gloss over with tears. He inspects the swelling of Thomas's jaw and the burst blood vessels in his eyes.

"We'll get you cleaned up real soon, Tommy, don't worry," Lance assures with distraction in his aspect. Manus is cruel. Lance has never seen a patient treated like this before. "It will get better, Thomas." Lance takes out a small rag from his pocket. He rinses it in the sink. He wrings excess water from the cloth and takes his place at the head of Thomas's bed. "This should make you feel better," he says, wiping dirt and blood from Thomas's face and arms.

Justice enters the room hesitantly. He holds fresh hospital pants, underwear, socks, and a shirt for Thomas to wear. He stands near the door, waiting for the courage to face the young man he had abused.

Lance gives him a look that conveys what Manus had done to Thomas was far worse than anything Justice had done.

Justice bites his bottom lip with his top teeth as he enters. "I raided the linen closet for you. Don't tell anyone. I just thought you might be more comfortable in these."

Lance is taken aback by his act of kindness.

As Justice lays the clean white clothes at Thomas's side, he notices the condition Thomas is in. The corners of his mouth point down. His jaw clenches. "This won't happen again, kid. Don't worry." Justice gives Thomas an encouraging pat to his thigh.

The way Thomas was treated is not usual practice. Restraints are only used in rare cases when patients are so out of control, it is necessary to keep them from hurting themselves. Both Justice and Lance knew Thomas was very much in control and should not have been treated in such a way. Thomas was made subject to the bonds he is in. And yet, he endures the inhumane treatment without raising his voice.

"Well, let's take these restraints off so you can get dressed." Lance unlocks the rusty belt and frees Thomas's hands. "That must feel better, huh?"

Justice hovers behind Lance as he starts on the leg restraints. He looks like he has something to say to Thomas but is waiting for the right time to say it. He has been up all night. The guilt of treating Thomas in such a way clings to him like a millstone around his neck. Why had Justice acted in such a way toward the defenseless teen? What had provoked him to be so cruel? He doesn't understand why he did what he did.

Justice retreats into the corner of the room as Lance continues to free Thomas's legs.

Lance tosses the leg restraints aside. They clank against the stained floor as they bounce off it. Thomas's ankles are raw. Lance helps Thomas to sit up slowly.

Thomas focuses his eyes on him. He gives Lance a peaceful look as he rubs the burns and tears on his wrists and ankles.

Lance notices there is something different about Thomas this morning. He doesn't know what it is, but the boy's eyes are not the same. The fear Lance saw in Thomas is gone.

Thomas rolls his head in a circle for relief. Justice nervously fidgets in the darkest corner of the room. Thomas finds Justice and fixes his stare upon him. He studies the orderly as if seeing into the very depths of his soul. Justice looks away uncomfortably. He does all he can to avoid eye contact.

"You're forgiven," Thomas says in a calm and raspy voice.

Justice looks at him. His forehead crinkles with embarrassment. "I'm what?"

"You are forgiven and loved." Thomas follows his words with a kind look on his face. "You are forgiven for everything."

Justice steps out of the darkness.

Lance gives his partner a cautioning look. Would Thomas's words put the large orderly over the edge once again? Lance shakes his head; he warns Justice not to pay any mind to what Thomas said.

However, anger does not motivate Justice to approach Thomas this time. He walks over to the young man with confusion in his eyes. He did not ask for forgiveness, so who is Thomas to forgive him? He wonders.

"What are you saying, kid?" Justice folds his massive arms in front of Thomas. He means to intimidate the young man while also hiding his own fear.

Thomas tilts his head curiously and slowly reaches his hand toward Justice's chest. The orderly flinches back in terror, but for some reason, he cannot pull himself away from the hand slowly approaching his heart.

"What…what are you doing, kid?" Justice asks in fear. His feet become cement on the floor. Chills race up the back of his legs.

Lance rises slowly in amazement. The scene before him is strange.

Finally, Thomas lays his hand directly above Justice's heart. A sudden surge of energy rushes into the orderly as if struck by lightning. His arms stretch wide. His back arches as his chest is forced toward Thomas's hand. His eyes close, and every hair on his body stands erect.

"My god," Justice gasps. Tears roll down the right side of his face.

"What the…" Lance reaches for the wall behind him, retreating from what he does not understand.

"I'm sorry, I'm so sorry," Justice cries as he is lifted by Thomas three feet into the air from the floor.

"That's…that's impossible!" Lance yells.

Justice floats higher into the air like a child's balloon in Thomas's hand. Thomas turns to Lance and says, "On the seventh day, God rests!" The lightbulb in his room and the fluorescents in the hall explode. Thomas turns his gaze to the painted window. Rays of sunlight melt the paint from the other side. True light enters the room, and they are immersed in it.

"You are forgiven, Joseph," Thomas says kindly, using Justice's God-given name. "You have been lost, but now you are found. It is time to rest." Thomas lowers Justice to the ground. He takes his hand away from the orderly's chest.

Justice falls gently to his knees. He weeps. His tears are no longer from pain. They are the result of letting the pain of his past go. His tears are now tears of joy. Thomas's touch did more than lift Justice off his feet. It did more than raise him to another plane. It expelled his every fear and wiped away his every doubt.

Lance's heart races and his hands shake as he walks over to the two cautiously. "What did you do to him?" he demands.

Ignoring Lance's question, Thomas kneels with Justice on floor. He lifts his chin, revealing a face red with emotion and wet from tears. Thomas looks at the scar covering Justice's eye. He raises his hands, extends his thumbs, and presses them firmly over his good and bad eyes. "The Leviathan's scales are his pride," he says quietly.

Thomas takes his thumbs away. Lance is in shock. Both of his partner's eyes are covered with two large fish scales. "What did you do to him?" Lance screams and tries to run from the room but falls in his escape.

"See!" Thomas demands and claps his hands together. The loud sound shatters the glass window. Even the bars vibrate.

Lance covers his ears and crawls into the corner of the room. He watches as Justice peels the scales from his eyes away. He drops the scales, and they float to the floor like feathers from a frightened bird.

Justice faces Lance. He opens both eyes. His sight is perfectly restored. "I can see! I can see! My god, I can see!" Justice screams for joy. His fingers dance above his eyes now that he can no longer find the scar that kept him blind. Now he is free. Now there is no reminder of the day Thomas's mother scratched his eyesight away.

"What the hell is going on here?" Lance screams.

Thomas effortlessly rises. He focuses his bright blue eyes on him. "It is hell that has been here for too long. It is hell that will soon be gone." Thomas reaches out his right hand. He turns his palm toward the ceiling and opens his hand. "I'm ready for my new garments now," he says angelically.

Lance stumbles to the table for his clothes. He cannot help but do as Thomas commands. Too frightened to take his eyes off Thomas, he reaches for the new clothes as a blind man would. Lance bundles the clothes together in his arms. He places one foot in front of the other and slowly makes his way toward Thomas.

Thomas reaches out for Lance.

"Here you go," Lance says, handing over the new clothes.

The smell of lavender and roses fills the air.

"Thank you, Lance," Thomas says and walks past the seemingly frozen orderly.

Lance's eyes are wide. None of this makes sense. It's like a dream.

Justice runs over to him. In his excitement, he embraces Lance and lifts him high in the air. "Its true, Lance! All of it is true!" Justice laughs and kisses his scared partner on the forehead.

"What's true, Justice? What?"

"He's never left us, he never forsook us, and he never needed to return. We only needed to remember!" Justice declares with a powerful voice. He releases Lance from his tight hug. "It's the beginning and the end, Lance. It's the beginning and the end."

"What are you talking about?" Lance persists. *What is he talking about? What beginning? What end?*

What has Thomas done to him? What did Justice learn under his hand? What mystery was revealed? Has Justice gone mad like so many others held captive in this dark place? Or has he found the very thing that will answer all the questions plaguing Lance's mind?

An answer is not given. Instead, Justice rips the keys of the institution off his belt. He throws them to the ground. He smiles as he exits. He will leave Legirion once and for all. Justice knows once he does this, he will never be able to return to the darkness of this place again.

"Where are you going?" Lance asks as his friend walks away.

"I'm going home," Justice says, never looking back.

The room spins wildly around Lance. His knees are weak. His stomach feels empty. His breath catches as he turns, only to be startled by Thomas standing tall behind him. He is clean. His white clothes are brilliant. His eyes are as intense as they are compassionate and kind. His hair shines. A distinct glow surrounds him.

Lance's lip quivers as he asks, "What's happening?"

Thomas looks above curiously and answers, "Change, Lance. That's what's happening." Thomas walks to Lance with feet that don't appear to touch the ground—as if he is floating, hovering, not walking at all. He places his hand on Lance's shoulder. His touch calms Lance momentarily. "Bring me to the others," Thomas says in a pleasant voice.

Lance looks into his eyes as if in a trance. "What others?"

"All of them. Bring me to them all." Thomas reaches for the keys Justice threw to the ground. The dirty black keys that hold the insane and tormented in their chains become as precious as gold in Thomas's hand. He will use the very keys that once trapped them to finally set them all free.

The mudbug becomes the dragonfly.

The caterpillar transforms and then gracefully takes to the sky.

In the winter it seems every flower dies, but in the spring the beauty their resurrection brings can move grateful tears from our eyes.

The beginning of every chapter is only the beginning that you must realize.

In the end, every heart will mend, and nothing will compare to the incredible journey that has been your life.

Regardless of what you are going through or where you have been, soon you'll thank God for the cocoon your hard times helped spin.

You'll rise from your sorrow, embrace the possibility of tomorrow, and realize you were never born to lose but to win.

—Thomas James

BORN FROM ABOVE

Thomas enters the narrow hall of Legirion with the keys of Justice in his hand. The rising sun's light enters from a small window at the end of the hall and paints the dirty tile floor with its golden rays. The light seems to follow Thomas as he walks down the sad corridor. This hall is long. The locked doors are many. But with these keys in hand, there is nothing and no one Legirion has locked away that cannot now be set free.

Thomas breathes in the stale air through his nostrils. His shoulders relax as he soaks up the moment. It is a cruel place that keeps them, not a place of rest or healing. He approaches the first door he will unlock. He exhales confidently as he jingles the keys in his right hand.

Lance steps into the hall behind him. Nervous pins and needles prick his hands and feet. There are security cameras in every corner. It will not be long before word is out on Thomas's escape. "What do you think you're doing?" Lance worries.

Thomas turns to him. His eyes are as brilliant as a diamond reflecting the sun's light. His face is as calm as a glassy lake. "I'm doing what I was born to do."

A single key is separated from the rest on the large ring in his hand. He raises it slightly above his waist and thrusts it into the keyhole, like a knife into the belly of an enemy. He unlocks it, pushes it open, and makes his way to the door next to it.

Lance's face drops as the door swings open with an eerie creak. "What did you do? You can't…you can't do that!" But he is too late.

A young girl exits her prison of a room with a smile inching toward her ears. She must be thirteen years of age. Her face is drawn. Deep bags under her eyes weigh her skin down, making her eyes bulge from their sockets. She reaches for Lance, but his fear prevents him from helping her. Instead, he runs after Thomas in hopes that he can keep him from opening them all.

"You have to stop, Tommy. You have to stop, or Manus will have your head!" he cries, but the orderly has no power over him anymore. Door after door swings open, and those trapped behind them exit with tears of freedom in their eyes.

Men, women, and children of all ages enter the hall with an excitement of earlier days. Their afflictions are many, but Thomas does not look upon their wounds, nor does he acknowledge their crazed ramblings and grunts and groans.

Their insanity drove them to do unimaginable things. One had gauged out his own eyes; another ripped off his own ear. Many were bald from years of pulling out their hair, and some had cuts covering their bodies. Nothing is as disturbing as their frail appearances though. Their skin is drawn tight over their protruding bones. Their bellies bloated from the gases that have no nourishment to digest. They are a pitiful bunch. But now they are free.

"Back to your rooms!" Lance screams as the crazed mob follows Thomas as rats would a Pied Piper. They walk awkwardly behind him, like zombies fresh from the grave. No one knows where Thomas is leading them. Not one cares why Thomas set them free.

"Everyone, get back to your room, or else!" Lance yells again. His threat is wasted on uninterested ears. His authority came to its end the moment Thomas took the keys of Legirion away. In a panic, Lance reaches for the emergency cord. He pulls it and brings to life the alarm. Cutting through the air like a bloodcurdling scream, the blast of the siren drives those behind Thomas into a panic. They shout and cry. Some fall to their knees, begging for forgiveness. They know they will be persecuted for trying to escape.

"That's it, Thomas, it's over! You have to stop before you make it worse for us all!" Lance believes he has the upper hand.

Thomas does not take another step. But he does not stop because he is told to. His head sinks, but it is not because he thinks all hope is lost. There is no fear in his eyes. No regret fills his heart. He only does this to find the key that matters most to him, one last key to make everything right. "There is still one door that needs to be opened," he says, taking the key in hand and pressing it into the last locked door.

The madness of those behind Thomas is beyond control. Fearing for his life, Lance stands in the gap between the rooms and the main cafeteria. He covers his face with his hands as the crowd jumps and shouts and pounds their chests.

"We have to go back to where we were, Tommy! We have to go back!" Lance pleads. "Someone is going to get hurt!"

Thomas will not be moved. He turns the key. The lock opens with a snap. He pushes against the large door and enters the room.

In the corner, a young woman sits fearfully on the cement floor. She hugs her knees and hides her face as Thomas approaches. She is his age, but she looks much older. Horrifically thin from years of a devastating eating disorder, it is a miracle she is alive at all. A tear runs down Thomas's cheek as his eyes rest on her piteously. He lowers himself to one knee.

"Betty," he says softly. "Betty, it's over now. Come with me." He takes her limp hand in his and caresses the top of it with his thumb.

After hearing the familiar voice of her past, Betty slowly raises her eyes to his. Her lip quivers, and her body trembles. "Tommy?" she asks in a barely audible voice. She cannot believe it is her old friend—the one she held hands with, got sick with. The one she said she would always love, until the lure of popularity drew her away. Oh, how lost Betty became in the six long years Thomas was away. Reduced to a starved, cowering patient who for years tried to take her own life, her arms are covered in self-afflicted bruises, her hair has fallen out in clumps, and a large scar at the base of her throat is where the institution force-feeds her.

But now her old friend is here to rescue her from this dark and horrible place. He is as pure as the driven snow, as impressive as a mountain's peak. But his actions are as gentle as a dove's.

"Come with me, Betty," he says, fastening his compassionate eyes upon hers.

"Tommy, is that really you?" she asks in an unbelieving whisper.

"It is." Thomas helps her to her feet.

"Why are you helping me?" Her knees wobble. Thomas keeps her from falling. She cannot stand on her own.

"We're two peas in a pod, remember?" Thomas smiles as he cradles her in his arms like a father would a newborn child. He carries her into the hall where the rest wait to see where Thomas will take them next.

Lance stands before him. "It's the end of the line, Tommy. There is nowhere to go from here. You hear that alarm? Soon this place will be swarming with orderlies and security."

Thomas heads for the main cafeteria.

"Don't even think about it, Thomas. That place is a trap. You go in there, and they will lock that room down so tight that no key will let you out. Trust me, Thomas. There is no way out of this place."

Betty's arms tighten around his neck as she clings to him. He stands in front of the impressive dining hall door. Lance's words ring in his head. But Thomas does not worry about his fate. His life has taught him the greatest lesson there is to learn. His life is beyond his control. He cannot choose the things that happen to him. He can only choose how he reacts. So there is no longer a point to worrying about this or that. There is no need to fear the future for his actions now, when all anyone of us has is the moment to begin with. He is doing what he knows is right. He is standing where others refuse to stand. He stands in faith. He will not fear what might happen if he does the very thing that can save them all.

He turns to Lance. Hope shines like two beacons of light in the deep blue sea of his eyes. "Come with me, Lance. Don't think. Just listen to your heart, and follow me." Thomas takes the key to the main dining hall in hand.

"I can't, Tommy. If you go in there, you're on your own."

Thomas looks to the group behind him. He looks to Betty in his arms. He looks above. "Not alone, Lance. I'm never alone." Thomas unlocks the cafeteria's door and rolls it aside so all can enter freely.

Lance jumps in front of the group. He uses his body to barricade the entrance. "You can't leave, Thomas. This is where you belong. Can't you see that?" Lance insists.

"I am not from this place. Those who belong here stay here, but I never have and never will."

Lance takes his hands from the doorframe and steps aside. The passage is clear. "It's your funeral," he says with a heavy heart.

Thomas boldly steps into the large dining hall. Many behind him refuse to follow suit. They would rather stay where they are than suffer or sacrifice anything to be free. Legirion is all they have ever known. Here they have drugs to keep them numb, promises that they will be well, men and women to tell them what to eat, when to eat, where to go, what to do, and what not to do. Here they can follow without question.

But with Thomas, they will have to lead. One by one they return to the darkness of their cells. They will wait for another savior, one who will whisk them away without ever having to struggle or suffer and give up a thing.

Lance watches as the crowd dwindles down to almost nothing. Only a small number of those Thomas frees are ready to follow him into the main dining hall. These five, including Betty, know they will be persecuted for wanting more than Legirion has to offer. They do not care. They want to be free. They want to know the truth of who they are and who they can be.

Thomas tilts his head sadly toward Lance. "You don't know what I am doing now. But soon you and the others will understand why it is I did what I did and said what I said. That is the day you will wish you had done it with me."

Thomas turns his back on Lance. He enters the large dining hall with Betty in his arms. And as the others follow close behind, a car's tires are heard screeching to a stop outside.

Two long black tire marks stain the street behind its wheels. Manus quickly exits. He runs to the entrance of the institution, forgetting to close the door. He screams into the cell phone he has pressed against his ear. "Lock it down! Lock it down!" Manus leaps up the stairs two by two. He lunges for the handle on the front door, but he is stopped by Jim Williams.

Jim hid himself well, waiting for the doctor's arrival. The anxious reporter has a smile on his face and, in his hand, a large dark brown folder. "Can I get a moment of your time, Vince?" Jim asks. He knows something Manus does not.

"Get out of my way!" Manus shoves Jim aside.

"Easy there, big fellow," Jim says, spinning around Manus, barring him once again from entering the institution. "You are going to want to hear what I have to say." Jim laughs.

Manus rolls his head impatiently. The sound of cracking bones is heard. His jaw clenches. His glasses begin to fog. "What is it you have to say, Mr. Williams?" Manus asks calmly and directly.

Jim hands Manus the folder.

"What's this?"

"Oh, you know what it is. These are your greatest hits, Doc. And don't you worry, I have copies just in case these get lost. Everyone has a closet that needs to be cleaned, Doctor. I just had no idea yours was so…full." Jim's smug look quickly turns to one of disgust. "Everyone underestimates the janitorial staff. But it *is* true what they say. They help clean up the mess, don't they?"

"Excuse me?" Manus is not amused.

"It's amazing what information you can get with fifty dollars and a handshake. Here, I'll spell it out for you. Your janitors don't think much of you. Nor do I, for that matter. You're sick, dude. But don't worry. Like you said, I'm sure no one will ever take a reporter like me seriously. But if they do, I don't think you will be sharing a magazine cover with any midget baby werewolves anytime soon. You'll be sharing a cell." Jim laughs as he turns to exit.

Manus's hand shakes with anger. His face is red as he loosens his tie. He does not open the envelope to see what's inside. He knows the pictures from his office better than anyone else. He simply takes off his glasses and calls for the reporter. "Jim, before you go." Manus follows after him. Dark storm clouds gather in the sky.

Jim turns. "Yes?"

"I just wanted to shake your hand. Would you do me that courtesy?" With a devious grin, Manus extends his left hand.

"Why?" Jim asks with butterflies in his stomach.

Manus's left eye twitches. "Well, I'm not going to force you." Manus sneers. "Perhaps you're a better reporter than I gave you credit for." He appeals to Jim's pride.

"Fine." Jim reaches for the doctor's hand. As soon as their palms meet, Jim sees the doctor for who he truly is. A loud crack of lightning shakes the ground beneath them. "Oh my god!" Jim cries in terror, noticing the complete blackness of Manus's eyes and festering sores in his decaying flesh. "Let me go! Let me go!" Jim screams, but the more he struggles to break free, the harder it is to do so.

"You think you know who I am?" Manus squeezes his hand until Jim's bones are crushed. Jim falls to his knees, crying out in pain. "How dare you accuse me? I am the accuser. I am the one who judges. Not you!" His voice steals Jim's hearing, but his words become tormenting thoughts in his head. "You're an insect. You are a pathetic, weak fool, and I am a titan! I am a god in this world!" Thick dark clouds blot out the sun.

Black blood rushes down Manus's neck, making its way into Jim's hands. Jim's veins visibly fill with the black blood, his veins under his skin taking on the appearance of dead branches of a burnt tree. His eyes cloud over, and Jim fights to breathe.

"You think you know the truth about me?" Manus asks with a sinister smile, revealing pointed daggers for teeth. "You're right, Jim, everyone has things hiding in their closet. Perhaps it's time I remind you of yours." Manus lets go of Jim's hand and gauges his two thumbs deep into Jim's temples. Blood oozes out from the holes, and Jim's eyes roll back.

"No!" Jim screams as memories of every horrible deed he has done in his life flash before him.

"I'll leave you to your sackcloth and ashes, you disgusting little worm," Manus whispers, releasing Jim and walking away.

Jim shakes all over. "No, no, someone, help me!" he screams, believing a swarm of flies is biting him. Like a madman, he flails around on the ground, scratching and tearing into his skin, trying to free himself of the flesh that attracts the flies.

Manus heads for the institution with a disgusted look on his face. He is greeted at the door by two staff members. They welcome him with opened doors and the look of relief on their faces. A great disturbance resounds inside their walls, one they cannot understand or control. But now their leader is here; now they feel safe.

"Where is Thomas?" Manus asks two of his nurses.

"In the main dining hall, sir. Security has them trapped there." One of the nurses, the shorter of the two, fixes her appearance for Manus's approval.

"And what are they doing?" he asks, walking like a giant through the halls.

"Sitting still, Doctor, in the middle of the room. They are just sitting and waiting."

"Waiting for what?" His head turns to them angrily.

"For you." The short nurse bites her bottom lip nervously. "Thomas said he is waiting for you."

A curious look takes over Manus's face. "This behavior will not stand." He growls like a lion seeking whom he may devour. "Tell security we have a riot on our hands."

"A riot, sir?" the older nurse repeats worriedly. "They are sitting still. They aren't harming anyone."

Manus snaps at her, a shark tearing into its bait. "Tell them to bring the gas and their clubs and to meet at the back entrance of the dining hall. Am I making myself clear?" he snarls. His breath makes the nurse nauseous.

"Yes sir," she answers, holding her hand over her mouth to keep from throwing up. She runs over to the phone with red eyes and makes the call.

Inside the dining hall, Thomas sits in the center with Betty's head resting on his lap. He speaks gently to those sitting next to him. "Old things are passing away. Soon everything will become new," Thomas says confidently.

Besides Betty, who is unconscious, those with Thomas are terrified. They want desperately to escape Legirion's halls but worry that if they do, they will be put to death for it.

"What will we do?" a scarred woman in her fifties asks with glazed eyes. Her delusions drove her to Legirion. Once there, she was never free from them.

"We will stand," Thomas says. "We will stand…to be free."

"How?" she asks with dreamy eyes.

"You know how to stand, Mary." Thomas looks at her compassionately. "You already know everything you need to know. We all do. We just forgot. We've fallen asleep. We have forgotten who we are, but I am here to remind you."

"Remind us what?" a young teenage boy named Jacob asks as the sound of marching is heard in the distance. Jacob jumps to his feet in fear. "What is that?" he screams.

Thomas looks toward the back of the hall. He rises slowly to his feet. He knows Manus will use force to take them from the dining hall. And as the sound of their adversaries close in, Thomas does not show fear. He takes off his white shirt and rolls it into a pillow. He places it under Betty's head and motions for the others to stand with him.

They stand slowly, their eyes racing around the room. What have they gotten themselves into? They worry.

"I said, what is that sound?" Jacob demands.

"That is the sound of everything standing in our way," Thomas answers as plainly as he can.

The loud marching suddenly stops. Manus and his minions are right outside their doors.

Thomas closes his eyes and turns his palms upward. "Now that you are with me, you will see and hear what others cannot. Be not afraid. You are more than you know. You cannot die. You cannot fail, for as I am, so are you in this world." Thomas opens his eyes, and a glowing light surrounds him. The bewildered group cowers as a protective circle of light closes them in together.

"I don't understand! What's happening?" the last member of the group asks, a girl in her early thirties who, after losing her son, lost her mind. "What is it we will see? Why is this happening? What are you talking about?"

"You are about to find out, Danielle," Thomas says with concern as the hollow sound of the door unlocking is heard.

The men with Manus shout and curse outside in the hall as he takes the key away from the door. The orderlies and security cannot wait to get their hands on the small group. They pound their fists into their hands and shove each other, as if readying themselves for war. Manus laughs as he tucks the dining hall key away inside his jacket pocket. He eyes the excited small army behind him. He knows these men will do more than simply contain the situation. They will punish Thomas and his group by taking their own frustrations out on them.

"Ready, men?" Manus asks, stirring their lust for blood. The men raise their clubs in the air and scream as Manus slowly presses against the large door. It slides opens with what sounds like human nails dragging across a chalkboard.

"Thomas James!" Manus's shouted words echo in the dining hall and strike terror into the patients' hearts.

"Stay with me," Thomas begs as the strange sound of locusts fills the room. Millions of them, chirping louder and louder, until the sounds of their legs rubbing together are all the small group hears.

"What's happening? What is that?" Danielle cries, trembling in fear. The noise makes no sense to those in the glowing circle.

Thomas takes a deep breath. He sticks his chest out for all to see. "If God be for us, who can be against us?"

Suddenly, the sound of the locusts stops. The group lowers their hands from their ears. Their hearts race, and with their breaths held, they move close to Thomas. This is but the beginning of the plagues. From behind the door, millions of black ants march into the room.

"This isn't happening, this isn't happening!" Mary yells as the ants crawl over everything in their path. The floor and walls are thick with them. The white room is covered by the blackness of their shells.

"Look!" Jacob screams. His finger points like a spear toward the door.

Manus is the source of the plague. The ants pour from his mouth, like polluted water from a broken main. He turns his head from side to side.

"I don't want this anymore!" Mary shouts, believing the ants to be a delusion from her past. But what the group sees is as real as the air they breathe. Thomas has given them power to see what others cannot. The evil that hides in plain sight is now as clear as the wild thoughts running through their heads.

The ants change into the appearance of hornets, and the group's eyes widen in horror. The hornets swarm like the winds of a tornado around them. They attack the protective circle of light but are repelled by its sheer brilliance. Inside Thomas's circle, the group is safe, but that no longer matters to them.

"Let me go!" Danielle cries as Mary vomits and Jacob covers his eyes. Thomas pulls her back as she tries to leave him.

"Stay with me!" he demands.

The hornets change into a hundred thousand frogs. They cover every inch of the room—except the small circle of the group. They croak and lash at the shield of light with their horned tongues.

"What's happening?" Jacob cries as Thomas fights to keep the group from leaving him.

Manus sees their division. He smiles as he walks toward them. The frogs separate with every step he takes, as if Moses himself had parted them down the middle. "Come to me, Jacob." His words are inviting, not at all the words of a man who would kill if he could.

"Don't, Jacob," Thomas demands, but the hooks of Jacob's fear are deep.

As the frogs turn to snakes and the snakes begin to slither past the protective barrier, the group's fear can no longer be contained.

The snakes enter. They wrap around the patients' legs and strangle every bit of peace.

"Stand with me!" Thomas yells at the top of his lungs. His voice is like a cannon shot. It bursts the heads of many snakes, but his words are not enough.

"I'm sorry, Thomas," Danielle says as she runs for Manus and Legirion.

The snakes clear her path. Manus smiles as she falls at his feet. He strokes her hair as if she were his pet and waits for the others to leave Thomas as well.

"No, Jacob," Thomas pleads with tears forming in his eyes. But the young man runs to Manus without ever looking back. Mary follows him with regret in her eyes. Betty and Thomas are left alone. The snakes hiss and strike as they circle the pair.

The small group is on their knees, ready to kiss the feet of the very man who locked them away.

"No!" Thomas cries. The frightening image of the thousand snakes disappears. Confusion sets in. The image of the reptiles is replaced by the orderlies and security guards crowding them. Reality sets in for the once-freed patients. Manus no longer needs to veil his intent.

"Lock her back in her room." He points at Betty as she lies asleep at Thomas's feet. "And bring him to me," Manus demands.

His men snap to attention. They walk cautiously to the eighteen-year-old as if approaching an angry giant in their midst.

Thomas stands his ground. "Those who love their lives will lose them," he says and stamps his feet into the ground. A loud crack of thunder is heard. The cement beneath them begins to shake. A deep crack races through the floor and splits the room in two. The guards fall to their knees as the foundation of Legirion is torn apart.

"Get up and bring him to me," Manus commands while many of his men turn and run in fear.

"Judgment begins now!" Thomas yells and stamps his feet again. The walls of the institution crumble to the ground. The remainder of Manus's men run from the institution, followed by all who work and reside there.

Manus now stands alone with Thomas's followers at his feet.

"They are with me!" Thomas demands with a voice that thunders like a mighty waterfall. He stamps his feet again. The ceiling of the building collapses around them. "They are mine!" he repeats, and his words become fire. Like a flamethrower burning down a field of thorns and weeds, his fiery words engulf Manus, leaving him bald, burned, and scarred.

"You can't do this." Manus drops the envelope Jim Williams had given him to the ground. He reaches inside his jacket pocket and pulls out a gun.

Jacob stands to his feet and runs back to Thomas, dodging the large pieces of the falling debris. Thomas's arms stretch wide for him as he once again stamps his feet. The entire institution splits down the middle as each side falls away, leaving Thomas in its center.

"Help me!" Jacob yells.

A loud gunshot is heard.

"No!" Thomas cries as Jacob falls dead in his arms. "No!" He screams with words that become four winds gathered from the four corners of the world. The mighty winds of his voice clear the debris that once made Legirion strong.

The pictures that fell from Manus's envelope are caught up in the winds' strong current. The images of every atrocity Manus had committed on those entrusted to his care are finally revealed. The pictures circle those in the room.

Danielle points as his molestations are made clear. "How could you?" Danielle demands with a fire growing in her belly. She rises to her feet and slaps Manus and spit in his face.

Manus cowers as the sharp edges of the pictures close in on his face.

Mary stands strong. Tears fall from her eyes as she realizes what a monster the man who had cared for them was. "You're a murderer, a liar, and a thief," Mary declares as she walks humbly back to Thomas.

"No. You all need me. You all come back to me or else!" Manus threatens as he points the gun at those who walk away from him.

"Those that hate their lives in this world shall keep them forever," Thomas says calmly as the rest of the group settles next to him. The winds of his voice are stronger. They blow the pictures of Manus and his evil into him. The images slice and cut him down with their edges.

"Help me!" Manus cries as he is sliced open again and again. He can no longer see those he imprisoned as his eyes are cut from him. The pain is so great. He slowly brings his own gun to his head.

Thomas leaves those with him to stand above Manus. "From nothing you came, and to nothing you will return."

Manus squeezes the trigger and falls dead at Thomas's feet.

The winds cease. The fire dies down. The group cries over their fallen brother, Jacob, as Thomas returns to them. The sky above becomes clear.

"No more wrestling with your demons, Jacob. It's time to wake up," Thomas says, plugging the gunshot wound with his forefinger. A bright ray of light shoots out from the other side. The bullet is forced from Jacob's mind. It falls to the ground next to him. Thomas wipes away the blood from Jacob's temple as the eyes of those in the group become wide, but this time it is not from fear. The wound disappears as Thomas breathes on Jacob. Instantly, air returns to Jacob's lungs, as does the beating of his heart. Jacob is alive.

"My god," Danielle whispers, almost falling to the ground in disbelief.

Thomas turns to the group. He gives them a smile. Who would believe the tale they now could tell?

"Where do we go from here?" Mary asks genuinely. After Legirion, what is there left for her?

Thomas reaches down. He takes Betty into his arms again. "You'll know where to go, and you'll know what to do. God is with you, and all will be well." As Thomas cradles Betty's sleeping body in his arms, he turns away from them and begins to walk.

The group joins hands and holds each other tight. They try to make sense of what has happened as Thomas walks toward the light shining from the glorious sun, which hangs over the dead woods of Lyons Belt in the distance.

As Thomas walks toward the dead woods, people in the street hold their heads in confusion. Each is scattered from their own homes. Thomas has shaken them all from their daily ritual. He has broken up many of their dwelling places. These lost souls now search high and low on the streets, like rats for a piece of cheese, for the things that were lost. They do not know what to do or what has happened. There is crying and wailing in the streets.

Many believe all is lost. However, for those close to Thomas, this mighty act of God brings hope.

Lance, Justice, and a recovered Jim Williams join the group inside what once was called Legirion. They too join hands with the others for support, wondering when they will see this remarkable young man again.

A child is born in dreams heard and spoken.

Life becomes death when hearts are broken.

In school there is no rest between life and death until eyes are opened.

Yet there is hope for the brokenhearted; there is good news to protect and share.

Be not afraid; dwell not on mistakes you have made.

All that seems wrong isn't; nothing is ever lost that is not one day found, everyone will know love; no one will miss it.

Hearts change when a new day is here.

It will be shouted from the rooftops, "Those that hate the most must be loved the most!" "The lost cannot see clear."

It can't be silenced; nothing shall stand in its way. Oh Lord, what a day it is when enemies betray with a kiss. Don't worry, my little butterfly, the day of the Lord is here.

I know who you are.

You are forgiven and loved, born from above.

Wake up, child of God.

—Thomas James

Wake Up, Child of God

A thick fog hovers above the open field leading to the dead woods called Lyons Belt. The tall trees that guard the forest from the sky stand eerily above the field. Not one falls from the earthquake that tore Bethel apart. Not one tree moves from its place. Lyons Belt is not affected at all.

The same cannot be said for the field or the town. Those in Bethel must wait for the sun to rise for the collateral damage to be realized. It is nearly dawn, but even with the sun's light to guide them, if the fog remains thick, it will be impossible for any to see the devastation the earthquake leaves behind.

The shift in the earth has separated the edge of the woods from Bethel and those in it. A deep sixty-six-foot-wide and sixty-foot-deep chasm surrounds the dead woods. A gap in the earth so deep and so dark that the woods become an island unto themselves. Like a moat surrounding a dark castle, the gulf protects the woods on all sides but for one small path. This path is the only way in and the only way out. It is a perilous passageway for all who dare to cross there. A way few will find in this dense fog.

An unnatural silence filters through the trees. Not even the wind whistles as it passes the barren branches of the dead trees. Time stands still in the field until the sounds of crackling of footsteps on fallen debris is heard.

"Whose there?" a woman's voice calls from the dark fog in the field.

"It's Allan. Allan Brooks. Who are you?" he asks, nervously loosening the top buttons of his Bethel Hospital security uniform. Allan cautiously steps into a small clearing in the fog. He looks around for the one who called out to him. He cowers back as her figure grows out of the haze.

It is Nurse Nancy. She steps into the clearing nervously, clutching her shawl. "Allan? What are you doing here, sweetheart?"

"I don't really know…I had a dream…and, uh…I was told to come here."

Nancy's jaw drops. For a moment, she cannot find her words. She tightens her grip on her shawl. "I had a dream like that too." They hear more footsteps approaching. Chills race up the back of Nancy's neck.

Allan's head whips around to find the source of the noise.

"Is there anybody there?" a familiar voice calls out from the darkness. The two can see his silhouette moving toward them, like a blind man in a foreign land.

Nancy grabs Allan's arm tightly. Their eyes focus on the figure as it gets closer.

Allan's eyes tighten. "Dr. Striphe, is that you?"

Colin enters the clearing, confusion painting his face. "What's going on here?"

Nancy places her hand above her racing heart. "We don't know."

They hear footsteps. This time there are many. The three turn from the dead woods to face the entrance of the field. A group walks toward them in the fog. Some are closer than others are.

"Something is happening," Colin says, catching his breath. "Something big."

Dr. Felicia Adams is the next to enter the clearing. She shivers from fear. "Did you have the dream too?" she asks in horror.

Colin swallows the lump in his throat. "Come here, Felicia." He wraps his arms around her to make her feel safe.

Flashes of light frighten the group.

"What's happening?" Felicia screams.

The bursts of light are quick and directed at the group. Allan raises his hands, shielding his eyes from it. "Who's there?" he demands as Jim Williams appears out of the fog with camera in hand.

"If this isn't a freaking weird story, I don't know what is." He snaps a picture of the frightened group as Justice enters the clearing from behind him.

With a peaceful smile on his face, Justice breathes in the early morning air and sighs. "You all woke from the dream too?" He laughs to himself and slaps his knee. "Life isn't what it used to be, is it?" His belly laugh attracts another walking aimlessly in the field.

"Justice, is that you?" Lance asks as he enters the clearing hesitantly. "I had a dream. Thomas told me to come here. He said here is where it would end and where it would begin."

The eyes of those in the group nervously meet each other. Together they slowly nod their heads in agreement.

"Thomas told us all the same thing," Nancy says as Jacob enters, still wearing the institution's clothes. Entering with Danielle, he holds her hand. Neither says a word. As they join those standing in the clearing, Danielle rests her head on Jacob's shoulder.

Mary enters behind them. She takes off her tattered institution slippers and allows her feet to rest on the cold earth. She looks at the many worried faces. "My name is Mary. Please tell me this isn't a dream too."

No one has an answer to give her.

"What's happening to us, Colin?" Felicia presses herself against him for security and warmth.

"Does anyone know what 'Here is where it ends and where it begins' means?" Lance asks as the last to enter the small clearing arrives.

It is John. The scars on his arms have almost healed. Color has returned to his cheeks, and hope rejuvenates his eyes. The former bully and drug addict steps forward, a new man with a solemn look on his face. "It means old things have passed away, and everything is being made new." A deep silence follows John's words.

The group huddles close together. Above them, thunder roars in the sky. A mighty wind rushes past them, and the fog miraculously rolls away like a retreating tide. The sky turns red as the sun peeks above the dead woods of Lyons Belt again. The group gasps. They tighten their grips on each other as a tall figure approaches from the dead woods. He walks onto the small path above the great gap in the earth.

"It's Thomas," Felicia says, excitement in her voice. The eleven run toward him and stop within feet of the small clearing leading to Lyons Belt. The path Thomas stands on is narrow. They fear that if they fall while trying to reach him, they will forever be lost.

"Nothing is ever lost that isn't one day found," Thomas answers their worry in an angelic voice. The trees behind him bow as he speaks. He stretches his hands toward them, inviting them to his embrace. "I know things have been hard for you. They have been hard for us all. But here is where it ends, and here is where it begins again."

The sun breaks free from the shadow created by the world. The light from it shines so brightly on the group, they have to cover their eyes. Behind them, it is as a desert wasteland. The earthquake devoured the town of Bethel and left its inhabitants with nowhere to call home.

"Why are we here?" Jacob cries as those with him take their hands from their eyes.

"To know the truth," Thomas says with a voice as pleasant as a love song. "To know who you are and what you must do." Thomas pauses and looks into each of their bewildered eyes. His words confuse them, regardless of how deep a chord they strike.

"What is the truth?" Allan asks nervously.

Thomas looks up. Eight mourning doves circle him in the sky. Behind him, Betty appears.

Felicia's eyes widen. "Elizabeth?" she cries. Her niece is more beautiful than the day she was born.

Betty takes Thomas's hand in hers and stands tall at his side. She smiles as they lock eyes with love for each other. Her frail frame has mysteriously changed. Her pale skin now exhibits a warm, rich tan. Her hair is full and seems to glow.

Colin looks at Felicia. A wide smile grows on her face as the wrinkles of worry in her forehead disappear.

The fog is gone. The darkness of night is stolen away by the morning light. The path to the woods on which Thomas stands is clear.

"What is the truth, Thomas? Who are we?" Allan demands again.

Thomas's head sinks. "You are dead, Allan," Thomas says plainly. "You are all dead, as are all those in this world. You just don't know it yet."

"Dead? What does he mean dead?" Danielle cries and falls to her knees. "How can we be dead?" She screams as Jim drops his camera. It shatters on the ground.

Their hearts sink as the horror of his words set in.

"How can that be?" Lance shouts.

They stare blankly at Thomas. Not one of them knows what he means.

How can they be dead when they have experienced so much pain? How can they be dead when they exist in such a dark place? How can they be dead when they all believe they are alive? And if they are dead as Thomas has said, where are they now?

Thomas raises his head high as a great leader would. "Many worry of a hell after leaving this world. Never once worrying about the hell they are already in." A tear leaks out of his right eye and runs down his cheek. "This world is a prison. You are its prisoners. A prison with many horrors, where there is weeping and gnashing of teeth. This world is the only hell you need concern yourself with. And we have been called to set man free from it."

"What are you talking about?" Colin yells. "What are you even saying?" He pounds his chest.

The mourning doves sing above Thomas as hundreds of butterflies appear from nowhere and flutter around the frightened group. Thomas closes his eyes and speaks softly to them. "You don't understand who you are or where you are."

"Who are we, Thomas?" Nancy begs.

"You are gods, Nancy. All of you are children of the Most High. But you died like mere men and fell as one of their princes the moment you believed you were human. But now it is time to arise, Oh God. Now it is time to wake up and judge the earth. Now is the time to live again and set those captive here free!" Thomas says with great authority. He opens his eyes. They are bluer than ever before.

Those in the group cannot find the strength to question Thomas anymore. His words, as terrifying as they are to them, ring true.

"A revolution is coming," Thomas declares. "A battle unlike any this world has known. A war so great all will be changed by it. And it begins with each of you."

Thomas takes Betty by her soft hand. He turns his back on the group and leads Betty into Lyons Belt. The moment his foot enters the dead woods, green leaves sprout from every barren branch on every dead tree.

Quickly a lush green canopy fills the woods as life returns to it. Fruit appears on many of the trees as well, and the polluted water running from the great river into Bethel's water supply becomes crystal before their eyes.

Those in the field tremble as Thomas leaves their sight. They look at each other but do not know where to go next.

"I don't know about all of you, but I want to find out who I really am," John says. Without fear, John follows after Thomas by crossing into the woods as well. He leaves the man he was for the man he can be.

The rest of the group look at each other. They collectively agree. As if there is no other choice that can be made. One by one they do the same.

As those remaining make their cross to follow Thomas into the woods, hundreds more imprisoned by Legirion appear behind them in the field.

EXHIBIT C:
Entered into evidence: 09/11/2022
Intercepted communication: Thomas James–Defendant

Dear friends,

I am writing to you because we face an even greater threat today than before. The world is quickly changing, and with each passing day, more of our lost brothers and sisters hear our voice and have found their way back to us. The glorious revelation of who we truly are that the principalities and powers of this world have fought to keep hidden is now being shared abroad. I applaud each of you for keeping your tongues until the time appointed. We have taken upon ourselves the great and terrible task of sharing so great a truth that if we were to reveal ourselves to the world too soon, it would most surely be our end.

I am filled with sorrow that I had to keep, until now, the deepest and most powerful message of all from your ears. This was for your own good and for the good of our brothers and sisters in bonds.

To the point of these words, my messenger has delivered to each of you pages that I have labored to write for many years. This work, which may seem to the world mere fantasy, hides the keys to unlocking the very secret of creation.

To those who are without understanding, these following pages will seem an idle tale meant to entertain, or the ravings of a delusional man. However, I assure you, this journey you are about to embark on will prove these words true.

It is of the utmost importance that you do not keep these pages to yourself. They are now meant to be shared far and wide. All must be made aware of this book. We do this with the hope that the blind may be given their sight again and the corruption of Dominion will fall.

I want you all to know how deep my love grows toward each of you. I know of your many sacrifices, and I have heard of your many trials, for which my heart breaks. We have been scattered as so much straw in the wind. Nevertheless, I eagerly and faithfully wait for the day we are reunited.

Wisdom tells me the end will justify the means, and our suffering will seem as nothing compared to the joy and power we inherit. I ache for the moment our purpose is fulfilled and the darkness holding mankind in chains is extinguished by our light.

I have not abandoned you. It was for your good that I went away, but know this: I have never left you, and I am always with you. The good work that has begun within you will continue until my revealing again.

We have fought the good fight within, and now that fight begins without. Now the truth will be shouted from the rooftops, and what a day this will be.

Your life is not what it appears to be. What will happen when the truth is poured out on a world that is deceived? To this question I have but one answer—change. The truth will change you, and my words are the instruments of this change.

We must stand firm and play the parts we are meant to play so we can be that change for those who cannot see. I have told you in days past how you will be hated, falsely accused, condemned, and hunted because of your ability to hear the words I speak, but be of good cheer, my friends, for we cannot fail.

We will overcome this world with good; evil will not overcome us. Regardless of bonds, persecutions, distress, famine, or war, we will always be free, liberated, at peace, full, and never wanting. We have within us so great a treasure that the reach of Dominion is of no effect.

Soon, very soon, you will understand that where you are is where you are meant to be, and where you are going is beyond your greatest dream.

Keep these pages safe. Keep these pages close; you will do as you are meant to with them. Never question, never regret, and never fear that you have been a failure. For every single instant of every single moment was of absolute necessity to bring you to right here and right now, reading these many pages that follow. A true account of my journey.

The past does not exist. The future does not exist. This moment is all that matters. This moment is a treasure. This is why it is called "the present."

Blessed are those that do not condemn themselves in what they allow. Blessed are those who do no harm. Blessed are those that do not fear what may be. Fear is the root of all suffering. Fear is the father of all lies and pain, reserved for destruction by the words hidden within the pages you are about to read.

The desire of your heart has been for this moment; the declaration of liberty is at hand. Let love be your guide. Let patience rule your heart. Let joy heal you in your time of trouble. Follow the path set before you even though it may seem a grievous thing. It will be your devotion to share what you find in these pages that brings you the purpose you so desperately seek.

For it will be your words and your actions that ignite this world once again in what is most certainly humanity's greatest and most terrifying hour.

Do not try and find me. Do not believe that the messenger is greater than the message. Do not think higher of yourselves than others, for blindness in part has happened to your brothers and sisters in bonds so you could play a role in setting them free.

For now, know how close you are to my heart. You may not see me, but I keep my eyes firmly planted on you. You are never alone for we are one.

As for this note, my messenger will see fit to release it to the world as a work of fiction when the time is right, causing no alarm among the masses until after the truth of this great work is revealed.

Trust your heart, trust each other, and know that when those who read these pages are gathered together, so too will begin mankind's ascent out of this grave called life.

Keep vigil, keep the faith, keep to yourself, and keep watch, for the hour is fast approaching.

Yours in the faith,
Thomas James

Made in the USA
Las Vegas, NV
24 June 2021